DEATH OF A HEALER

A Novel by

Paul Henry Young

Printed in Canada

For information address:
Durban House Publishing Company, Inc.
7502 Greenville Avenue, Suite 500, Dallas, Texas 75231
214.890.4050

Library of Congress Cataloging-in-Publication Data
Young, Paul Henry, 1950

Death of a Healer / by Paul Henry Young

Library of Congress Catalog Card Number: 00-105930

p. cm.

ISBN 1-930754-04-3

First Edition

10 9 8 7 6 5 4 3 2 1

Visit our Web site at
http://www.durbanhouse.com

Book design by:
B[u]y-the-Book DesignóM adeline Hˆfer & Jennifer Steinberg

To my family

ACKNOWLEDGMENTS

My appreciation to Joan Wassilak, Patricia Darby, and Susan Wilson for their dedication over the past seven years to the typing (and retyping!) of this slowly evolving manuscript; to Bob Middlemiss, editor and mentor; and to John Lewis, publisher and visionary. Quotations taken from Etziony M.B., The Physician's Creed, C. Thomas Publisher, Springfield, 1973.

DEATH OF A HEALER

I swear by Apollo Physician and Asclepias and Hygieia and Panaceia and all the gods and goddesses, making them my witnesses, that I will fulfill according to my ability and judgement this oath and this covenant;

To hold him who has taught me this art as equal to my parents and to live my life in partnership with him, and if he is in need of money to give him a share of mine, and to regard his offspring as equal to my brothers in male linage and to teach them this art—if they desire to learn it—without feed and covenant; To give a share of precepts and oral instruction and all the learning to my sons and to the sons of him who has instructed me to pupils who have signed the covenant and have taken an oath according to the medical law, but to no one else.

I will apply dietetic measures for the benefit of the sick according to my ability and judgement; I will keep them from harm and injustice.

I will neither give a deadly drug to anybody if asked for it, nor will I make a suggestion to this effect. Similarly, I will not give to a woman an aborted remedy. In purity and holiness I will guard my life from my art.

Whatever houses I may visit, I will come for the benefit of the sick, remaining free of all intentional injustice, of all mischief, and in particular of sexual relations with both male and female persons, be they free or slaves.

What I may see or hear in the course of the treatment or even outside of the treatments in regard to the lief of men, which on no account one must spread abroad, I will keep to myself holding such things shameful to be spoken about.

If I fulfill this oath and do not violate it, may it be granted to me to enjoy life and art, being honored with fame among all men for all time to come; if I transgress it and swear falsely may the opposite of all of this be my lot.

The oath of Hippocrates
(Sixth Century, B.C.)

1

The conditions necessary for the Surgeon are four: First, he should be learned; Second, he should be expert; Third, he must be ingenious; and Fourth, he should be able to adapt himself.

It is required for the First that the Surgeon should know not only the principles of surgery, but also those of medicine in theory and practice; for the Second, that he should have seen others operate; for the third, that he should be ingenious, of good judgment and memory to recognize condition; and for the Fourth, that he be adaptable and able to accommodate himself to circumstances.

Let the surgeon be bold in all sure things, and fearful in dangerous things; let him avoid all faulty treatments and practices. He ought to be gracious to the sick, considerate to his associates, cautious in his prognostications. Let him be modest, dignified, gentle, pitiful, and merciful; not covetous nor an extortionist of money; but rather let his reward be according to his work, to the means of the patient, to the quality of the issue, and to his own dignity.

Guy de Chauliac (1300-1370)
Father of Surgery

Jake watched the anesthesiologist over his surgical mask. It was already starting to itch. Later it would get moist from his breathing. Above him the OR lights burned bright. Around him the surgical team moved, a ballet in green gowns, each knowing his job. Except for Hudley. Instruments gleamed on Martha's tray. He could count on her, this totally dedicated head nurse who would barrel through the OR doors, the last drops of soapy water running off her arms. A rock of efficiency. Her green gown was wrinkled but sterile. She wore size six rubber gloves. Her eyes moved from her surgical instruments to Jake to the anesthesiologist. Her mask hid a good face, a down home country face with its ready smile. Head OR nurse for the University of Minneapolis Medical Center said it all. Jake's own mask hid a concern about the patient. One of those irony things, those bittersweet things. But watching the anesthesiologist had pushed it all back behind intense concentration. Now he waited on the gas-passer who minutes before had cradled a phone to his shoulder and breathed stock quotes through his mask. "Listen, we ought to get ten thousand shares. Yeah. Ten…" All the time injecting several brightly colored anesthetizing agents, in sequence, into a clear plastic tubing. And all the time with the patient nervously staring up at him.

Mitchell M. Malone was an attorney-at-law. He had worked overtime to become the most notorious medical malpractice lawyer in probably the entire country. He posted incomes of well over five million a year. He ran commercials that underscored his high profile reputation and slick talking personality. He was also president of NAPILA, the North American Personal-Injury Lawyers Association. His specialty was to round up litigation against hospitals and associated physicians, and then to manipulate each fingered defendant into unwittingly criticizing the care delivered by the other.

But while arguing a case against a St. Paul ER physician and his hospital, a case dealing with an alleged failure to properly diagnose and treat a patient who had suffered a massive disabling stroke—Malone had collapsed. He had been rushed to the emergency room. Paramedics were told by the lawyers that Mr. Malone had been arguing with a defendant's expert witness when he suddenly complained of a severe headache. He then vomited and collapsed into a state of unconsciousness. Jake had been walking through the ER corridor.

◉▨✠

The anesthesiologist gave the nod. Jake placed the attorney's head into a vise-like holder that would prevent unwanted movement. Martha nodded for one of the team members to hand Jake an electric shaver. Silver and gray hair were placed in a sandwich bag and taped to the front of the chart. For the mortician. Just in case.

Jake motioned for the prep nurse to cleanse and prepare with antiseptic the shaved area. Then he went to the stainless steel sink just outside the room to wash his hands. Hand washing is always a ritual, a time for the surgeon to collect his thoughts, envision each detail, rehearse every step. What problems could come up? How would he handle them?

"Dr. Gibson, my name's Timothy Knoxmann, sir. I'm a fourth-year student assigned by Dr. Hudley. I've never been involved in a brain operation before and—"

"Tim."

"Sir?"

"Lesson one. I need some quiet time. This is going to be a touchy one. Scrubbing is a good time to go over things."

"Yes, sir."

Jake's eyes crinkled above his mask. "But I'm glad you're here."

"Thank you, sir." Knoxmann rejoined the observers.

It was routine for the chief resident to perform the initial opening. Jake handed Hudley an immaculately whetted, stainless steel scalpel. Hudley began the cut, breaching layers of scalp. A couple of bleeders sprayed down the front of his gown. Bright red blood squirted from the cut tissue edges and streamed from the wound. It trickled into a large black trash bag attached to the sterile drapes beneath the attorney's head. Jake watched what he had come to expect: sloppy work and poor technique.

It had been the same earlier looking at the angiogram. Dr. David Hudley was late.

"Where you been, David?"

"Nobody beeped me. Sorry. So what we got?"

"A couple of berry aneurysms, a giant basilar bifurcation. And an eight millimeter left P-Comm. Any idea which one bled?"

"Guess it could be either one. Does it matter?"

Jake's face colored.

"Look, nobody beeped me, all right?"

"So which one bled?" Jake again pointed to the films.

Jake had kept his anger down. Several years of effort with Hudley had revealed only a marginally dedicated physician. He never had it quite together, academically or technically.

"You know, this should be a damned medical student's case. This guy has no chance at all. And look who it is. Malone, for chrissakes."

Jake had massaged his throbbing temples. "Get him up to ICU. We'll hope for some sign of improvement overnight to his brain function." He turned to leave. "And by the way, I already gave a pretty good dose of steroids. Let's not order any more tonight." With that, Jake had gone to see the family.

Martha slapped the drill into Hudley's hand. Jake mapped the placement of the opening as a quartet of nickel-sized holes were bored through the attorney's calvarium, near the junction of the left forehead and temple. Then Hudley connected the openings with an air-driven craniotome. The sound of the skull being sawed shrieked in the room. Bone dust and tiny droplets of blood spattered the surgeons.

Jake watched as Hudley loosened, pried up, and lifted away a portion of the attorney's skull bone. About the size of a sand dollar. He watched it slip from Hudley's grasp and tumble towards the terrazzo floor. Jake caught it, handed it wordlessly to Martha. Their faces were impassive behind their masks. Martha guided the cumbersome operating microscope into place. Overhead lights were dimmed slightly. Video monitors were illuminated and positioned. With Martha beside him, Jake began the journey into a man's brain.

Malone's wife was in her fifties, trim and robust, blond and expensively dressed. Bethany Malone was used to getting her way.

"Dr. Jason Gibson?"

Jake nodded.

"Doctor, my husband must have the best of everything." Her words were flat, an edict handed down.

"Everything possible will be done for your husband, Mrs. Malone."

"And that includes what?"

"We'll perform a CAT scan of the brain in order to find out what happened. If he's suffered a hemorrhage around the brain surface, like I think he probably has, then we'll do a complete blood vessel study, an angiogram, to find the source of the bleeding." Jake looked into her eyes. "Mrs. Malone, we'll find a way to pull him through."

Some of the tension left her, then arrogance firmed her up. "Please be certain your best is good enough."

A summons to ER Critical Care had taken him away.

◎⊞✠

For two hours Jake worked through less than a one inch gap alongside the attorney's brain. He employed long forceps as he worked through the opening. Occasionally he would ask a nurse to raise or lower his seat. He focused the microscope with a mouth switch, his hands free to work the delicate instruments. Martha was close by.

"I need some temporary clips. I don't think this is the one that bled yesterday. We'll clip it now anyway."

Martha knew that meant temporarily blocking the main artery that supplied nearly half of the blood to the attorney's brain. She placed two gold-embossed clips, one at a time, into Jake's open right hand. He exactly positioned them, one on each end, along the pulsating blood vessel. Martha motioned for the circulating assistant to yank the string on the electric timer mounted on the wall. Jake had thirty minutes before the clamps had to be removed. Otherwise the attorney would suffer a disabling stroke, his language center devastated due to a prolonged absence of oxygenated blood. Jake could feel his heart thumping as he worked. Inside twelve minutes, he had applied a permanent titanium clip around the first aneurysm's neck.

Temporary clamps were released to restore blood flow to the left portion of the cerebrum. Green-gowned figures watched, tense. Jake punctured the wall of the blood-engorged sac with a tiny needle. It immediately collapsed with only a feeble spurt of blood. Tension lessened. Jake yawned nervously. He got up from the commander's seat and stretched his shoulders and neck. His upper back muscles remained tight. He tried to restore circulation into his buttocks and feet. "Okay. Now the bad one."

The second aneurysm was clearly the one that had ruptured and seeped blood. The bleeding point would now be sealed over with only a thin and fragile blood clot. If it were to be disturbed, it would issue a massive and probably fatal hemorrhage.

"Get word to the patient's family. Things proceeding well."

Then it was before him. An ominous pulsating blister.

"Oh, my God." Jake had not anticipated anything this bad. Beads of perspiration popped out on his forehead. He began to work on isolating the inflated sack that was threatening to burst at any moment. The aneurysm was so large and its walls so thin and translucent that streams of heme could be seen flowing inside it.

He was in that other dimension now, where all concentration, skill and confidence, where all his years of repetitive practice and training would come to bear. Just a few fractions of a millimeter either way, and a human being would either live a full life or die. A sudden spurt of blood would signal failure.

Martha motioned for a "Do Not Disturb" sign to be hung on the door. The thermostat in the room was lowered. The observers watched in silence; afraid to cough, sneeze, or move. Only the anesthesiologist was unaffected. He sat and read the newspaper.

The silence was broken by an ugly thud. One of Hudley's operating clogs had fallen from his foot as he shuffled in his seat.

Jake looked to a nurse to wipe his forehead, willing Hudley's bumbling out of his mind.

"Okay" Jake said. "I think we're about ready for a clip."

He swallowed behind his mask while Martha firmly placed a clip into his hand. With an exact snap of the wrist he closed its blades gently around the neck of the aneurysm.

Schwooshshshshsh…

A sound of sucking blood.

Lots of it.

It echoed around the room.

"Shit!"

Gushing blood filled the entire wound opening and began to pour from the head, running off in different directions. It saturated the drapes. It pooled on the floor. Jake's heart pounded mercilessly while his sweaty hands trembled.

"More suction, I need more suction!"

The green gowned figures watched as a man's life slipped away.

Jake positioned a suction device against a cotton swab at the leak point. He tried to suppress the bleeding enough to visualize the size of the break and how best to fix it. Blood spurted, hitting the side of his mask. Martha passed another swab. After a few seconds, he could visualize the site of the break.

"I have a feeling this clip is just a little bit—ah—too short."

Martha was there.

"All right, give me the next longer one."

She placed an empty applicator instrument squarely into his hand. Jake first slowly released and then completely removed the first clip. Bleeding dramatically increased. He lost sight of the aneurysm.

"Blood pressure is falling!" The anesthesiologist stared up from the patient. "Sixty systolic. I'm going to start a unit of blood."

"Hang on. Don't give him any hemoglobin just yet."

Martha plopped a proper sized clip into his open palm.

"Come on, baby." It was a prayer to himself. "Almost—almost—okay. Just a little bit further, come on, come on, come on—good. All right. Yes."

He slowly let close the spring-loaded blades of the clip to re-embrace the neck of the aneurysm. He leaned back, sucking on his mask. "Thank you, Lord!"

Martha provided salt water irrigation to squirt around the origin of the aneurysm. This removed the pasty clotted blood that had encased the area. Carefully Jake inspected the blood-filled balloon. He checked around its base to be certain that none of the important surrounding arteries or nerves had been inadvertently damaged.

"Okay," he said, looking closely again at both sides of the clip, "everything looks good."

Eyes watched him over surgical masks.

"The parent artery is intact. And there's no branches trapped in the clip. We did it."

For the first time in hours Jake looked at the clock.

"All right then. Shall we puncture the aneurysmal sac, or just leave well enough alone?" But everyone knew he was talking only to himself. "No, we've gotta be sure."

Martha was already placing a tiny needle into his hand.

Jake punctured the aneurysm at its dome. It immediately collapsed beneath a gentle leak of its contents.

At once the atmosphere in the room changed from great tension to joviality and anticipation. Like kids after school, the operating team loosened up with talk about spouses, kids, hobbies, movies and vacations. The anesthesiologist told lewd jokes, some about his wife, some about other patients who had gone through. Tension bled away. Jake knew fulfillment and relief.

Jake backed away from his headquarters at the microscope and with a flip of his mitt motioned for Hudley to prepare to take over. To a nurse he said, "Inform the family that everything's gone well. Tell them I'll be out to speak with them very shortly."

Jake stayed around for a few moments monitoring Dr. Hudley, who had begun to stitch the brain-covering layers in preparation for replacing the detached piece of skull bone. He needed to pull away from the operating room environment, but in truth it was difficult for him to leave Hudley alone to close the wound.

"Thanks, Martha. Thanks, everyone. Great job."

Jake saluted as he pushed the operating doors open and disappeared down the hallway. First stop, empty his bladder.

In a quiet doctor's lounge Jake stood next to his open locker for a few minutes. The phone was pressed into his shoulder. He rubbed his eyes and temples while he waited for her to answer. There were droplets of blood on his operating shirt and on the side of his forehead. When she didn't answer, he cleaned up before going to meet the family.

◎▩✠

In the waiting room were Mrs. Malone and her family. His smile uplifted them.

"Everything went great."

Jake was introduced by Mrs. Malone to other members of the family. Then he summarized the operation.

"We were able to clip both aneurysms without a great deal of difficulty. There was a bit of bleeding from the larger one, but I don't think that will cause any great problem. I'm confident Mr. Malone will make a very good recovery."

Jake approached Malone's daughter, Shannon, who was standing noticeably apart from the others. She was wiping at tears. He put his arm around her.

"We clearly have taken a giant step towards his full recovery. He must continue to recover from the initial bleeding, and a number of problems may come up over the next few hours to days. But fortunately, our ability to deal with all of these is now dramatically improved."

Mrs. Malone smiled, claws sheathed. "Thank you, Dr. Gibson. Everyone has been just great—and Dr. Hudley's the best. He assured me that everything would work out okay. I just knew that with him on the case, you'd find a way to pull my husband through."

Jake kept his smile in place. It was quite a feat coming off a difficult operation. What the hell had made Hudley promise such a thing? After a few minutes he excused himself and headed back for the doctor's lounge.

In the O.R. the lights remained bright. They reflected an operation completed, a certain clinical disarray, a presence of blood and used instruments. Martha waited and worried. She took a ragged breath and spoke to one of the circulating nurses.

"Summon Dr. Gibson."

Hudley flashed at her, his eyes angry.

"Dr. Hudley, I'm concerned that something's not right."

"Not right?"

"During the repair of the dural covering over the brain. As the last stitch was being passed—"

"Yes, what?"

"I thought I saw a spurt of bleeding arising from the surface of the brain. Should it be the case—"

"It would be possible in a few hours for a clot to develop. I don't need a lecture from a nurse. Everything is fine. Really, I can handle this."

The anesthesiologist was back on the phone. He nodded assurance to Martha that the patient was fine.

As Hudley began the closure of the scalp layers he kept up a commentary to Martha. She stood her ground, watching his work carefully.

It was the anesthesiologist who ended it. "Look, the guy's vital signs are stable and he's even beginning to wake up. Let's cut this crap."

Two doctors against a head nurse. Martha watched as the bone and scalp flaps were replaced and secured with layers of sutures. Should she have bucked them and insisted on informing Dr. Gibson?

She watched Hudley leave.

She listened as the gas-passer talked more stocks.

She worried.

2

Jake rounded second base. He had laced a blistering line drive between the outfielders. The ball came back to the infield on a wicked bounce. The TV repairman tried to nail the brain surgeon in his headfirst slide.

Perched on third, with hands on his knees, Jake took a few deep breaths. He readjusted his cap. He glanced at his teammates hooting on the bench. He felt good, like playing with his younger brothers and sisters in their large Catholic family. Good times, when you were going to live forever and played your heart out. And he had some of that here. The other players couldn't care less if Jake was a world-class brain surgeon. They were playing ball, and the repairman's nod in his direction had to do with that. On that diamond, Jake was free.

The beeper echoed across the field. Knocking the infield from his cleated shoes, Jake signaled with his cap for Ben on the bench. He watched his best friend locate it within his athletic bag and disarm it.

Who was calling? A critical patient? Possibly Malone? Or some workman's comp refill for backache medication? Or Jeanne, could it be Jeanne?

An aluminum bat striking a softball turned his head. A long fly out to left. He scored and jogged directly to the weathered wooden bench. Wiping his forehead, he dialed the hospital on his cellular.

Each ring tightened him up. Emergency or frivolous? Peace of mind and fear of failure rocked on some inner fulcrum. He paced behind the bench.

Midge picked up the phone.

"Dr. Gibson, I'm concerned about your patient, Mr. Malone. He seems to be less alert and responsive."

"What are his vital signs?" Jake sat on the bench and began to remove his spikes.

"They're fine. But somehow he just doesn't seem right. He's a lot sleepier than when he first arrived from the recovery room. I don't know." She hesitated, tension in her voice.

"What is it, Midge?"

"It's a gut feeling. I've just got this gut feeling that something bad is in the works."

A commotion went up for a home run and Jake covered his ears.

What to do.

A false alarm, with Midge the overzealous observer?

Or—

Midge Stone was in her late twenties, exceptionally attractive. She had shoulder length hair, blond and stunning, against her Scandinavian features. She offered dignity and grace and a very sharp mind. She had worked in the neuro-ICU for some time. Even had a special interest in stroke-afflicted patients. Over the years, Nurse Stone had been propositioned by many of the physicians around the hospital, married and unmarried. Which is why she liked Dr. Jason Gibson. Jake inspired the best in those around him, he was caring and soft spoken. She would kill for his smile, always checking it for something more than friendliness. So far, no luck.

"Okay, Midge. Give him a dose of Mannitol and order a head CT stat!" He raised his voice against ball-game spectators. "Give me ten minutes, maybe less."

Jake made his way up the gravel path past the cemetery and the family plot to the parking lot in his stocking feet. The kid in him looked back just once at the game.

Jake's black jeep seemed less out of place than usual on the doctors' lot. He shoved his cap in his back pocket, dusted off his pants, and ran for a secluded rear door. It offered a seldom used back stairwell that jarred memories. He moved fast by the stairway windows that overlooked the flat roof of the hospital. That's where it happened.

◉❖✠

Mrs. Kathleen Kincaid had been brought to the emergency room following a minor traffic accident. She had sideswiped an oncoming vehicle. She was admitted with only a mild concussion and a few minor scrapes and bruises. But something was peculiar; she laughed about the nearly fatal accident.

Less than an hour after a detailed psychiatric evaluation, she was face down on the bedrock of the cafeteria. She had thrown a chair through a plate glass window on the eight floor and jumped. Jake brushed gravel from her mouth, applied mouth to mouth, but she was gone, pupils empty.

Enter Malone, big time lawyer, fueled by the husband's huge personal injury lawsuit, a big chunk of it aimed at him, the attending neurosurgeon.

◉❖✠

Jake was bounding upstairs, heading for Malone. There had been a 4.19 million dollar settlement. Jake shoved the memory away.

Just inside Malone's room Midge was fidgeting, the chart in hand had updated lab data. Jake pushed by and positioned himself at the patient's side. He pinched Malone and gave a loud command for him to stick out his tongue.

Early in his neurosurgical career, Jake learned the importance of this primitive task. An individual's ability to protrude and deflect the tongue upon command depended on proper functioning of diverse parts of the brain. All the way from the lower parts of the conscious-regulating brainstem to the highest levels of the thought-commanding cerebral cortex. For years, he had taught his residents proper tongue agility as a quick and easy bedside test of intact brain function.

Malone made only a feeble attempt to open his mouth as though he wanted to speak. But he was unable to protrude his tongue.

"His wife still around, Midge?"

"I don't believe so."

"All right. See if you can find her for me. I'm gonna run down to x-ray to check out the CT scan." With a check of lab data and vital sign information presented to him by Midge, he snapped the chart closed and returned it to the tabletop rack. Then he was moving fast for the x-ray suite.

The radiologist slapped the films onto a row of view boxes. "He's got a huge parietal lobe hematoma. There's a lot of shift."

Jake stared. "I don't understand. Where did this come from? I don't see any way a blood clot like this could've resulted from the operation."

"Then it doesn't make any sense."

"No, it doesn't." Jake dialed Martha's number. She picked up immediately. "We've got a big problem with the patient from today. I don't know how or why, but he's developed a monstrous intracerebral clot, parietal lobe even. I just can't figure what—"

"Oh, God, Dr. Gibson. I knew it! I should have informed you. I'm so desperately sorry. I know what happened. Dr. Hudley caught a stitch on the cortex when he was closing the dura. It caused a spurt of bleeding."

"Of course, Dr. Hudley."

"He insisted everything was okay, he overruled my calling you."

"Good God."

"It's totally my fault, Doctor. I should have brought it to your attention."

"Okay, now we know what we're dealing with."

"I don't know what to say, Doctor."

He caught her tension and anguish. "It's not your fault, I should have stayed and supervised the whole thing."

"I'm sorry, Doctor, I wish—"

"Look, we need to reoperate on him right away. I could sure use your help. Can you make it in?"

"I'll be right there."

Martha untied her apron and dabbed her eyes with it. She left the dishes and hastily combed her hair and brushed her teeth. In his ornate study, her husband was surveying the business section of the evening news. Howard, soured on her working at all, sat in his favorite chair which backed up on the foyer. He puffed and fingered an imported cigar. Martha rushed past his shadow on her way out the door. Smoke roiled in her wake.

"Operator, get me Dr. Hudley, stat!"

If anyone was to blame it was himself for tolerating Hudley's ineptness. And it had to be Malone. Tension cranked up as he waited. The phone got sweaty in his grip.

"Dr. Gibson, I can't seem to locate Dr. Hudley anywhere. I've tried his beeper and there's no answer up in the call room."

Jake swallowed his anger, carefully modulating his speech. "Okay. Keep trying."

That was when he saw Bethany Malone rushing along the hallway in his direction. It was obvious she knew something was wrong. He stepped towards her. "Mrs. Malone, your husband has regressed over the last hour or so. A blood clot is collecting inside his brain."

"Dr. Gibson, I don't understand." Hard eyes held his.

"We need to operate immediately."

She took in his softball togs, like they were a personal insult. Jake folded his arms across his t-shirt.

Her eyes never wavered. "My husband's going to die, isn't he?"

"We must—"

"You're going to lose him, aren't you?"

"Mrs. Malone—"

"God, why can't you guys just say it like it is!"

Jake tried again. "We don't know exactly what to expect from this clot. Certainly, after I take a look and get it out—"

"Oh, no you don't."

What?"

"I want a second opinion." The claws were out now.

"Mrs. Malone, every moment counts, we have a serious problem which needs to be dealt with immediately—"

"And I say I want a second opinion, Dr. Gibson. We need to wait."

"Mrs. Malone, please listen to me. This blood clot will continue to grow and pressure the brain around it. Your husband can slip into a coma at any time. It would be wise to remove the clot before that happens—"

She got close to him, her stare glacial. "A second opinion. Do you understand?"

His beeper went off. Jake retreated.

At the doctors' locker room he met up with Martha, who was just arriving.

"Go ahead and get everything ready." He brushed past.

She hesitated in the doorway watching him, giving him a chance to talk.

"Can you believe it? We have to wait for a second opinion." He opened his locker and began undressing.

"Whoever they get will agree."

"But too late, way too late. We don't have time for this. This whole thing really…"

Jake continued to ventilate as Martha looked on.

"I would have bet on boxers."

Jake looked down at his colored briefs.

"Dr. Gibson, call Neuro-ICU. Stat!"

Jake snatched a phone and dialed.

Martha watched, ready.

"Dr. Gibson, come quick." Alarm spiraled down the wire. "He's just dilated his pupil and his blood pressure's falling."

"Shit!"

With a worst case scenario unfolding, Jake slammed down the phone and hurried past Martha and down the corridor. He adjusted his pants and white operating room clogs as he went.

Martha rushed away to change her own clothes and prepare the O.R.

◎※✠

Back in the ICU, Jake's stomach knotted at how unfavorable the situation had become. Malone had slipped into a deep coma and was on the verge of herniation. Which meant irreversible pressure being exerted on the deeper parts of the brain. Areas that control breathing and heart rate. Within minutes intracranial strain would very likely be fatal.

"Midge, tell the O.R. we're coming down at once."

"But, Doctor, we have no documentation from his wife. The chart—"

"I'll take care of it." His eyes went into her. "Do it, Midge. Just start moving him to the O.R." He headed out of the unit. "I'll speak with the wife right now."

He found her in a far corner of the waiting room sipping hot coffee and chain smoking. She was talking with Dr. Hudley.

"David, I've been looking for you everywhere."

Hudley got up and looked to Mrs. Malone.

"Mrs. Malone," Jake said, "things are deteriorating very rapidly. Your husband has slipped into a coma. We must get him back to surgery right away."

Hudley moved toward the door and left without a word.

Jake watched him leave. He had to let him go. Mrs. Malone was the challenge.

She stubbed out a cigarette, leaving its lipsticked butt in a full ashtray. "I will not grant you my consent. I want that second opinion." She looked to the empty doorway. "Dr. Hudley agrees."

Jake kept it all in, girding up for a balanced delivery of his words. "Mrs. Malone. Any chance at waiting is over. We must perform surgery now to save his life."

"In your opinion, doctor."

Dear God in heaven.

Jake turned on his heel after Hudley and to get to the operating room. He went through the doors in a rush. Malone had just arrived.

"Okay, everybody. Let's get going. Now!"

It was not his regular team. It was no ballet. But he had Martha, and the rest were trying.

Martha was opening sterile instrument packs even as she directed the part-time evening O.R. crew to find needed equipment.

Someone from the prep team was removing Malone's head dressing and reprepping the freshly stitched wound with an antiseptic.

A befuddled on-call anesthetist was inserting an endo-tube into Malone's airway. With her other hand she administered drugs into an I.V.

All the while a late-shift orderly and Frank, the neurosurgical P.A., were securing Malone onto the operating table with several broad leather straps.

Someone got the bulky ICU bed from the room.

Beat…

Beat…

Beat…

Jake ran for the scrub sink and cleansed his hands, all the while pacing. Frothy iodinized water spewing down his O.R. shirt and pants.

Back at the table he found Martha had already assumed her usual tabletop position.

The phone rang.

"If that's Hudley tell him to get his butt down here." Jake was putting on his gloves.

The anesthetist waved the phone. "It's Mr. Brickle, the hospital administrator."

Jake continued to drape the sterile field.

"He wants you to stop what you're doing immediately."

"Tell him I'm busy." Jake kept her at his back. "Martha, give me the knife. Let's get going here."

"No, Dr. Gibson. He wants to talk to you. Right now." The anesthetist dangled the phone over the sterile field.

"Son of a bitch!" Jake was sterile, but he angrily grabbed the phone.

"Listen, Chad, this guy is dying. I need to operate on him now, right now. What the hell do you want?"

Chad Brickle, University Hospital administrator and chief spokesperson, was quick and slick. "I just received a Stat call from Malone's daughter, Shannon Malone? I believe you were introduced to her. You are aware she's an attorney in her father's firm? She tells me the family has refused to grant permission for this operation."

"Chad, unless you get off this phone right now, this patient is going to die." Jake's words were spoken quietly. The chill of them froze the surgical team.

"Understand this, Jason. I'm on your side. But I don't think you understand what you're getting yourself into with this particular patient."

"Right now, my only concern is to keep him alive."

"Then consider yourself warned—"

"You're off the hook, Chad. Now let me work."

The room was ghoulishly silent. The operating team members glanced around nervously. Except Jake. The anesthetist glared at him for a moment, before settling back into her chair. Better document everything.

When he held out his right hand to Martha, the knife was placed firmly into his grasp.

Jake started to cut.

3

I have had three personal ideals. One, to do the day's work well ...The second ideal has been to act the golden rule...towards my professional brethren and towards the patients committed to my care. And the third has been to cultivate such a measure of equanimity as would enable me to bear success with humility, the affection of my friends without pride, and to be ready when the day of sorrow and grief came, to meet it with the courage befitting a man...and if the fight is for principle and justice, even when failure seems certain, where many have failed before, cling to your ideal...

William Osler (1849–1919)

Jake eased himself down into the hot tub. Water and steam bathed him, smoothing out knotted muscles, drawing tension from deep within. As steam swirled he draped a face cloth over his face and shut out the world. No light. Just swirling water caressing him, slowly loosening him up. It took longer for his brain to settle, to calm beneath his skull. Images jangled. Sliding for third, Ben watching him as the cellular beeped across triumph and innocence. Midge with her gut feeling, Martha distraught over not reporting on her fears about Hudley's stitching. Then the opposing team… Jake watched them cartwheel behind his eyes, the face cloth soothing but not enough. Mrs. Malone, claws out, Chad Brickle doing his verbal dance. *You're off the hook, Chad, now let me work…*

Jesus.

Water swirled and caressed, easing it all from him, calming the jangle. Salig burst through the calm as he had burst into the surgery. *Well, Dr. Gibson, what have we gotten ourselves into today?* Jake twisted against the water, rinsing the face cloth, slapping it back over his face. Jeanne. Think of Jeanne…

And she was there, her deep blue eyes finding his soul, hands soothing in their touch, brown hair against his cheek, a hint of her perfume. The face cloth grew heavy and cloying and he dragged it from his face. Steam coiled and whorled before him. He had phoned her from the doctor's lounge, wanting her voice, a soothing affirmation borne on her words, like oil on shattered nerve ends. But she hadn't answered. So he had hung there in the lounge, blood spattered, with his empty core. But it was all pretty much academic anyway. Jeanne was Ben's wife, her belly contoured over their baby growing inside her.

The pounding on his front door jarred him. He sat quite still in his ethereal world, Jeanne vanishing on fragrance. Then he heaved himself up, pulled on his crumpled scrub pants which he had worn home, too tired to change, and grabbed a towel. It was an uncomfortable walk, from the deck through the townhouse, wet and chilly. And who the hell was it anyway…

Martha was standing there, holding newspapers that had piled up at his door.

He was holding his towel, the outside chill welting him up in goose bumps. "Martha?"

"I'm sorry to bother you, Jake." Her eyes were focused on his. "May I come in?"

Jake stepped back. Not in all the years of working together had he encountered Martha outside the hospital. Not once. And she had never called him Jake. He watched her. Her face seemed naked without a surgical mask. Free of hospital surroundings she looked vulnerable. He had never seen her like this, never known her like this.

She managed a smile. "I guess I caught you at a bad time."

"A good time really. I was in the whirlpool easing out all the kinks."

"There were plenty of those today."

Shivering, he ushered her in. "Mind if I jump back in?"

"No, not at all. You wouldn't have a spare swimsuit or something would you?"

Jake grinned, one hand clutching his towel. "Well, nothing with a top." He watched her, quizzical, wondering what was going on.

"Then I'll dangle my feet. How about that?"

"Sounds good."

"Got any cold beer?"

"Sure."

"Why don't I get us a couple while you put on swim trunks or something."

"Okay." Jake found his trunks, a new pair with the tags still on. His strenuous heart-sucking, brain-bending day had taken a new turn. Curiouser and curiouser. Back at the tub he found Martha dangling her feet, chilled beer in hand. Wordlessly she passed him his beer. He popped the can open and settled back into the hot, therapeutic, swirling waters. After a moment, he decided he'd better get back the initiative.

"What's going on, Martha?"

She met him head on. "A number of things."

"Like what?"

She sipped her beer. "God that's good."

"Like what?"

"Who was that guy who barged in tonight?"

Jake sat up.

"Everett Salig."

"You handled him well." She mimicked him. "Meet the legendary Dr. Everett Salig, self-anointed world expert!"

"I sounded like that?"

"Oh, yeah. Lots of anger. Bitterness, maybe. But you were good. Didn't miss a beat getting that clot out. Smooth. Salig scuttled out quick."

Jake said nothing. He remembered Midge waking him not once but twice beside his patient's bed. Good things had gone good. But he shouldn't have fallen asleep in that chair.

"Why are you on the outs with him?"

Jake shifted to face her. "I'd rather know why you're here, Martha."

"Come on, what's with Salig?"

He swirled an arm across the water, steam rising, and retrieved his beer. "What's with Salig?" He took a swig and watched her. "In a nutshell, here it is. I was doing a fellowship with Professor M. Yul Kordesch, a brilliant doctor. My mentor. Even back then, the best in the world. The guy was amazing. The well-to-do from all corners of the globe sought him out to operate on them, or members of their family." He finished the last of his beer. "Anyway, through Kordesch I got this chance to work with Salig on a research project on brain tumors. I did the grunt work. Took almost a year gathering, collating, researching. When it was done, I passed it on to Professor Kordesch for review. In fact, I went over it with him just before I left Switzerland. He made the decision to leave Salig's name off. Seemed like the proper thing to do. The jerk hadn't contributed a damned thing." The empty beer can crunched in his hand.

"A month later, Kordesch was dead. The entire draft, pictures and all, disappeared."

"And?"

"Several months later, my work came out under Everett Salig's name. He took credit, got the whole ball of wax."

"Oh, my God. But surely you contested it, talked with the publisher—"

"Oh, sure. I got quite a scolding for trying to take credit for a brilliant man's work."

Martha sipped her beer. "So what was it called, the book I mean?"

"The Salig International Classification of Brain Tumors."

Martha's face went white. "Dear God, that was you?"

"That was me."

"That was published over ten years ago."

"Yes."

"And you've carried this for ten years."

"Oh, yeah." Jake's smile was bitter.

"And then the sonofabitch breaks in on your surgery tonight."

"He published two other landmark texts after that. Oddly, the professors associated with both of them also died suddenly. I guess if I were paranoid I could build things on that."

"I'm sorry, Jake. Really sorry."

"Hey, nurse, how bout another brew?" He lifted up. She blocked him.

"Stay where you are, doctor. I know where the icebox is."

Jake leaned back and closed his eyes. The pulsating jets. Those tense muscles. Jeanne was there, just for a moment, then she was gone.

Martha returned. She knelt behind, and began to massage his neck.

"You're hired. Charge by the hour?"

She pushed deeper.

Jake opened his eyes. "Why you here, Martha?"

"Well, I could say it's because I worried about you, the risk you took with the surgery. But that's only part of it. And I could say it was me fumbling the ball, not telling you about Hudley's botched closing."

Jake elbowed himself up. "But?"

"But . . . I guess I can't hold it in any more."

Jake waited.

"I—I care about you, Jake."

"Martha—"

"I've cared about you for a very long time. Tonight is the end of a bad day when I was responsible for putting a patient at risk. And my life with Howard is sterile and empty, and hey, now the beer…" She let loose her hands to graze his back. "You are the kindest, most considerate man I've ever met. What you did earlier tonight showed unbelievable courage. You know you'll be hauled on the carpet tomorrow. Malone's wife, Chad Brickle, God knows who else." She found his shoulders. "I just want you to know how strongly I feel about you."

Jake lay back, Martha's fingers caressing beneath swirling waters. Jeanne was there, of course, behind his eyes, some love beyond reach, like trying to touch an exquisite porcelain doll through surgical gloves. Then Martha was close, so close, and he took her in.

4

It was still his room. The pastel walls, the thick carpet, the generic furniture and piles of medical journals sliding sideways under their own scholarly weight. Bedside reading for lonely nights. But now, the room held memory of another's presence. He stared across at the dented pillow next to his. Martha's lingering fragrance mixed with the musk of her, the warmth and enfolding flesh of her, the breath of her.

Jake lay still. He took it all in. Jeanne wove into his thoughts of Martha, and he tried to sort out his feelings. It was not easy. His life had been of parallel worlds. Worlds in different orbits. Medicine here, a dominating presence tapping off all energy and thought; and Jeanne over there, a forbidden avenue to whom he could turn for solace. Words and insight and kindness, these at least were available to him. But Martha. She had come into his life cradling old newspapers. The nurse personified, passion and candor setting the stage. God, it had been so long, so very long. Self denial for medicine had exacted a terrible price.

But there was a patient to take care of right now. Jake threw back the bed sheet and flung himself into his day.

He put his car into its familiar curve into the hospital parking lot, tires grinding over patches of gravel, then he hit the brakes. A yellow Corvette resembling Hudley's was in his spot. His Firestones squealed. Jake found an unassigned slot and parked. It was going to be a tough day and an irritating one. Like his phone call to the ICU this morning over his bagel and cream cheese. *There's no one available to talk to you right now, Dr. Gibson.* He shrugged it away along with the lax security at the parking lot and went to see his patient, Mitch Malone, litigious lawyer extraordinaire. Embedded in Jake's stride was the postoperative anxiety he always experienced. Carefully he overlaid it, sealing it away.

The ICU was quiet under the subdued hum of equipment and the beep of monitors. Nurses moved around on practical shoes designed for long shifts. At Malone's room he hesitated briefly then went in.

"Good morning, Mitch."

The lawyer was sitting up in bed having breakfast. His head was wrapped , left eye swollen nearly shut.

"Good morning. You the doctor?"

"That's right." Jake watched him sip his apple juice, the pale eyes not leaving his face. "You know what's happened to you?"

"Some of it. Not much. Nobody talks around here."

"You were in court. You suffered a burst aneurysm. Yesterday morning we operated to fix a couple of dangerous weak spots, one of which had bled. Unfortunately, a few hours after surgery, you developed a serious complication, a blood clot."

"Those are bad."

"Right. We took care of it last night. Looking at you this morning it looks like you came through it fine."

"So, you're a brain surgeon?"

Jake nodded. His life frisked by Malone's look. *The sonofabitch doesn't even know who I am.* It ran like a ticker tape behind Jake's eyes, a familiar and gut wrenching playing out, his first brush with the legal system. Naive and blind trust in Truth. They sliced him up good. Malone's penthouse office, a court reporter, a gathering of lawyers in good suits, a scattering of yellow legal pads. Even the hospital's attorney had dodged around truth for accommodation. And Jake was under the microscope: *Any trouble with drugs or alcohol, Dr. Gibson?*

Jake talked straight, head down against it all, cleaving to the truth. Not just for himself, but for the hospital staff, the psychiatrist and nursing staff defendants, even the hospital itself. Absolute truth to shed light on how Mrs. Kincaid had ended up face down and dead on the cafeteria roof. 4.19 million cut from the hospital and Jake. And the sonofabitch didn't even remember.

"Wait a minute. It's coming back." Malone fingered his head dressing. "A good sign, I guess."

"Coming back?"

"We met before. The Kincaid case."

Jake watched him.

"You're Jason Gibson."

"Yes."

"I'll be damned. You must have done a good job on me, I don't have much pain. In fact, I feel pretty damned good."

"Good."

"So what now?" Malone pushed up in bed.

"Now? Well, you need several weeks of rest and recuperation. You've been through two serious operations. Fact is, you almost died last night."

"Bullshit. I'm up and out of here." Malone pulled irritably at the IV stuck in his arm. "I've got to get back to my court case—"

Jake picked up his bedside chart and studied the stats and graphs. "Has Mrs. Malone been by this morning?"

Malone suddenly got interested in his liquid breakfast. He didn't look up as Jake left.

At the nurses' station Jake added a progress note to Malone's chart and gave a few orders. It hit him then. Sidelong glances and whispering. The atmosphere was wrong. He looked at his watch. Almost 7:30. Time to put in a call to Martha in the OR, see how she is. And get ready for the weekly M+M conference. Last night's surgery decision was sure to come up.

"I'm sorry, Dr. Gibson, Martha called in sick. She won't be coming in today."

He was stunned. Martha was *never* sick. For a moment a fresh and raw private life entered his disciplined hospital life. He retreated to his office. There he sat quietly. He listened to his inscribed pewter clock tick, a gift from last year's graduating residents, pushing Martha from him. Time for questions later about whether she was upset with him, genuinely sick, or anything else. Stay focused. The M+M would commence upstairs in a few minutes. The Malone case. And he could corner Hudley.

◎⊠✠

The conference room was crammed with surgical house staff coming off morning rounds. Students also were there, primed to talk about what they had seen on the wards, to be critiqued on clinical observations, to have their developing instincts prodded for progress. To see also how they handle pressure. Jake was given the cold eye he had experienced at the nurses' station and during his walk down the hallways. Furtively he checked his zipper.

Jake took his customary seat in the first row center. Dr. Wilson entered then, accompanied by Dr. Hudley. Jake got up, but Chairman Wilson stepped in.

"Jason, could I speak to you for a moment—in private?"

In the hallway Wilson's voice was low and venomous. "Jason, what you did last night was irresponsible and unconscionable. What in the hell were you thinking?"

Jake watched the tightly drawn face, his own words bottled up in surprise. Of all people, Wilson's lashing out at him was unexpected. Concern yes, disagreement, yes. But this?

"You nearly cost that man his life, and you really pissed off the hospital administrator."

"Chad's an opportunist." Jake said bluntly.

"Chad Brickle was doing his job. You should know he wants me to immediately suspend your privileges."

"Jesus Christ—"

"And failing that, he wants a letter of resignation on his desk."

Jake's anger coiled like a snake. But he kept it at bay.

"How could you get the department involved in this thing—"

"Vince, the patient is doing fine. And I did what I had to under the circumstances. And another thing—how come no one has approached me about the circumstances of this case? The nursing staff appear to know, residents are giving me the fish eye—they know."

Dr. Vincent Wilson was a gut fighter used to getting his way. "Dr. Hudley has filled me in. There's nothing more to discuss, especially here and now."

Jake fought off the wicked stares of those entering the conference room.

"The hospital executive committee is investigating this matter and will make its recommendations. Until then, why don't you take some time off?" Wilson moved towards the conference room.

"Time off?" Jake's tone was bitter.

"You're leaving for Washington this afternoon, aren't you? Well, why not lay low next week? Stay in D.C., go sit on a beach somewhere."

"Sit on a beach."

"God knows you need a vacation."

"Sit on a beach." Jake said again, staring into Wilson's bifocals.

The chairman stared back, then abruptly turned and went back into the packed conference room.

Sit on a fucking beach. Jesus Christ.
Jake went directly to Chairman Wilson's office and waited.

It did not go well. Vincent R. Wilson had been Chairman of Neurosurgery at the University Hospital for over 25 years. Only person around who had his initials on his hubcaps, V.W. had trained Jake. The sole resident under his tutelage on the tenure track. Jake was the heir apparent. He laid it out for his department chairman. He talked at length about Hudley, his borderline professional skill, the caught stitch and inevitable bleeding, the attempt to get a second opinion because of Mrs. Malone's insistence. Jake outlined how it came down to saving a life.

There was some reaching out on Vince's part, Jake could see it. But there was something else going on, a hidden agenda, the maneuvering.

"You know, Dr. Hudley warned me that you would try and find a way to blame it all on him."

Jake pushed back in his seat, anger barely controlled.

"Vince, that's bull. You know that—"

The knock on the door was ugly, not to be denied. The door swung open before Jake could reach for it. Martha's husband, Howard Crane, lunged in. He was off balance at seeing Jake. He stood there, handsome and tailored in his business suit. The congested blood in his face detracted. He caught his balance and addressed Wilson.

"Dr. Wilson, there is something I want you to know." His eyes found Jake. "About a member of your department."

Jake stood up. "Mr. Crane—"

"Shut up, you lousy son of a bitch! Just shut your damn mouth!"

Chairman Wilson stood up.

"Dr. Wilson, my wife got home at 6 a.m. this morning after spending the night with this asshole." Howard Crane had control now. "She's decided to leave me. She says she wants a divorce."

Jake hung there, watching his private and professional worlds collide. Then he did the only thing he could. He left. Back in his office he slumped in his chair. He thought back over his career, more accurately, his passion to serve, to use his skills for mankind. That was not too high sounding a phrase for what he did. The years of study, the dedication, the never wavering commitment to his fellow man, money always second in a money first world. The pewter clock ticked away his life. Around him diplomas and awards caught the light. *Physician-Educator of the Decade* from the AMA; the *Most Acclaimed Surgical Disciplinarian in the Country*, that one from the American College of Surgeons; and the International Congress of Neurosurgeons award, *Premier Neurological Surgeon—Under 40—in the World*.

And family pictures, well framed and permanent. Smiling, kindly faces of support within the closed-in walls of his office. He smiled back. Maybe he should have been a blue collar guy, like Henry Hofmeister, security guard. Salt of the earth, Henry Hofmeister, loving granddad, toucher of lives. Jake reached for the letter on his desk. An elegant invitation imprinted with the presidential seal.

Dear Dr. Gibson,

As a member of the President's Select Commission on the State of American medicine, you are to be commended for meritorious service to the people of the United States. It is with great anticipation that I inform you of the commission's presentation date before a Joint Session of Congress.

It is my honor to personally welcome you and your spouse (guest) to the White House for a special recognition dinner to be held the evening prior.

Richard Mauser

President of the United States

The phone rang.

"Dr. Gibson, this is Martha."

Relief flooded through him. "Martha, are you all right? Where are you? I wanted to—"

"Jake, I can't talk, not right now anyway. I just wanted to let you know I'm going back home for a while. I just wanted to say goodbye. And thanks."

"Martha—" But she hung up.

He tried to find Hudley. He prowled the phone lines for him, but he wasn't around. Slimy bastard. He dialed Jeanne's number. She answered, her voice dancing brightly down the wires.

"Hello."

Jake shoved aside the President's letter. "Hey, lady. How are ya?"

"Hiii! Jake!"

Jake settled back into his padded chair. "How ya feelin today?"

"I'm okay. Yesterday was a pretty good day."

"Yeah, you sound better than you did the last time we talked. Sorry I didn't get to talk to you yesterday. What did the ultrasound show?"

"They think it's a girl. But I don't know. This one sure feels a lot different than the first."

"Well, I wouldn't put any of those boy names on hold just yet."

"It really doesn't matter. As long as it's healthy."

"Yeah, I suppose so."

"Are you okay? What's wrong?"

"Nothing, I'm fine."

"Jake?"

"I'm okay."

"Jake, what's wrong?"

"Should've realized."

"We know each other too well. Out with it!"

"I'm okay, I just had a pretty tough day yesterday."

"All your days are tough. You thrive on it. Let's have it, Jake."

"Okay, yesterday I operated on a patient. A man with a ruptured aneurysm. He developed a complication. And I had to operate on him again last night."

"Ben said you got called away from the softball game. Everything ok?"

"He's doing fine."

"Why don't I believe you?"

"No, he really is recovering okay. Actually, I think he came through the whole thing a lot better than I did."

"What do you mean?"

"He was dying and—well, I went ahead with the surgery. Without the family's permission."

"You did what you had to do, right?"

"Yes. Unfortunately, a few others don't quite see it that way."

"Why? What are they saying?"

"Everybody's maneuvering. There's probably gonna be an inquiry. I wouldn't be surprised if I was reprimanded."

"That's crazy! You're the best surgeon down there."

"Thanks, but—"

"No, don't thank me. I'm sure they'll figure the whole thing out. And if they don't, I'll come down there and knock a few of them over the head."

Jake grinned. "Now that I'd like to see."

"Hey, when are you leaving for Washington?"

My plane takes off in a couple hours." He looked at his watch. "I'm just getting ready to leave here to drop by my place. I have an errand to do on the way to the airport."

"I'm gonna miss you while you're gone."

"I'll miss you, too."

"Please be careful."

"Tell that to the airline pilots and taxi cab drivers." Jake was breathing easier. That honeyed chuckle from his dreams.

"Well, Washington, D.C. is a pretty dangerous place."

"I know."

"I don't want to lose my best friend."

Silence. There were so many ways to go. He could give her the loving feelings in simple detached words and she would know, she would draw to her their true meaning. You've been in my life forever, Jeanne; you occupy my thoughts in sterile bedrooms; you're there when I cave in in sweaty greens and drink stale coffee; you're just beyond the windshield on sunny days and in the dark and wet of rain...

"Jake?"

"Yes, I'll take care."

The phone droned its emptiness in his ear. Getting Martha's address from a secretary, Jake left by a side door.

Back in the hospital parking lot, the yellow Corvette was gone from his parking slot. Now there was a silver Rolls Royce.

A fully outfitted maid greeted him at the massive entrance and directed him into the foyer. He watched her walk away on quiet step, moving in a world far removed from doctors and nurses and their tread. Steps for all occasions. He looked around, and for the first time realized just how successful and powerful Martha's husband was. Howard had gotten himself a mansion: marble floors, fine woods, antiques. How odd that Martha could come out of this each day and plunge herself into the stress and challenge of an O.R. This was another facet to Martha beyond the nurse persona.

Martha appeared at the top of the stairs. She wore a casual loose fitting silken jumpsuit. She stood for a moment, caught in chandelier light, a creature withdrawn under silk, her eyes puffed and red.

"You shouldn't have come here."

"We have to talk, Martha."

When she came to him she took his arm and guided him into her husband's study. A smell of tobacco hung in the air.

"I have something I need to say to you, Martha. What happened last night was my responsibility. I know it's caused irreparable damage. I'm so very sorry—"

She still held his arm, and now she squeezed it until he stopped talking. "Look, Jake. There's nothing to be sorry for. I came to you, I knew what I was doing. It was a night I'll treasure always."

Jake stared at Howard's chair, taking in its heavy leather and bulk. Everything else in the room imploded around it.

"Martha, I don't want to come between you and—"

"You're not." She released her grasp. "I was leaving Howard long before last night." She pushed the words out. "I'm going home. Back to Mascoutah. To my parents' place. I need to be away for a while." She looked away. "Once I'm gone, I'm sure things will settle down for you. And you'll be able to get your life back to normal."

"I doubt it. I've been suspended."

Martha's eyes came back. "Over what happened last night? I thought Malone was doing fine."

"He is."

"Then I'm confused. What's with the suspension?"

"Our friend Dr. Hudley gave Wilson and others an earful. Something's going on, Martha, behind the scenes I mean."

"Wouldn't be the first time." Martha's voice was sour. "Look, you don't have anything to worry about." She took his hand. "You're one of the finest neurosurgeons in the world. I'm sure everything will work out in the end."

"I don't want you to leave."

"I know. But I have to."

"But why? You say leaving Howard has been a long time coming—"

Her hand came up and touched his face. "Dear Jake. You don't see it, do you? Master of medicine, prince of control, gifted beyond belief—you don't see it."

Jake watched her eyes.

"I'm in love with you, Jake. Have been for a very long time."

"Oh God, Martha."

"Last night was what I wanted. Something to take with me. I'll remember it always." She pinched him. "You in a swimsuit."

Jake managed a grin. "Different from greens."

"Much."

"You're a helluva nurse, Martha. How will I replace you?"

"I want to be more than that, Jake."

"You are. You know you are."

She pushed back on a rustle of silk. "Look, I'd better keep packing things, get out of here."

Jake took in her words.

She forced a smile. "I'll be okay, Jake."

"I know." He turned to leave.

"Thanks for coming, even though you shouldn't have. I said too much."

"No you didn't, Martha."

He retraced his steps to the foyer. The big front door swung closed behind him.

He stood there, his feet anchored around unsaid things, around unfed emotions, around disjointed words with brittle edges. Medicine no longer a refuge for rousing passion. He banged on the door.

When it opened he brushed by her, then gathered her in his arms.

"I didn't even kiss you."

"Jake."

He swept her up and kissed her, last night catching up with them on some lost echo.

"Jake, I'm not asking for anything—"

"Finish packing. There's a change in plans."

"Jake!"

"How would you like to meet the President of the United States?"

5

I have weighed in a nice and scrupulous balance whether it be better to serve men or to be praised by them, and I'd prefer the former.

Thomas Sydenham (1624–89)

The White House offered its elegance and magic from the moment they drove up. The famous facade and portal and, inside, the sudden restrained quiet. History lived here, embedded in the walls, in the sweep of curtain and stately oils and busts of famous men. Chandeliers, a cushioning of steps on carpet. Neither Jake nor Martha spoke. They followed appointed staff who moved past the West Wing with ease. She clung to his arm. They saw the Secret Servicemen, elegant in their tuxedos, but apart, living in a world of suspicion and threat, while Jake and Martha lost themselves in the sumptuous world of high social ceremony.

The formal dining room was packed. Two dozen of the country's top doctors and their guests.

He accepted champagne from a passing waiter.

"Excited?"

"Are you kidding? I'm supposed to be on a plane home."

"I'm glad you're with me."

"It's overwhelming, Jake."

Jake squeezed her hand.

They were shown to their seats. Around them wait staff moved; above them chandeliers glistened with soft light. On their table gleamed silverware and crystal and china. Napkins were enfolded in gleaming rings.

Jake looked around. There was hubbub here. Surgeons, many world famous, settled in their chairs. A chink of a water glass, a resonant voice used to authority lifting on the air. He glanced at Martha and took her hand under the table. "I'm a little nervous about this."

"Why?"

"My speech tomorrow. It'll ruffle a few feathers."

"You're on a Select Commission, Jake. You're not alone in your thinking on modern medicine."

"I know, but—"

When the President and First Lady entered the dining hall and moved to the head table the impact was immediate. Everyone stood on command. All thoughts of newspaper bickering, disagreements, petty squabbling amongst politicians and the press fell away. Here was raw power. President Richard Mauser smiled and nodded, a focal vortex in which he was obviously quite comfortable. When everyone was settled he spoke from the podium. His distinctive voice carried on its regional accent.

"Ladies and gentlemen. It is my special privilege this evening to welcome you to the White House. It is certainly an honor for me to be in the presence of what may well be the finest group of doctors ever assembled. Your accomplishments occupy volumes. Let me personally express to each of you, my deepest appreciation for your willingness to take the time to assure a healthy future for the medical profession in the United States."

All eyes remained fixed on the most powerful man on earth.

"I know your consensual report is based on many hours of meetings. Let me assure you all that your ideas will go a long way towards assisting this administration develop an innovative reformation plan for the healthcare profession. After reviewing your list of key recommendations, I was impressed by your willingness to support, on behalf of your profession, all of the proposals made by this administration. Please accept my heartfelt thanks for all of your efforts."

Jake again found Martha's hand. Even while listening to the President he felt her comfortable presence beside him, the warmth of her. When he glanced at her he found her smiling at him.

"Over the next few months I look forward to the opportunity to meet with many of our era's healthcare leaders. Including, I hope, most of you present this evening. I especially look forward to your presentations tomorrow morning before the special congressional committee."

There was polite applause. Jake made a crease in the tablecloth with his thumbnail.

"What are you thinking?" Martha whispered.

"About you, dedicated professionals like you, who are not getting acknowledged tonight."

"We're used to it."

"Well, I don't like it."

"It's enough for me that you recognize us, Jake."

"Ladies and gentlemen," the President continued. "I know of no generation of American physicians who have contributed more to medical science than yours. To recognize dedication of this degree, I recently sent Congress a bill to establish a special annual award, complete with stipend, for excellence in health professions technology. Perhaps our first recipient is present with us this evening."

Jake winced at Martha. He knew she would have the same thought: such an award would bring the weasels out of the woodwork at the NIH, all knocking themselves out to be first in line for that Presidential Medallion. Salig stealing his research on tumors and publishing it as his own would be child's play compared to the scramble for the medal.

When the President finished his opening remarks Jake rose with the others. He looked at Martha. "I'm going to try and have a quick word with him."

"What—now?"

"Others are. Just a quick word."

"Hope he doesn't catch your Air Jordans." Martha grinned at his shoes.

"Be right back."

Jake stepped to the podium. He waited for a famous heart surgeon to finish his comments, then he slipped in and faced President Mauser.

The President's distinctive smile softened the impact.

"Mr. President, as a member of your select commission, I am grateful for your sustained support for change in the health professions."

The President's dark eyes drove into him and found his guest badge. "Well, thank you Dr. Gibson. And I for one am glad to have all you fine physicians on the commission." The eyes carried a humor. "How did my little speech go?"

"Your speech?" Jake was momentarily off balance. "Why, fine, Mr. President."

"Hit the high spots, did I?"

"Yes, sir."

"Good." The dark eyes lost some of their humor as he looked around. "You must forgive me, Dr. Gibson…"

"Oh, of course, Mr. President." Jake stepped back as other tuxedoed bodies pressed forward.

Martha's eyes never left him.

"I thought I was going to meet him." Martha poked his leg under the table.

"Wrong time. Notice how only docs went up to him?"

"I did."

"After dinner. There'll be a better chance."

"It's okay, Jake. Just getting here is something I'll never forget."

He looked at her then. How different and wonderful she looked. Martha, her features so often hidden behind a surgical mask. Martha, always there with the right instrument, always slightly ahead of him, there for him. Martha, watching the surgical team, constantly monitoring. Gifts and talent beyond price. And now here she is, so close, a hint of perfume, the cut of her long black dress. Her dark hair flowing in waves, her smile. The exquisite woman out from behind the mask. He watched her use a fork tine to crease letters into her linen napkin. I-A-E-J-L-Y.

She leaned over to him. "I always especially just love you."

Jake squeezed her hand again. "I need you, Martha."

"I know. And that's enough."

He wanted to say something else, something that would indicate a deeper commitment, but the words wouldn't come.

Keeping her hand, he again rose from his chair. He made his way back to the right hand of the President of the United States, Martha in tow. A moment to remember.

Over pheasant and roasted potatoes, they moved on to lighter talk, all offered with wine and French words. Later, in the comfortable quiet, Martha toyed with her cherry cheesecake.

"Penny for them." Jake said.

"What?" Martha looked up, startled.

"Your thoughts."

"Oh. This china. It reminds me of my mother's. Never cherry cheesecake, though. Mom makes these marvelous cobblers."

"You love her a lot."

"She's the best, Jake."

"I have a mom like that. Homemade soup, apple pie, none better."

"Helps you keep faith."
"Yes, it does."

The ride back to Georgetown was serene. Jake had the limousine driver take the scenic route along the Potomac. A full moon reflected on George Washington's favorite river. Martha lowered the window a little. A faint breeze ushered in from the Chesapeake. Soft jazz on the radio. She leaned back, content.

"Going back over it all?" Jake said.

"Savoring it, is the word."

"Quite a night."

He put his arm around her. She smiled.

"I think I could get used to this." He pulled her head to his shoulders. "It's amazing. I've been searching for something so long, and never realized how close it was."

They found each other's eyes under the D.C. skyline.

Jake closed the door to their hotel room and took Martha in his arms. He kissed her then, drawing in the warmth of her, the soft breath of her. She pressed into him, contouring her body against his. "Oh, God, Martha..."

A natural flow of movement and emotion, kissing and clutching. They fumbled with each other's clothing, seeking out flesh and intimacy. Hungry mouths exploring, fingers caressing, a slow build of urgency.

He lifted her to bed.

"I love you, Jake."

She drew him down onto her.

"Martha—"

"Don't talk. Just make love to me."

For a moment Jeanne was there, a shimmering presence behind his eyes, then she was gone.

Congress gleamed in the morning sun, its rotunda white and elegant. Tourists streamed across the steps like some multicolored skirt. Cameras winked in the sunlight. Flowers bloomed, catching the light breeze. There was dark wood, seasoned by time and oratory as ideas were debated throughout the years. A forging of a country. People moved here, too. Older people, mostly men, bearing the passage of time on their shoulders. This was their habitat. Voted in and sometimes voted out, they served their terms and for the most part did their best for America.

Against a background of fitful coughing, the muffled bang of iron and wood as chairs were lifted, Dr. Jason Gibson sorted his notes at the long table in the speaking well of the house subcommittee room. The house members were seated up front. Far up in the gallery was Martha. It gladdened him to know she was there.

The subcommittee chairman tapped his microphone. "Members of the committee and invited guests, it is my special privilege to introduce the members of the special Health Care Commission. These members are here today as guests of the President. They will be presenting their views on the state of American medicine."

A rollcall of distinguished names followed. Physicians and surgeons who had made their mark, their contributions imprinted in library resources and computer data banks around the world.

"Most of you are probably familiar with the career of Dr. Jason P. Gibson. Author of over twenty books and almost two hundred papers. He has taught at nearly every major medical center..."

Except Harvard, Jake mused to himself.

"He has operated on hundreds of prominent heads of state, some of whom have honored us with their presence here in Congress. He has operated on entertainers, sports celebrities, corporate leaders, and professional people from around the world. I would like to add as a personal note that he is a hero and a friend."

Jake rose briefly from his seat.

In the gallery Martha watched him, remembering the man of last night's passion and the man before her now: rather elegant, but with a saving grace of youth and idealism to him, the best surgeon she had ever seen. She loved him beyond all explaining.

It was Jake's time to speak. He stared down at the podium, realistic enough to know that there were factions, splinter groups of opposing views. And he knew there were those who supported his own views and were there for him. But here, in front of the gleaming chrome of the microphone, he knew a first unease. Opposing factions included the very powerful...

"Mr. Chairman, like the other members of this commission, I am most appreciative of the very kind recognition that we have been afforded this morning. But it is with a keen sense of urgency that we present to you our concerns about the future of our great discipline..."

So far so good.

Ladies and gentlemen we work in an era in which the fundamental principles that sustain the profession of medicine are being threatened. We have moved from the foundational philosophy that caring for someone in need is among the most elementary of human instincts. And an individual's need to be cared for is the most cardinal of human rights."

Photographers moved in, kneeling, fiddling with their cameras.

"As we are all aware, the last several decades have witnessed an unprecedented explosion in health-related technology. We can

only marvel at the number of lives that have been saved by these miraculous advances…"

Jake blinked to the flashes of cameras.

"Still, these devices have altered, or as some might say, 'mutated' the current professional oath of medicine, such that it currently reads 'dedicated to providing care for a price.' Capitalism has been woven into the very fabric of medical care. To transform the acquisition of care from a right to a privilege, and the delivery of care from a privilege to a right. It seems today, more often than not, we hear 'How are you going to pay for this?…'"

He paused and looked around.

"Rather than 'How can I be of help.'"

A first slight stir in the audience, like the gentle breeze outside brushing against flowers, bending them. Members of the audience moved uncertainly, occasionally glancing at each other as cameras clicked.

Jake stood erect, his hands gripping the podium. His words, like those uttered by generations before him, spoke out for truth and justice.

"We must ask ourselves: who is responsible for this blue-chip metamorphosis in medical care? Are the instrument and equipment manufacturers whose huge profit margins propel them higher on the list of profitable corporations each year at fault? How about the mammoth health insurance industry that invests far more time and effort into bottom-line profits than quality assurance? We know that HMOs frequently deny coverage for treatable conditions…"

The tension tightened Jake's stomach. How much easier it had been, stretched out on the bed with Martha, reading through his speech, listening to her supportive observations. Clutching the last page he had looked at her, eager for her support. Then they had moved into each other's arms, loving and entwining under harsh lamplight. Even as Jake now spoke, a hint of her perfume came off his pages.

"Then of course let's not forget the profit-at-all-cost hospitals. The big national chains and their newfangled alliances. Ringing up large cash surpluses in the seeing of patient care. And what about our dutifully elected public officials and government agencies? Who respond far more readily to lobbyists and their own special interests, than to the plain and simple welfare of their constituents."

He was hot now, and the press smelled blood. Television lenses focused in. In the audience of physicians and dignitaries there was the first grumbling. Most of it came from the commission members' table. Lastly, from the instincts of political survival, came disgruntlement from members of the House. The good Dr. Gibson was to be cut from the herd. His self-inflicted wound came from naivete.

Jake pushed on. His throat was dry.

"The most important issue facing American medicine today?"

He paused and looked around.

"I believe it's profitability. The future of medicine demands that we restore its foundation of caring. We must stop its economic erosion. We must patch up the deep fissures caused by greed..."

The House members shuffled about in their seats. Several stood up. Jake took water as he watched them walk away.

"To reach these goals, I present a short list of recommendations.

First, consumers must retain the right to obtain the highest quality care regardless of their ability to pay.

Second, practitioners must hold dear the special privilege of their calling. As such their compensation derived exclusively from the direct rendering of patient care... At a level consistent with the Oath of Hippocrates.

And third, corporate entities providing health services, insurance, equipment, supplies, pharmaceuticals—must be not for profit... We cannot permit the future of U.S. healthcare to be bartered away on Wall Street and sold to the highest bidder..."

Martha stood and clapped. It was only a scattering of applause. Most of it from the visitor's gallery. Jake gathered up his speech and yielded the floor to another commission member. Sitting at the long table and listening to the next speaker, Jake was handed two handwritten messages. One was from the House subcommittee chairman. The other written in the left handed scrawl of the President of the United States. Jake read the President's first.

'Thanks again for your many worthwhile contributions, but your services will no longer...'

The chairman's message was shorter.

'Well done, Jake. It's in the record, and it's on tape.'

Jake smiled. He looked up at the gallery. He found Martha. Casually he stuck out his sneaker. The white swoosh on the side. She loved it and she got it. Just like throwing tea into Boston Harbor.

6

Jake woke up sensing the different rhythms, the different feel to his bedroom. Martha's black evening dress lay rumpled by a chair. He felt her presence beside him, her steady breathing, but those thoughts fell back against a rivulet of worries. The speech at Congress had gone both good and bad. He had most certainly lost the President's support, and others in his own rank. But he had said what needed to be said. The alarm clock ticked beside the bed. Then the real thought eddied in: the hospital. He couldn't shake the thought that something was going on behind the scenes, some adroit maneuvering he was not privy to.

"Penny for them," Martha murmured into her pillow.

"Just restless, Martha. Sorry to wake you."

She turned, bouncing the bed a little, then her eyes settled on him. "What are you restless about?"

"The Malone surgery. Hudley popping up then disappearing at critical times."

"We've gone over that. You did what you had to do to save a man's life."

"I know, but I just don't feel good about things. Something's going on."

"You're a good man, Jason. It'll all work out." She kissed his brow. "Go back to sleep."

The knock on the door was loud. "Who the hell's that at six-thirty in the morning?" Martha was still asleep, the back of her head bending into the pillow beside him. He shut off the alarm before it could let out its brash wake-up call. Gently he lifted the sheets and swung off the bed.

He pulled the door open to a dank daybreak.

"Dr. Jason Gibson?"

Jake stuck his head out, taking in the raincoat and wrinkled collar. "That's right. Is there an emergency?"

"Dr. Gibson, I have been retained to deliver this to you personally."

A subpoena. White, clean, not wrinkled. Jake stood there in his Viking's shirt and baseball cutoffs. He watched the man walk away course and unshaven, double-parked, engine running. Perhaps to deliver another subpoena to someone else. Disgustedly he shut the door.

Halfway up the stairs, he encountered Martha. Dwarfed inside one of his dress shirts.

"What is it, babe?" She was rubbing her eyes.

"Some kind of subpoena. Looks like Malone is suing me."

"Well," Martha said drily, "at least your instincts were right."

He unleashed it over the bannister. They returned to the king-sized satin sheets.

He was at the hospital by 8:30 a.m., and after a quick unsuccessful call to Jeanne he headed for the ICU to check on Mitch Malone. There he found Midge, holding court just inside the door, her manner honed to the tension.

"The good Dr. Hudley transferred him to the floor yesterday." She exchanged a pointed look with the nurses standing around her.

"How's he doing?"

"Frankly, he's fine. He has no deficits. But he's obnoxious, talking forever on the phone, bellyaching to the staff."

"Nothing you couldn't handle."

Her Scandinavian eyes seized his. "I heard you spent—how shall I put it?—an exciting weekend in Washington."

"Very educational."

"I bet it was."

Jake sidestepped her look. "One thing, Midge, I have a greater appreciation for the nursing staff. Let's have coffee some time, I'd like to pick your brain on a couple of things."

"I'd like that."

Jake smiled. "Time for Malone."

"Rather you than me."

On the neurosurgery ward Jake could not find the hospital chart in the rotary rack. He checked the cluttered counter top with no luck. The ward secretary was new. "I need Mr. Malone's chart."

"Oh, Dr. Hudley, the physician in charge, placed that chart under strict limited access. No one's supposed to have it." Her green eyes left him. Too new on the job for this.

Jake scanned the names of doctors with approved privileges. His name was scratched out. "Mr. Malone is my patient. Give me his chart." It was his OR stare.

She handed him the chart.

Jake reviewed the record as he headed for Malone's room. Everything appeared in order. Malone had already been up and about with no noted problems. His brain swelling and anti-convulsant medications were being progressively weaned, and his craniotomy wound was healing quite well. Overall, the nursing staff appeared to be voicing far more complaints than the patient.

A large handwritten sign was on the door: NO VISITORS.

Jake knocked and went in. He was not surprised to find Malone next to his bed in an oversized recliner. He was talking on the phone as he poked with his fork at a gourmet breakfast. Jake was amazed to find Hudley, sitting on the hospital bed, working studiously on a stack of unbound papers. Jake flipped the chart closed, placing it on his hip. It was tempting: challenge Hudley now. . .But Jake let it go. Such a confrontation would not be good in front of his already irascible patient.

Malone hung up and reached for his coffee.

"Morning, Mitch. You look much improved."

"That's right—thanks to Dr. Hudley, here."

"I see you're mobile, using the phone." Jake said.

"Right. And with Dr. Hudley's permission I'm going home today and will be back in the office next week. A light load, of course."

"Now look," Jake began. "It's important we go slowly here—"

"Listen, Gibson. I don't think you're in a position to give me advice. Got the subpoena yet?"

Jake pushed a response out. "Yup."

"Good. The guy knew his job. You doctors are hard to catch."

Jake looked at Hudley. "I think you owe me an explanation —"

"He owes you Jack shit!" Malone shoved the plate aside. "This whole thing is very simple. Through your negligence and carelessness a life threatening complication occurred in a defenseless patient." The lawyer's words were fluent, courtroom seasoned. "Your actions necessitated a second and dangerous operation—one that was performed against the family's wishes. It's plain to me, Gibson, that you're guilty of gross malpractice, and that I and my next of kin are in line to receive adequate compensation."

Jake shook his head. "I can't believe what I'm hearing here."

"Oh, believe it, Dr. Gibson, believe it. You have the subpoena."

"I acted in your best interests."

"Really, well you'll find my claims are supported by several expert witnesses." Malone stretched his neck towards Hudley.

Before Jake could respond, Malone's nurse entered. Her professional calm did not quite succeed; her face showed some fear. "Dr. Gibson, Dr. Wilson's secretary just called. You're wanted in his office immediately." She turned to Dr. Hudley, affably. "There's also a call for you, long distance from Washington State, I believe. He says he's returning your call and that it's important he speak with you."

"We'll settle this later, Dr. Hudley." Jake also left a fed-up look with Malone. Outside he stopped to gather himself. He bit his lip and headed for his boss's office.

He walked right in. There were few preliminaries. Nothing about the Capital Hill speech.

"Sit down, Jason."

Jake sat and waited.

"Jason, you and I have been colleagues and friends for a long time. I consider myself one of the people who had a role in making you the surgeon you are today. And there's little doubt you're one of the best around. Maybe even the best." Wilson sat solemnly behind his desk, hands enfolded. "I remind you of that because of the distasteful news I must give you."

Jake forced a grin. "Couldn't be worse than what's happened already today."

Dr. Wilson did not smile. "Jason, I want you to know first-hand that I am totally on your side. You have my full support, and in the future—"

"In the future?" Jake leaned forward. "What is it?"

"I did try to reach you in Washington—"

"What is it?"

"I must suspend your hospital privileges—"

"What!"

"—indefinitely. I'm sorry, Jason, I really am, but I have no alternative."

Jake stood up.

"A civil lawsuit was filed late Friday against the medical center. On behalf of your patient, Mitch Malone. Claiming negligence on your part in his surgeries. I imagine you've already been served?"

Jake stood stone-faced.

"The initial impression of the university's legal experts is that this action is probably not defensible. As a result, I have been instructed by the dean to suspend your hospital privileges. Indefinitely."

Jake's face reddened; his head pounding. "Vince, this whole thing is preposterous. You must be aware that Malone's making an excellent recovery? What I did was right and you of all people should know that." Jake presented his reservations about Dr. Hudley. He omitted nothing.

Wilson's face congested in anger. "So it's your belief that one of our very own staff physicians purposefully caused this man's blood clot?"

"I didn't say that, Vince." Jake sucked down his anger and gathered his thoughts. "All I know is that ever since Mitch Malone arrived at this hospital door, David Hudley has behaved very strangely. Something's going on, Vince. And I don't know what it is."

"Paranoia doesn't become you, Dr. Gibson. In any case, every detail of this sordid affair will be examined by medical staff committees. For the moment, there is nothing else I can do." The chairman sat straight in his tall leather chair, rapping his fountain pen. He searched around for more neutral talk. "By the way, local television stations have been calling. They want to interview you about your Washington speech. I told them you were too busy."

Jake curled his lip. He was ready to leave as the office door was shoved open. Again it was Howard Crane, again the malevolent voice. Jake braced himself.

"Sorry to barge in like this again, Dr. Wilson, but I need to drop this off." Crane shoved a crisply folded document into Jake's hand. His voice was very low and controlled, far more threatening than his earlier shouting. "I wanted to deliver this to you personally, Gibson. I'm suing you for every last penny you have, you son of a bitch. I'm going to destroy you!"

"Better get in line, Howard." Jake slipped the document into his coat pocket and left.

Back at his office, Rona, his personal secretary, was waiting. She spelled out her reassignment by Dr. Wilson. Effective tomorrow.

"Wait one damned minute." Jake threw the subpoena onto his desk. "This's crap! I—"

Rona was wiping her eyes.

"—listen…I'm sorry." Jake found the back of his rocking chair. "I don't know where any of this is headed." He rubbed his forehead. "Proper arrangements need to be made."

Rona took a seat in front of his desk. Her auburn hair tossed over her shoulders. "Your office appointments and operations have been canceled, your patients reassigned." She dabbed at her nose with a tissue. "I feel so helpless."

Jake began rocking, finding a calm in the familiar movement.

"One more thing," Rona got up to leave. "Your buddy, Ben, called earlier. Your softball game for tonight has been canceled."

"That's just great." Jake's smile was bitter.

There was silence. Jake looked at the bronze bust of Asclepius across from his desk.

Rona watched from the door.

"How many years have I been addressing the freshmen med students on their first day of class?"

Jake stared at the statue. He orated the words, words indelibly etched into his professional soul. "Future physicians and compeers. You are about to embark on a journey that is unequaled in the chronicles of medicine. From this day forward, you will be afforded the opportunity to care for fellow members of the human race with the most sophisticated technology in history at your ready disposal. No healer in history has been given the opportunity that is to be yours every day of your lives. You must cherish and respect this invaluable privilege. And at the same time do everything in your power to defend the unalterable rights of your patients. Generations of Asclepians have composed our profession's enduring responsibility."

Jake looked to Rona, but she had quietly slipped away.

Jake tried to reach Jeanne, his soul mate. He tried to reach Martha. As he put back the receiver Adam von Hecklinghausen walked in. Adam was a nearly deaf and partially paretic middle-aged man who had worked in the hospital receiving department for years. Jake had operated on him and three of his brothers, all of whom suffered from a rare hereditary disease, one that produced recurring tumors on nerves that ran along the base of the brain. While still a resident Jake had recognized the hereditary nature of this previously unrecognized disorder. It became known thereafter in medical literature as "Von Hecklinghausen's Disease'.

"How are your brothers doing, Adam?"

"They're all doing great, thanks to you." Adam offered several cardboard boxes. "Rona asked me to get these for you." He waited, his eyes troubled.

Jake shook hands with him, trying to sound upbeat. "Give my best to your brothers, Adam."

Alone again, Jake shut his office door and shuffled the boxes around his desk. He began gathering up his personal belongings.

The figurine from the interns, the brick from his trip to Germany and Hitler's Berghof. And the cross. He picked up the old wooden cross given him by his grandfather, running its smoothed comforting shape against his hand. He was still drawing strength from it when Midge came in.

"Doctor, we need to talk." She quietly closed the door behind her and sat down in front of him.

"Okay." Jake glanced at his watch.

"Not around here."

They made their way to Midge's brand new red Spider, cranked it up, and headed for the park. They pulled in against a spruce and birch lined path and got out.

"Been here before?" Midge asked, as they began walking. "There's a pond with lily-pads and a fountain down the way."

"What's on your mind, Midge?"

She lit a cigarette. "You've been canned because you've been pissing too many people off."

Jake managed a smile. "Nothing new there."

"No, think it through. I have. Follow the trail, Doctor. First, you're popular with patients and staff. That threatens people in high places… Second, remember the Hot Line?"

"Of course."

"Thanks to you, they set up a 24-hour stroke hot line, right into the neuro ICU. Anyone in the community could call and speak directly with an experienced neuroscience nurse for information on stroke, for comfort, for anything that would help them through the worry. A hundred inquiries a day we got! People began to learn about the warning signs of stroke, how to help themselves a bit."

"And it was canned because of excessive professional time." Jake said.

"Like hell." Midge blew a smoke ring. "It was canned because it was keeping too many paying patients out of doctors' offices."

They were at the fountain, feeling its cool spray.

"You're a nice guy, Doctor. Perhaps too nice. You didn't see that?"

Jake sat on the stone ledge. He looked out into a grassy area where a couple of young boys with caps were tossing a baseball back and forth. "Okay, what else?"

"Third. Neurosurgeons in this town don't get along. All they do is bicker and work against each other. You tried to encourage cooperation. And Jake, you failed, right? Why? Because everybody's out for number one. These guys are making big bucks, right? You were messing with a good thing and coming across as a show-boat." Midge flipped her cigarette butt. "There's not a doctor in this town who would lose a night's sleep if you were forced out."

As they resumed their walk Jake thought about it. Was it that bad with his so-called colleagues? He couldn't believe it. In fact he wouldn't believe it. There was Hudley, but every hospital had its Hudleys. And Mitch Malone and Howard Crane were out-siders drawn into his life by circumstance. But it all nagged at him. "Thanks, Midge. I appreciate the input and your concern for me." He touched his hand to her shoulder. "I really do."

She kissed him then, soft and quietly on the mouth. "You're too good for your own good, Doctor. And I'm jealous as hell about Washington."

Jake felt his face redden. "I think we should be getting back. I've things to do."

It was a couple of hours before he drove home from the hospital. Too much was going on, too much grist for the straining mill. He thought it all through as he drove, the wipers rhythmically swiping at the drizzle. From Washington to loading up cardboard boxes. A double whammy of subpoenas, first delivered on his own doorstep, then next in Howard Crane's angry hand. Martha, healer of torn spirits, love abiding. Jeanne, holder of his heart while married to his best friend. And Midge. Feisty, tough, savvy, practical Midge there for him. But he couldn't believe all she said. He needed time and distance from this day. He needed to talk with Jeanne, and he needed to let Martha know about Howard's visit to the boss's office.

Once he had his front door open he knew Martha was gone. The rhythms had called into the usual loneliness; the moods were different, shades of gray and barren. He barreled through the kitchen and upstairs. He found her letter beside the bed.

My Dear Jake,

The last few days have been the absolute BEST of my life. I think you know how wonderful you are, and how much I love you...

He carried the letter to the kitchen while he got himself a beer. A new kind of loneliness impinged on him.

Unfortunately the world around us will not leave us alone. I know the trouble that my coming into your life has caused...I must go away...to my parents, to get a grip on myself.

I'll love you always. IAEJLY.

Martha

He dialed Jeanne's number. The relentless ringing went on and on. Finally he hung up.

7

All my life I've tried to make science and research the basis of our national endeavor, but I have always known full well that there are values higher than science. The only values that offer healing for the ills of humanity are the supreme values of justice and righteousness, peace and love.

Chaim Weizmann
(1874–1952)

Early October saw the leaves changing and the first of them beginning to fall. Soon the limbs would be stripped, not unlike the way Jake had been stripped of his professional contacts, his circle of confidants, his very fabric of relationships so necessary in the pursuit of good medicine. He was out, banished. Like autumn leaves relationships had curled and withered. He was down to family and best friends, like Ben and Jeanne. He stood on their front porch and rapped on the door. But it was Jeanne he wanted. Jeanne, keeper of his soul, who always understood.

Her shadow moved behind stained glass, then she was there, holding back the door. She captured his emotions as she always did: short brown hair with those subtle highlights that offered

gold tints in the sun; the intelligent and incredibly blue eyes…
The eyes watched him now as Jeanne stood aside to let him in, her
pregnant belly pushing out against her yellow maternity dress.
Jake kissed her lightly on the cheek and squeezed her hand as they
walked to the couch. The couch was a familiar retreat for them, a
place where they could move easily into trusted confidences and
shared fears.

"What is it?" Jeanne said.

Jake's mouth compressed around his words. "It's all getting
to me."

"The subpoenas."

"The subpoenas, and being ostracized. I'm cut off from my
world, Jeanne, the place where I thrive and compete, and try out
ideas, and nurture my skills—having meaning in my life." He
looked out at the old sycamores lining Ben's yard. In his talks with
Jeanne he had seen them grow, move through their seasons.

"Sleeping okay?"

"Not really."

"Are you ready for the attorneys?"

Jake shrugged. "I just plan to tell the truth."

Jeanne took his hand. "Sometimes how we express the truth
can help or hinder."

"Truth is truth, Jeanne. It stands on its owns, unambiguous."

He looked at her, then reached out and ran his hand over
her belly. It was an unusual touch, a meld of the physician and the
man. And Jeanne responded in kind, sucking in her breath and
closing her eyes.

"And we have a truth here, Jake. Standing on its own,
unambiguous."

"Jeanne—"

"You know how I feel about you."

Jake leaned back and stared at the corner table with its
portrait of Ben and Jeanne, smiling into the camera at their future.
"The road not taken," he said.

"We have our friendship. Ben understands that; many men wouldn't."

Jake stood up. "Shouldn't have come here today, Jeanne. I'm off-balance."

"Jake, listen—"

"I just feel so cut off."

"Not from people who really care about you, who believe in you."

Jake took her in his arms and kissed her gently. He turned to leave.

"It'll work out, Jake."

"I know." He forced a smile.

The phone rang.

"Hello?" Jeanne's arm entwined with the phone cord, the hint of auburn in her hair catching the sun. "Hey, what's goin' on? Caitlin's down the street and I was just thinking of taking a nap. What time do you think you'll be home?" Blue eyes offered sunlight and sadness. "Okay. Well, drive safely."

Jake waved and let himself out.

◎◈✠

It was not a good drive home. Jake tried to set aside his thoughts about Jeanne, the cross currents of emotion about Martha—even Midge's impulsive kiss—and focus on his other problems, his legal predicament. But it was difficult. He found himself double checking himself: maybe he should have spent more time chatting with colleagues in the doctor's lounge; maybe he should have joined the right clubs; maybe he should have participated more in golf games and adroitly worked out business deals, all to the swing of a nine iron.

Maybe, maybe, maybe. But that wasn't him. He had never been a game-player, using the mantle of medicine to justify shady deals, slipshod professionalism, and slick relationships. When he arrived home his mailbox bulged with a manila package. Rona had sent him a backlog of correspondence from the Neurosurgery

Department. He dumped the contents on the couch and spilled out colorful greeting card envelopes, mass mailings, and the inevitable letters asking for donations. The greeting cards pleased him. He had always encouraged patients to stay in touch by sending yearly updates on their health status. He made it a point to read every note, sometimes responding in special cases. Kind words to him cushioned some of the troubles he was facing.

The letters asking for donations were always difficult. Not the glossy brochures geared to appeal, but the personal letters, the nurse who needed help with a sick parent; the blue collar worker laid off, trying to get his car running again. These touched him and he always responded. And there was one from St. Anthony of Padua Capital Fund Drive. Monsignor Joseph McMurphy had died on the operating table, an event from years before that seared Jake's soul.

Whether from guilt or altruism or anger at the events he was dealing with, Jake wrote a check for $5,000 to St. Anthony's. It cleaned him out.

But in with greeting cards and mass mailings and personal embarrassed requests there was another letter. Out of state. A doctor's clinic imprint.

Depositions for the pending litigations were set for the same day, October 31. A week prior an attorney assigned by the malpractice carrier solicited Jake to set aside an entire day to review his testimony.

Trevor Callahan was an unfortunate stereotype of the upwardly mobile lawyer. He was young, his taste in clothes beyond his income, his veneer of experience obviously thin. Rolex and ring gleamed in the plush office light. It was not a good beginning for Jake to provide depositions for the pending litigations.

"Get you anything, Dr. Gibson—coffee?"

"No, thanks."

Callahan cleared his throat. "Okay then. Let's get started. I've been appointed by your malpractice carrier…let's see, that's

MoMedico Mutual…in the upcoming malpractice litigation." His eyes were serious behind his wire rimmed glasses. Lamplight reflected from them. When Jake said nothing he continued.

"My first responsibility is to inform you that—um—the limit of your coverage is—ah—only two million. In this suit the claimant, ah—Mr. Mitchell Malone, has listed damages in excess of ten million dollars. And that, by the way, does not include punitive awards."

Jake looked around the office. Diplomas and plaques, not unlike his own. A family photo, wife and two kids smiling. A silver plated paperweight. All of it not unlike his own office—except Jake's identity was now in cardboard boxes. "Tell me, Trevor, what kind of car do you drive?"

"Car? Actually, a Porsche 911. A convertible." He grinned self-consciously. "Wind in my hair, the open road…"

Jake filed it away. This guy was loyal to the insurance company. But for the next several hours Jake went over every detail either from medical records or personal recollection. With each accounting on Mitch Malone's treatment the lawyer reinterpreted it into a comfortable legalese. A little rephrasing here. A little interpretation there. At no time was there a distortion or a lie. Just a comfortable couching of facts aimed at a jury for positive response. Finally the key element came up. Malone had been operated on without family consent and totally against next-of-kin's wishes. Callahan's glasses winked at him. "We do appear to have Malone's verbal permission, just before his second surgery. This nodding of the head to you, his affirmative—"

"It didn't happen that way." Jake raised up in his chair. "I never sought informed consent from the patient. He was far too sick to understand what was happening. I merely—"

"Dr. Gibson, we need—"

"No, listen to me. I merely asked him to stick out his tongue as part of an examination. That's what he responded to. In fact, by the time I had made the decision to proceed with the second operation as an emergency procedure he had already slipped into a deep coma."

"My point exactly, Dr. Gibson!" Papers shuffled under slender fingers. "In his sworn deposition, Mr. Malone himself admitted that he didn't have any recollection of what occurred that night. In fact, no one from the Malone family was present when you spoke with him, were they? Now, I've spoken to several of the ICU nurses attending to him, and at least one of them is willing to corroborate your account—"

"Look, Callahan," Jake overrode him, getting ruffled. "I only asked him to stick out his tongue—like this!"

The lawyer jerked back in distaste, comical in his reaction.

"But he couldn't do it, see? All he could muster was a clumsy movement of his mouth as he tried to speak."

Callahan studied his pencil. "Look, Jason—may I call you Jason? You must understand all this in legal terms. What is important is that which can be proven. If we can support with an eye-witness that an event happened a certain way, then as far as the court is concerned, that's the truth."

Jake thought about Jeanne, her thoughtful eyes carrying concern for him. *How we express the truth can help or hinder...* And he's said what: that truth was truth, unambiguous. "Callahan, I won't lie for you or anyone else."

"Then you'd better realize something. You're in an indefensible predicament."

"I'll testify to truth only." Jake listened to his own voice. It sounded stuffy, stubborn, pugnacious. Not good, but that was where he was. "I'll testify to nothing more, nothing less."

Callahan doodled on the legal pad.

"Whatever happened to the truth, the whole truth, and nothing but the truth, so help me God?"

"I wish it were that simple."

"You lawyers are amazing."

"Only doing my job."

"Jesus, Callahan!" Jake closed the files in front of him. He thought about walking out.

"Ok, let's move along. This second deposition, Howard Crane."

"That's personal, it's got no bearing on Mitch Malone."

"One last thing, I'd suggest you draft a letter of resignation from the university and submit it to your department chairman before trial."

Jake rubbed his temples.

"It would be in your best interest, Jason." Callahan said quietly. "Malone is an expert at raising a flap between doctors and hospitals. If you are no longer associated, then he'll have a much more difficult time of it."

Jake gathered up his papers and files and walked towards the door. He took a stick of licorice from a canister.

Jake shook his hand and left.

He would have preferred old green scrubs for the Halloween deposition, but he compromised with an easygoing Hawaiian shirt and khaki slacks. He stood out compared to the lawyers in their white dress shirts and custom-tailored dark suits.

"A suit would've been nice." Callahan said.

While the lawyers talked to each other in exclusive tones, Jake shook hands with the video engineer.

At that moment the sliding doors to the conference room were forced open and Mitch Malone entered. He blended in with the lawyer ranks.

Callahan leaned his way. "You must hate him."

"No, not really."

Callahan stared.

"He does look well." Jake said.

When the proceedings were about to begin Jake was asked to raise his right hand and was sworn in. For the next six hours he was grilled by an unlikely adversary, Malone's daughter Shannon. She was sleek in a tan business suit. Jake watched her prowl in front of him. The first woman to graduate summa cum laude from both the medical and law schools at Harvard. Her father sat placidly alongside, taking notes on a yellow legal pad, occasionally tossing an expressionless look her way. He glanced from father to daughter and back again. She possessed the genes and brains to make the perfect malpractice attorney. He remembered his arm around her shoulders at the hospital. She had been the only one who had cried.

This was another incarnation. Her line of questioning was aggressive, well conceived, and though preposterous, completely believable. It rang like truth off the conference room walls. It was during a break that she came up to him, softened around the edges.

"I never got a chance to thank you, Dr. Gibson, for everything you did for my dad. I want you to know that I appreciate the courage and conviction you displayed. To do what you did, that took real guts."

"Then why are we here, Ms. Malone?"

Her eyes hardened. "Because from a legal standpoint you're a damned fool."

He watched her hang there. He found a measure of sympathy for her. Truth can be a hard taskmaster, and she was on the rack. "I gather I can count on more of your aggressive questioning."

"You gather right, Doctor."

She hit him hard: Jake had deliberately produced a deadly blood clot during the initial operation; he had undertaken the subsequent operation without consent; and all this was done to kill or disable Mitch Malone for a prior malpractice case against him. As an added benefit, he had hoped to pass the blame onto an understudy who had blown the whistle on him. Jake found himself answering each interrogatory, each attack, speaking honestly, thoroughly, talking forthrightly. He even overrode his own attorney's repeated objections. He gave unambiguous truth. They had a field day.

And the day was far from over. It was Howard Crane's turn. Malone sticking around for another crack at him.

"I understand you've declined legal counsel in this matter," Malone said, speaking entirely for the records. "Is that correct?"

"That's right."

"I'm sorry, you'll have to speak louder for the court reporter."

"Yes, that's right."

Then it began, a nightmare fabricating a nonexistent relationship and a froth of imaginative happenings. Jake answered every question and with each one felt himself enmeshed in a web. It went on for hours, with Malone boring in for details. But it was the silent Howard Crane that got to Jake. The eyes never left him.

All told, the two depositions took ten hours. Jake turned his back on them and walked out into the coolness of an autumn evening.

She came on the heels of Halloween, of children's laughter and the rustle of candy sacks.It was dark now, a cloudless cold October night.

"You're supposed to say Trick or Treat."

Martha smiled, but her eyes were wet. "I brought a suitcase."

"I'm glad."

8

They sat across from each other the following morning. The kitchen was bright and airy, the aroma of fresh coffee, strong and bracing. He watched her across the table.

"What?" Martha said.

"Nothing. Just that you came right when I needed you. There I was, knee deep in Halloween kids."

"It was close to midnight, Jake. They were already in bed."

He smiled. "I'm already romanticizing it."

"I was stupid, Jake. That letter—"

"Let it go, Martha. I'm just so glad you're here."

"So, how'd it go yesterday?"

"What, the inquisition? How'd you hear about that?"

Martha's eyes widened.

"Oh, sorry."

"Let it go, Jake. It's over. And I have the papers to prove it."

Jake looked at her.

"So, how'd it go?"

Jake frowned. "I was there all day."

"You look tired."

Jake smiled but bitter. "Well I've been busy. There's the children's free clinic thing, doing physicals a couple of hours a week, and the high school science lecture thing; and then there's the—"

"Jake, it'll all be over soon."

He looked off and nodded.

"Have they set a trial date yet?"

He shook his head.

"So now what?"

He studied her eyes. He handed over the envelope, the one from out of state with the clinic imprint, the one that had arrived with the junk mail, the letters for donations.

"Mt. Pleasant, central Washington State?"

"A resort area. They need a neurosurgeon."

"What about here, have you given up on straightening out things here?" Martha said.

"I'm just looking at it. No commitments..."

Martha put down her coffee cup and looked worried. A part of Jake was missing. Unavoidable to her. An essential part. A part tied to Jeanne, who had recently given birth to a son. Last night Jake had told her that Jeanne and he no longer confided in each other. But it was what he didn't say.

The doorbell rang.

Jake got up and answered the door. The postman dropped off a registered letter. He tore it open and read it. Back in the kitchen he handed it to Martha.

Dear Dr. Gibson:

By unanimous decision, the Regents of the University of the Minnesota Medical Center hereby 'revoke' your privileges as faculty member and staff surgeon in the Department of Neurosurgery. This action is "permanent and irreversible", and is effective 'immediately'.

Forthwith, David G. Hudley, M.D., is promoted to Assistant Professor of Neurosurgery. He will assume your clinical, research, and teaching responsibilities. Be advised that to ensure a harmonious transition, the Twin City Sheriff Authority is prepared to supervise your removal of personal effects from university premises.

Martha placed it gently on the kitchen table. Her face was drained of color. "Dear God…"

Jake managed smile. "It's Hudley. It was always Hudley."

The blue and red police lights filled his rearview mirror. Jake pulled over and waited. He kept the motor running while he cursed under his breath. Too much lead foot. Suspended hospital privileges and jabbing memories of Martha in his bed can do that. He watched while the officer called it in. Why was it taking so long?

"Would you mind getting out of your vehicle, Dr. Gibson?"

"Look, Officer, I'm sorry I was a bit over the speed limit, I'm —"

"Now, if you please, sir. Step out of your vehicle and place your hands on the hood."

Jake watched the eyes. A surgeon always watches a person's eyes. These told him a lot: angry, ready for trouble. Jake got out. He leaned against the car. "Am I under arrest?"

"Yes, you are, sir."

"Mind telling me why?"

"Well, I should think you'd know why, Dr. Gibson."

"I don't."

"That's a little hard to believe, considering you've got over two hundred outstanding parking tickets."

"Hey, now—look!"

"Sir, keep your hands where they are."

"Wait a minute, I—"

A knee pinned his backside against the car. His hands were snapped into cuffs.

It was some time later that he was placed in a holding cell. There he waited, trying to keep calm while he tried to figure things out. First off, he had no parking tickets…

The sheriff's deputy came by. "Our records indicate you have collected over two hundred tickets over the last several years. You are now under arrest for failure to pay the fines."

"There must be some kind of mistake. Are you sure have the right man, Dr. Jason Paul Gibson?"

"Yup."

"On Navajo Lane."

"Yup."

"Then, there's a mistake." Jake said quietly.

"Nope, you're the guy."

"Look, I'm a physician and there's no way that—"

Jake read his look. "Ok, I need to straighten this out. Just how do I get out of here?"

"You'll need to make arrangements to post bond."

"Okay then, I need my wallet back."

"You can't do it yourself. You've gotta phone somebody."

Jake kept his temper. The humiliation was tougher. He made his call and waited for his father.

He presented himself a few weeks later for his court date.

"How do you plead?"

"Innocent, your honor. With an explanation."

"Go ahead."

"Your honor, none of these tickets are mine. I haven't gotten a ticket in years. There has to be a mistake. Maybe a glitch somewhere in the computer system?"

"Is this your proper name?"

"Yes, sir."

"Is your birthday correct?"

"Yes."

"Same address?"

"Yes, sir."

"Well, I don't see a mistake. Perhaps you simply forgot getting these tickets."

"No, your Honor. As I said, no tickets in years."

"Well what about this one?" The judge handed him a parking citation placed on his abandoned car while he was detained.

"Okay, your Honor. I—"

The judge's eyebrows arched. "What's your occupation, sir?"

"Brain surgeon."

"Oh really." The judge smiled. "Where do you work?"

"University Hospital." Jake retrieved an identification card.

"Okay, so you are a physician." The judge removed his glasses. "You know, in my experience, doctors are the worst offenders. Always rushing around here and there. They seem to accumulate these sort of things in a hurry."

Several weeks later Jake and Martha sat on their bed.

"So you ended up pleading guilty." Martha said.

"Had to."

The bed was strewn with the contents of a manila envelope: lengthy computer print outs; driving records, and a videotape.

Martha scanned the sheets. "It's all street meters."

"More than that, it's all meters fronting on our hospitals."

"But who used the spots?" Martha asked.

"That's the tricky bit. Remember anybody bragging about not paying tickets?"

Martha gasped. "David Hudley. Oh my God!"

"Part of his man about town routine."

"Unbelievable."

"Turns out his wife is a clerk at the Traffic bureau. She switched numbers."

"Jesus…"

"Cost me almost a thousand bucks."

"What about this other stuff?"

"Obsessive-compulsive side: a video of my parking space showing no need to park on a meter; my driving record which is good… The judge thought I was crazy."

"You're not paranoid, Jake. People are out to get you."

"That's what I've been finding out lately. Too idealistic for my own good. Getting in the way of the money."

"Sounds like you've been talking to Midge."

"Just once."

"Good for Midge."

"She was curious about our time in Washington."

Martha's eyes darkened.

Jake tossed over the Washington State postcard. "This place is looking better and better."

"Mount Pleasant. Picturesque."

"Let's go out. Take a look."

"Me too?"

"You too."

They found each other across the bed, mashing down printouts and driving records. They knew a first freedom from the ugly litigation and double dealing at the hospital.

◎▩✠

Mount Pleasant lived up to its brochures. Jake and Martha toured the center of the town and enjoyed the Swiss architecture motif with the hand-painted stucco exteriors and fresh flowers filling boxes on the window sills. There was a heavy scent of pine that welcomed them. They were far from Minneapolis. Back at their room there was a message from Dr. George Black. Please call 555-1111.

"That's odd," Martha said. "How did he know we were here?"

They had purposefully not told anyone they were looking out of state.

"Small town," Jake grinned. "Mayberry without Andy Griffith." He grabbed the phone and dialed.

"Do you know much about Dr. Black, Jake?"

"Some. He developed an innovative approach to work on brain tumors along the base of the skull. Showed how it was possible to remove them by operating through the roof of the mouth. Got written up in Time magazine—Dr. Black? This is Jason Gibson calling. I'm answering your message. Yes…yes… Mount Pleasant's beautiful. I don't know if we've actually met but I did have the opportunity to attend your presentation at the I.B.T. Meeting in Minneapolis a few years—yes, the transoral surgery…" Jake winked at Martha.

Martha brought her ear close to the phone and pressed Jake's hand.

Black's voice was throaty, confident. "I received a call from the chief of surgery at the clinic who was asking about you. Look, I have an extremely busy referral practice here that includes most of central Washington State. My partner and I have been covering this area for the last seven or eight years. Is it true you're looking to leave Minneapolis?"

Martha squeezed his hand harder.

"Well…"

"I've spoken with my partner, Jim Wright. We both agree that your credentials are outstanding! Mount Pleasant would be fortunate to have you."

"Well, thank you."

"If you could spare the time tomorrow morning, I would like to arrange a visit with you. Your hotel is only twenty minutes or so from my ranch. I'd love to show you around. It's really a charming place. What's your schedule look like?"

"That sounds wonderful," Jake said, carefully closing his own hand over Martha's. "My fiancé is with me. We'll look forward to the tour."

Martha's lovely eyes widened.

"Okay, then. I'll see you both tomorrow."

Jake hung up just before Martha bounced him onto the bed. "Fiancé!"

"If it's okay with you."

"Dr. Gibson, that has to be the most laid back proposal a girl ever had."

They found each other then, drawing close to each other; Martha pulling away from Howard and a desolate relationship, and Jake with his thoughts about Jeanne who was married to Ben and beyond reach. But what Martha and Jake had would work, it would heal things, and they would grow together. It was much later that Jake was leaning back on a squashed pillow.

"What're you thinking, darling?"

Jake shrugged. "This town. Looks too small to support a neurosurgeon. Probably one of those towns with an overload of docs who come for the good life."

"Want to take a look around?"

"Yeah. Let's drop by the clinic. Our appointment's not till one. I say we go check it out with a little surprise visit."

"No surprises in this small town. Black's probably already talked to them while we were rolling around in the sheets."

Jake kissed her. "It was worth it."

"I should damn well hope so!" She pinched him and they tussled around.

"Okay." Jake said. "Let's get this show on the road."

The clinic was two story with small design patterns echoing the town's alpine architecture. Inside, the pleasant smell of pine wafted on the air. They met briefly with the clinic administrators, medical staff and a couple of local civic leaders who were involved in the national search for a neurosurgeon. The conversation was light and down home, their pride in the facilities obvious and enthusiastic. Afterwards Jake and Martha got into the rental car and pulled away to other quiet streets.

"So what do you think, Jake?"

"What do I think? I have doubts that they can support a full-time neurosurgeon. What they got here—twenty thousand people?"

"The brochures say twenty-five."

"Even so. Not enough."

"So now what?"

"Let's stop by the hospital."

They found it modern and well equipped, but hardly the caliber needed for world class neurosurgical procedures.

The drive back to their hotel was quiet, both Jake and Martha lost in thought.

◎▦✠

Dr. George Black arrived an hour late, pounding the air with his car horn. He was behind the wheel of a dusty Lincoln continental, a vehicle that looked out of place. He motioned for Jake and Martha to climb into the back seat as he shuffled x-ray folders and office charts to create space. The whole car interior was untidy. A faint smell of urine came off the upholstery. Martha gave Jake her Operating Room look, shorthand messages with her eyes, while she leaned forward and shook hands with Black. The doctor was a distinguished looking man, a contrast with his car's care. He had a round face and fine wiry mustache very similar to Everett Salig's.

As they drove through that brisk November morning, Dr. Black made it obvious that the view of the countryside, the pine trees, the snow on distant mountains, were not of interest. He brandished a file of IRS 1040 forms. "These are from last year. Go ahead, take a look."

Jake took a look, angling the files so that Martha could see. The good doctor had a net income in excess of $2,000,000. He spent the rest of the day showing them his ranch, treating them to lunch at the club, displaying his empire. It meant that Jake and Martha did not have time to talk to each other until the end of the day when George Black dropped them off at the airport.

As the single engine plane banked away for their connection in Seattle, Jake turned to her. "Well?"

"I have a queasy feeling."

"Like when Hudley fumbled that stitch?"

Martha took his hand. "Just a feeling. How about you?"

"It's odd. When we first got into his car, I had a sick feeling. Like something bad was going to happen." Jake shook his head. "I don't know. But Black is sure keen on having us come."

"So you'll try for other positions."

"Of course. I'll check it all out."

"Good."

But over the following weeks when Jake made his inquiries around the country, the offers were suddenly no longer available. It was becoming apparent that only Dr. George Black and his partner, Dr. Jim Wright, were interested in him.

It was a biting cold night just after Thanksgiving that Jake was given little choice but to accept the position. He and Martha were watching television to a cozy fire when the hospital ugliness surfaced. An expose told the story in punch-prose that a university surgeon of some repute had attempted to murder a well-known local attorney as a result of the attorney's involvement in a prior malpractice suit against him and the teaching hospital.

Jake was on his feet, anger taking him, his hands curling into fists.

Martha clung to him, restraining him.

Shortly afterward the phone calls began. Ugly calls, cowardly calls in the middle of the night. Screamed obscenities. They had to unplug the phone. Next day's newspaper splashed the same distortions. Reporters began hanging around the front door. But the worst hit far closer to home for Jake. When his mother and father called on St. Nicholas Day they let it slip that members of the family, even the little kids, were being harassed.

On their second trip to Mount Pleasant, Jake and Martha had dinner with Drs. Black and Wright and their spouses. They were treated to humorous but sinister stories. But during dessert Jake committed to joining the practice and moving to Mount Pleasant. "I'll begin my practice shortly after the first of the year," he said.

For Martha it was a case of supporting her man. But the final knife thrust was the worst: word quickly spread that Dr. Jake Gibson, late of the White House and fancy speeches about fair medical practices and taking care of the sick, was running from his detractors to a private practice in the middle of nowhere. The guy was obviously guilty. He'd given up the fight to clear his name. He'd sullied the entire profession.

Goodness is found in good families. The kindnesses and nurturing of enjoined lives lift the spirit. With caring families, loving families, no assault, no vindictive cries can destroy them. Jake Gibson came from such a family, a family of ten, with kids still young enough to enjoy Christmas and look to bright futures. And his family were gathered for the Season's loving rituals, and this for Jake included a traditional lambchop breakfast and the family gift opening. He watched with a childhood contentment as Martha was drawn in on the festivities. He had watched her go to the fireplace and touch the stocking with her name on it. It hung next to his. Both had been carefully knitted by Catherine Ann, his mom. In fact, all the stockings which stretched around the fireplace had been created by her, and they spanned decades of love and achievement by their owners, from good report cards to brain surgery. It was into this security and warmth that he spoke.

"The past few months have been difficult for me."

The words fell into a respectful quiet; kids put down toys and avoided rustling gift wrappings.

Jake smiled at them. "But, it's going to get sorted out, and I'm already looking to the future, to moving on. There are things I want to share with you." He glanced at his young niece—his godchild- who immediately scampered away and came back with a small awkwardly wrapped package.

"I wrapped it myself," Jake said, looking at Martha.

He watched her open it. He watched her lovely eyes as they found his. "I can't be laid back out this, Martha. Will you marry me?"

It was a simple ring, a gold band with a small stone setting.

Then she was in his arms. Her words nearly whispered. "Yes. I will marry you, Jake. I would love to be your wife." She was distracted then as pudgy little fingers explored the ring on her hand, poking at it. She beamed at Jake before she bent down and let the children see it close up.

◉❈✠

The week after Christmas was spent at Martha's home in Southern Illinois. Martha's mom and dad had lived their entire married life in the same house situated right on Main Street, just across from the town's water tower. Harold was a retired factory worker. He had inherited the two-story, wood-frame residence with barn and acreage. Strikingly dusted with a couple inches of new snow, the country home made it difficult for Martha to emphasize to her parents the immeasurable beauty of central Washington state.

Jake settled right in, enjoying the feel to this home imbued with the years of a good marriage. Martha took him to many of her favorite places: St. Francis, the church in which she had been baptized, her old grade school, the malt shop. And there was the playhouse out back built by her dad.

"Dad is so good with his hands, Jake."

"I can see that. You must have had a lot of fun in it."

"I did. Me and Lisa."

"Lisa?"

"My best friend when I was growing up. She just moved back from Iowa. Her husband's an ER doc."

"Must be something in the water down here." Jake said. "Turning out good medical types."

She pinched him.

Jake and Martha were married in an unadorned civil ceremony, attended only by Martha's parents, Harold and Ann. They came from there strong and ready and committed to each other. An aura of hope descended. It was New Year's Eve, prelude to their future. But neither knew what events lay in store.

9

You should never forget that to most persons a fit of sickness is an important event, the physician is associated with all its recollections, and you will best secure the confidence and regard of the patient and his friends, by having aided in beguiling its wearisomeness, diminishing its discomforts, relieving its anxieties, dispelling its fears, and raising its hopes. Your duty to your professional brethren, not to the least part of what is worthy of your deep consideration, may be summed up in the words of the Golden Rule: "May your manhood be irreproachable and your character unimpeachable."

Aaron Hart David, M.D.
(1812–1882)

That first month of January began with a beguiling joy. Jake and Martha just married, loving each other in special ways, each overcoming a sense of loss but looking now to the future together. And they were in Mount Pleasant, itself beguiling with its alpine motif and pungent scent of pine. But it was only days before the facade began to slip, before the idyllic became a nightmare. It happened quietly at first, with Jake and Martha getting closer, spending time over coffee discussing the new job and its daily events; spending time in bed growing closer still. In the final outcome it was their medical skills that saved them—those and their deepening love.

At first, it was the peeling back of the surface veneer that provided Mount Pleasant with its luster. Jake would bring home information and experiences; Martha would go out and scout the town, planning for them both.

"Way too many physicians, Martha." Jake said over breakfast.

"And the town can't support a neurosurgeon."

"Not really. But it is work. I got stuck with bills yesterday."

"Bills? For what, for heaven's sake?"

"Office renovation, furniture. Fancy stuff I don't need and didn't order. But I have to pay up as one of the associates."

"You got stiffed." Martha said.

"I got stiffed. And there's something else: everybody seems to be in the fancy office business, and you know what that means— a constant pressure to keep waiting rooms filled to provide a cash flow to support it all. The competition is fierce, even more it's—"

"It's what, Jake?" Martha poured him another cup of coffee.

"I'm hearing things. There's an ophthalmology group, for instance. They run a free bus service for the elderly to get them into the clinic."

"The cataract trade."

Jake nodded. "It's slick. But the fee collection is slicker. The ophthalmologists do the consultation and surgery, then they farm it out to the local physician for follow-up. Everybody gets a piece of the action—with kickbacks , of course."

"That's sick."

"There's more. A lot of these guys milk workman's compensation for all they can. Inflated charges routinely paid."

"And what about your associates?"

He looked up.

"What are you not telling me?"

"Not telling you? Well, it's gossip but—"

"But what?"

"There's talk about George. People call him a devious, cheating and stealing bastard. I discount it, but someone said he's a pathological liar. And supposedly, Jim Wright's not much better."

"Do you have first hand experience of this?"

"Well, it's only been a week, but Black's always late for office appointments, he gabs on the phone while patients are kept waiting, often hours at a time."

"That's hardly pathological."

"No, it isn't."

"What else?"

Jake got up and found his jacket. "Talk tonight, okay?"

"I'm not just your wife, Jake."

He stopped at the back door. "Meaning what?"

"I'm a pretty competent surgical nurse."

He kissed her then. "Let's give it a month. See how it goes. With lawsuits waiting back in Minnesota, I'm not exactly Mr. Cool myself."

"I'll see you tonight, Jake. No giving it a month. We talk. It's too important for both of us, and you're not going to carry any load on your own."

Jake smiled and kissed her again. "We'll talk in bed."

"For a while anyway." She smiled back.

But after Jake had left, Martha sat for quite some time at the kitchen table. The coffee grew cold.

Jake's first hospital patient was a young outdoorsman who had jounced a snowmobile while drag racing in the fog on a frozen lake. He had suffered a broken and dislocated neck, with resulting near-total paralysis of his arms and legs. After a few days of observation, Jake operated on him, removing a crushed cervical vertebra and replacing it with a bone graft from his hip. Something never attempted in a Mount Pleasant Hospital.

A few hours after surgery, Jake received a phone call from George. "The procedure went well," Jake said, finishing his review. "In retrospect, I probably should have operated sooner. As it is, he's still pretty weak in his hands and legs."

"Yeah? Well be sure to bill him for both the removal of the vertebrae and the fusion. In fact, double the normal charges. He's certain to end up as a legal case and they pay very well. Every little bit helps, Jake."

Jake hung up without comment.

The next day Black requested a consult. A middle-aged engineer had suffered a generalized epileptic convulsion, whereupon a CT-scan was obtained.

With the patient sitting on the exam table, Black queried. "What do you think this is?"

"Either a calcified tumor—" Jake pointed out the high density of the lesion. "Perhaps an oligo—or a cavernous angioma."

"I certainly think it should come out, don't you?" George patted the patient on the back. "You do it. I'll assist."

Jake sensed that the patient was being coerced to agree to surgery. Later he spent over an hour with him and his wife. But she had her mind made up.

That same week Jake removed a niggling mass of blood vessels from just within the patient's cerebral cortex. The operation was so uneventful and snappy that Black showed up too late to have his name listed on the operative ledger. In the recovery room, in front of several nurses, Black complained bitterly. "Why do you work so rapidly? Now I can't bill as a surgical assistant. In private practice, you'd better wise up. And quickly."

Jake glared, but said nothing.

The man awoke from surgery without difficulty. The next morning, he was up to the bathroom, without assistance. Plans were made for mobilization and discharge over the next few days. That evening, Black paid the patient a visit. Shortly thereafter, the man was discovered in his bed, completely unresponsive.

Jake rushed back to the hospital to see for himself. The patient appeared to have suffered a horrific brain insult. Yet a CT scan showed nothing. No swelling, bleeding, or any other sign of a problem.

The patient remained in a deep coma. Without any explanation.

A few days later the patient's wife sent a threatening letter to Jake. She demanded payment of $500,000 in lieu of being whacked with malpractice litigation. She pointed out that a "renowned neurosurgical expert" supported the claim that her husband had been operated upon "inappropriately." A conservative observation period should have been undertaken. When confronted, Black denied any involvement in the planned legal action. On that very day, his signature was notarized to a document, fully supporting that medical malpractice had been committed.

And so things began to cycle down, with earlier surgical procedures coming back in malignant repercussions: and something else, something dark and violent and frightening.

A 12-year-old was struck by a bus while delivering newspapers. The child suffered a devastating head injury. Upon arrival in the ER, he was already in a deep coma. The CT-head scan showed a cluster of angry bruises at the poles of the hemispheres, and a great deal of swelling.

Jake determined that if surgery was performed, the little leaguer would be left in an aphasic, disconnected state for the rest of his life. He made the calculated decision, after lengthy discussions with the child's parents, to undertake medical management. The kid's best chance for functional recovery.

The first few days were rocky. Even with drug-induced paralysis, blood-gas manipulations, high-dose steroids, hypothermia, and osmotic diuretics. Then after several days, the kid began to improve. By the end of the week, he was nearly waking up.

Wright was on-call that weekend. He walked in and promptly operated on the boy, removing a large chunk of the child's skull and most of his left temporal, frontal, and occipital lobes. The "A" student was left with no chance to recover.

Jake arrived at the hospital Monday morning to find his patient's head wrapped with kerlix and a kling. Wright was sitting at the nurses' station.

"Why in God's name did you operate on this kid?" Jake was beside himself. "What were you thinking?"

"I felt it was time to bite the bullet. Just get it over with."

Jake screamed at Wright. "The kid was making progress. He was beginning to wake up. For God's sake!"

"Hey, listen—" Wright looked up from his chore of recording billing information. "I've never understood all that stuff. All those damn pressure numbers. Our job is to cut. To get things like this over with quickly. You'd better get with it!"

The youngster never regained consciousness. Wright's bill to the family for a two-and-a-half-hour surgery was $12,800. And he never made any effort to visit the ravaged child or speak to his parents.

◎❖

Jake and Martha lay in bed sharing a mutual warmth. Beyond the curtains, they could see a clear night sky and its stars. A stack of JNS journals gleamed in the moonlight. "So, where the hell were you, Jake?"

"What?"

"It was nice, your body is nice—but where is your mind, where are you?"

Jake rolled back onto his pillow and stared at the ceiling.

"It's been weeks, Jake. I don't want to go on like this anymore."

"Martha, let's just leave this alone. I need a break."

"No! I'm in this too. What's going on?"

Jake's words came slow. "Ok, I told you about the snowmobile accident. The fusion and graft work."

89

"Yes. And George Black's hustle for double billing."

"Right. And remember the engineer, where I talked to his wife about options?"

"Of course."

"He went into a coma following the surgery. After a surprise visit by George."

"And how are things now?"

"He's still in a coma."

"Dear God." Martha found his hand.

"And then I had a 12-year-old kid that—" Jake hesitated.

Martha's voice was gentle. "So what happened?"

"What happened?" Jake's eyes glistened in the darkness. "What happened was Wright took out half his brain."

"Oh Jake—"

Jake stared ahead.

"What did Wright say?"

"He said I'd better get with the program."

"My lord!"

"That's not the worst of it, Martha. I'm being sued."

Martha was quiet for some time. When she spoke, her voice carried a surprising strength. "We'll handle the litigation," she said. "But as of now I'm going to find out all I can about George Black. This is a small town. There are ways to find things out."

"Well, we know he's a devious cheating bastard."

"And he probably is pathological."

10

It was Martha, small town girl who understood how small towns worked, who began digging up information on Drs. George Black and Jim Wright. She discounted some as hysteria, the sort of witchcraft mumbo jumbo that lay people attribute to the medical profession because they are afraid of its power over their lives. But what was left was a trail of devious maneuvering, especially on the part of George. There was a history of suspension of George's license to practice medicine; the last time because he permitted his physician's assistant to do brain surgery unattended. And, according to the wife of a dentist as she loaded groceries into her station wagon, just before Jake's arrival many of George Black's hospital privileges had been canned. These were withdrawn and not for the first time by the local medical staff: deficiencies included inadequate record keeping, inappropriate patient care, and malicious antagonism in his dealings with other physicians and staff. Martha watched as the dentist's wife swung down the rear door with a soft thump. But she asked nothing else. Who knew the network the dentist was in?

Her next chance came a few days later at the post office. An elderly man in a broad sun hat was sending off a large box to Nigeria. "Someone's getting a nice treat," Martha smiled brightly as she bought stamps.

"It's for my son, a couple of changes of clothes. He's a missionary and keeps going around in the same old pants."

Martha laughed. "He's obviously focused on the Lord's work."

"Yup."

"Are you a minister?"

"I was. I'm retired now." He hesitated. "Took early retirement. Things were getting hard."

"Oh, I'm sorry."

"Had a back problem. Didn't do too well after surgery."

"Back surgery can be bad."

"True enough. But this doctor, well…"

"Oh? I've just moved here, I don't—"

"Black. George Black." The elderly man pushed back his hat. "Stay away from him. He's slippery. Heard he's got another new doctor in town to speak up for him. Keeps getting suspended but always comes back. At board meetings at church, we lay bets on it. Well, have a nice day…"

◉⊡✦

Jake and Martha sat at the kitchen table, falling into their easy rhythm of review and planning. Martha finished quietly. "You realize, George plans to convince the hospital board that he's turned over a new leaf. And just to show his good intentions, why, here's the well respected Dr. Jason Gibson…"

Jake was quiet for some time. "Tomorrow," he said, looking at Martha. "Tomorrow I go see him. Have it out."

Jake pressed the wooden crucifix inside his pocket, withdrew his hand and went into George Black's office. George looked up at him as he quietly closed the door behind him. "We have to talk, George."

"Oh?"

"In a word, things are going on around here that I don't like."

"Is that so."

"It's right across the board, George: excessive billings, inappropriate surgeries—

George stood up behind his desk. "So you want to quit, is that it? We ain't noble enough for you."

"I know I can't continue in this practice. I made a mistake coming here-"

"Really, Gibson? Then just where in hell do you plan to practice your oh, so noble profession? Doesn't seem to me as if you have much of a choice. Nobody'll have you! You get that, Dr. High and Mighty? Nobody wants you."

Jake was ready to just walk away, but his instincts told him to hold on.

"You better wake up fast, my friend," George said, coming around from behind his desk. "There isn't a single place in the whole country that's open to you. There's not another job around that you can run to. Fact is, I'm the only real advocate you have." George stared deep into Jake's eyes. "Did you know your own chairman has given up on you?"

"That's bullshit."

"Really?" George pulled open a file drawer and offered Jake a letter.

December 8
Mr. Marty Sorrentino
Administrator – Mount Pleasant Hospital

Dear Sir:

I'm writing in response to your request for a recommendation regarding Jason P. Gibson M.D., former professor of neurosurgery in my department. Unfortunately, I find it virtually impossible to provide a favorable impression of this colleague. In fact, I have recently withdrawn my support for his continued membership in the Cushing Society and for his renewed credentials before the American Board of Neurosurgery.

Sincerely,

Vincent R. Wilson, M. D.

Jake swallowed down the bile rising in his throat, handed the letter back to George, and left the office.

The next few months took on a slow rhythm of surgeries and stressed exchanges with George and Jim Wright. Money drove all action and Jake had to fight against it, which drew him deeper and deeper into a web of hostility and ugliness. His only defense as the nightmare unfolded was to perform excellent surgical procedures then get home and talk to Martha, his anchor, his sounding board against doubts about his own stability. Jake would explain what was happening. Sometimes over a glass of wine before dinner, sometimes in bed with the quiet dark, looking at the ceiling. Looking at the night sky beyond the curtain, they did not know how much worse things would get.

———————————

◉❈✠

There was Andy, age 10 years, trying out his new roller blades. Thrown into a somersault onto his helmetless head. His mother, who had witnessed the accident, later reported to Jake in the ER that her son seemed to lose consciousness for a few seconds, but then quickly was able to get to his feet. Complaining of some headache, he was alert enough to untie and slip off his roller blades and drag them back to their driveway where he left them with the rest of his things.

Once inside the house, he complained of an increasing headache, and shortly thereafter became drowsy. At that point, his mother called 911. By the time the ambulance arrived some nine or ten minutes later, he had become very sleepy and was barely rousable. Paramedics noted that his left pupil was larger and less reactive to light than his right. By the time they got to the emergency room, he was nearly comatose, his breathing rapid and irregular.

With Andy's left mydriasis and right hemiparesis Jake suspected at once an acute left-sided epidural hematoma: a blood clot was forming between the dural covering and the skull, with resultant brain compression and progressive herniation. When Andy arrived in the operating room, his ER stretcher changed hands without stopping. Jake was already pushing the surgical team, such as it was.

"Let's get this started!" He called to the waiting attendants just inside the sterile zone of the OR corridor. As they got ready, the enlarging clot was causing additional compression to the boy's vital brainstem respiratory control centers. By the time Jake had changed clothes and entered the room, Andy had been intubated and positioned on an OR table in preparation for the procedure.

Jake pointed with his index finger to map out the area of interest on the skull. He directed the shaving, prepping and sterilization procedure while he scrubbed his hands. As Jake dried his hands on the sterile towel he knew a first fear: this was not the Minneapolis team; this was not Martha smoothly arranging and readying the surgical instruments. Jake spoke into the frenzied activity.

"Okay, everybody, have we gotten ourselves together enough to do this? Are we prepared to start? Is everybody on the same page? Can we get this thing going or not?"

There were blank and confused looks. There was scurrying and fumbling, perhaps stampeded by his words. There was the banging of sanitized trays and the clang of dropped metal as delicate instruments crashed to the floor.

Holy Mother help me!

Jake snatched a #21 scalpel and empty handle from the scrub nurse's poorly laid out table, assembled the two, and with one precise movement sliced through all layers of scalp. He made a lengthy curved cut that extended like a question mark from just above the boy's left ear, across the side of his head, there to end at on his forehead just behind the hairline. Bright red blood spurted from the tissue margins. An inexperienced surgical assistant found the hemostat clamps for Jake to place along the cut edges. The scalp was fully opened and its layers retracted to expose a large enough portion of the underlying skull bone. "Now we're getting somewhere," Jake muttered behind his mask. "Okay, let's have the power drill." Jake held his opened hand out impatiently. The drill would place the lifesaving holes.

"Sorry, doctor, it's not in the room. I think it's still in the sterilizer."

"All right. Hand me a Del Rico perforator." Jake said, prepared to use an archaic but commonly available alternative tool.

"Doctor, that isn't available either—"

"What! Listen, this kid is dying by the minute." Jake glared around at the masked faces, his empty hand still outstretched. "I need to get a hole in his head and right this damned second!"

"Sorry doctor, it'll be at least fifteen minutes before the power drill is sterile. It's still being flashed."

Jake closed his eyes against the madness, the stress slicing across his shoulders. "I want something right now," he said, controlling his voice. "I want something to make an opening in this kid's skull. Where in God's name is your trephine?"

It was an eternity before the nurse in charge responded. "We don't know, doctor, no one can seem to locate it."

Sweat trickled down Jake's temple. "All right. Get me a small bone chisel and a mallet."

Dear God.

Seconds later a set of crude carpenter's tools were unwrapped and handed to him. Jake chiseled away a small opening in the side of Andy's skull. After a few repetitive, clinically precise chops, dark red blood spurted through an irregular hole in the bone.

"Walter Dandy would be proud." Jake sucked in against his wet mask. "Now, do you think you can find me a simple duckbill rongeur?"

It was an ancient instrument, but in the hands of a master. Jake enlarged the initial lopsided aperture from the size of a nickel to the size of a silver dollar. Then, using a large-bore suction device, he began to withdraw thickly clotted blood.

"Watch his blood pressure," Jake shouted to the inexperienced anesthesiologist. "The severe compression of the brain up here is just about to be relieved."

Jake could feel his own horrific tension subsiding as he secured a hemostasis around the slightly oozing edges of the wound. Using an ancient Bovie electro-cautery he buzzed a group of tagged subcutaneous bleeders. A small cloud of smoke ascended in the room, briefly curling over the youngster.

That was when the drill arrived. Jake ignored it while he got on with the job. He completely removed the clotted blood and identified the tiny actively oozing meningeal artery on the surface of the dura. Jake reached outside himself to relieve his frustration. He found it in teaching.

"This is certainly the source of the brain clot. See how the skull fracture tore this conterminous blood vessel? That's how it bled and eventually formed a clot just underneath the skull."

His words drained off some of the stress in the room.

As soon as he finished, Jake headed for the waiting room. The honor student was already beginning to wake up in recovery.

"Wait a minute. We don't understand," the child's mother stammered. "Another doctor called in and told us that my boy… our son…" Her body was shaking. "That there was no chance he would ever…" The child's father was forced to continue. "He said that you weren't able to get the clot out quickly enough."

That night, Jake worked in his office catching up on paperwork, trying to tap off his anger and frustration at the malevolence in life. A heavy rain was falling, and there were flashes of lightning. It was around 2 A.M. when he shoved aside patients' files and notes on office visits and got up to leave. That was when he saw it, something positioned under file folders, a gleaming edge catching lamplight. As he lifted files and journals to look underneath, he found the stainless steel skull perforator. There was a handwritten note attached:

> *Hey, Big Shot Brain Surgeon—were you looking for this? Some things are just never around when you need them. Sort of underscores the value of keeping your mouth shut, right?*

Several bright flashes caromed against dark cloud and rain sluiced down. Thunder reverberated on the panes of glass. The lights went out. Jake had not experienced genuine fear often, but he felt it now. Sick to his stomach, he got up and left his office. He felt his way along the hallway. He went by George Black's office, then stopped suddenly. From inside came a muffled static voice. Lightning offered a jagged light in the darkness, then thunder rolled. Jake shook his head and left the deserted building.

A vile day, a perverted day, of imagined voices and nightmares to come. He needed Martha and her warmth and her abiding love. He was ground down to that: he needed.

11

The knife is dangerous in the hands of the wise, let alone in the hands of the fool.

Hebrew Proverbs

In the repugnant scheme of things, Jake fought back with what he had: good medicine. He had gifted hands, and with them he reached out. He reached out to the Asian woman; he reached out to the construction worker; he reached out to the timber-cutter. And he watched all his efforts end in ugliness, maltreatment, and finally, a horror so bestial and obscene that it all ended for him. But for now, as he struggled to pay six figure insurance premiums while he faced lawsuits in Minneapolis, and while he fought off the wife's threatening letter and demand for $500,000, Jake worked on.

The Asian woman spoke little English. She was brought into the ER early one Saturday afternoon with worsening headaches and loss of vision. These were discovered to be secondary symptoms to obstructive hydrocephalus. She had been infested by parasites months earlier from contaminated meat. Parasite ova were within the fluid spaces of her brain. Her presenting signs were produced by a buildup of spinal fluid pressure within partially blocked and dilated ventricles. There was high risk of death if even a single parasitic ovum was released. The caustic fluid resulting in dangerous meningeal inflammation and life-threatening swelling throughout the brain.

Jake picked and poked through the cisternal spaces surrounding the hind-brain. With meticulous care, he searched for each and every one of the infectious ova. The brain stem-regulating centers that controlled most every vital bodily function were dangerously close at hand. Painstakingly, sweat trickling down to his mask, he dissected free each ovum and removed it. He had what he was after: the entire CSF pathway was freed of obstructing material.

Immigration officials yanked her from her recovery bed. A minimum-wage seamstress with two boys, she was deported. The authorities had been alerted by an "anonymous" tip. The tip came from a "civic minded" local physician who had filed a report with the sheriff's department.

The construction worker was forty-five years old, and he came in by appointment with his wife and attorney. His complaint was severe lumbar pain, brought on by a lifting injury suffered at work. As Jake reviewed the patient's spinal x-rays, he realized that the problem was of a congenital nature, certainly unrelated to any traumatic lifting event.

Jake looked up and smiled. "You have a condition called spondylolisthesis, a slippage in alignment between two of the vertebrae in your lower back. Probably something you were born with."

The lawyer was having none of it. "Dr. Gibson, my unfortunate client never had any problem with his back before he was hurt at work. I don't think you fully realize the terrible trauma this poor man has suffered. I know he'll never be the same again. Certainly, he won't ever be able to return to any sort of gainful employment."

Jake set aside the lawyer's comments and described the possible treatment options. And in fact, the patient did return for office visits, each of which coincided with his employer's requests that he return to work. It was the attorney who made the determination that an operative treatment was in his client's long-term best interest.

During a two-and-a-half hour surgery, Jake was able to successfully fuse the involved motion segments, and he performed it using only a two-and-a-half centimeter incision. The otherwise well built man was discharged and remained pain free for several weeks. After tilling his garden one day, however, he began to complain of recurrent shooting pain in his lower back and leg. A follow-up evaluation which included spinal films showed a perfect positioning of the fusion mass with nothing amiss. Despite Jake's efforts to give it time, the construction worker was having none of it. His lawyer insisted on a second opinion.

It was Dr. Jim Wright who gave the second opinion, advising that Dr. Gibson's surgery had been "fuddled", and that an additional procedure would definitely be necessary to make it right. Subsequent surgery by Dr. Wright left the patient with a disabling paralysis in one of his legs and severe, unrelenting pain. The resultant disability and chronic pain syndrome were related by the construction worker's attorney to Jake's misguided operative intervention. A million-dollar-plus malpractice lawsuit was initiated without delay, to supplement the patient's several hundred thousand dollar claim for permanent and complete disability.

Martha smiled at him across the breakfast table and handed him a letter with the address written on it in an old fashioned hand. But behind the smile, she watched him as a trained nurse would watch: Jake was stressed; and from their last time together, held in his arms, she knew he was gone from her. Warm arms, but distanced as they tried to embrace the whirl of problems upon him.

Jake took the letter. "Someone else suing us?"

"Nope. It's your mom. She says they are all thinking about us and know that things will work out."

Jake smiled and set the letter aside. "Good. I'll read it later."

"I have more news from town, it's not so good."

"Okay. Lay it on me." Jake sat hunched over his coffee cup.

Martha hesitated. "We could—just pull up stakes. Get out now."

"What've you heard, Martha?"

"Okay. George is on what they call around here his seven year cycle. Every seventh year, he declares bankruptcy. He never has assets, just huge debts. As that seventh year approaches, he picks up as many loans as he can."

Jake slowly turned his cup, watching the dark brew wet the cup's insides.

"He has incredible success with a down on his luck doctor routine. The only people who aren't fooled are the town's lawyers. George can't find a lawyer within fifty miles of here who'll talk to him. In the recent litigations he has faced, he has been his own lawyer."

"And people say he's pretty good at it."

Martha nodded. "Bingo."

"What else?"

"A sexual discrimination charge brought by several female employees. Physical contact, seductive manner inappropriate to a clinical setting."

"He talked his way out of it, I'll bet."

"Yup. Swayed a mostly male jury."

"Why am I not surprised?" Jake shook his head. "What else?"

"He has closed door agreements with the administrator at Mount Pleasant Memorial Hospital—"

"How the hell did you learn that?"

"Wives, Jake. Professional wives. While we look over cauliflowers and get our nails done."

"Jesus."

"You know, I found out that was the first hospital in the Expercare chain. My cold bastard of an ex-husband got his start there." Martha shoved her cup aside and put her elbows on the table. She stared at Jake. "Here's the worst of it. Every time a paying patient is admitted into the hospital by your group, a kickback is placed into a special account. Every day the patient is hospitalized, an additional contribution is made to the fund."

"So that's why they keep patients in the hospital so long."

Martha nodded.

"Don't tell me. Only Black and Wright have access to this fund."

"Right."

"How much are we talking here?"

Martha shrugged. "Holiday travel for families, thoroughbreds for George's horse ranch, a chalet in Switzerland for Jim Wright." She hesitated. "And the wedding."

"Whose?"

"George's youngest son. He married Lawrence Hamel's daughter—"

"The philanthropist, the millionaire in discount pharmaceuticals?"

"That's him. At the same ceremony, George Black exchanged vows with the guy's wife."

Jake's eyes drove into her. "Wait a minute, how could he marry—"

"Seems old man Hamel died unexpectedly of a massive heart attack."

They sat quietly for a long time. Outside birds sang. Clouds drifted over stands of pine.

Jake leaned back and rubbed his face. "That's it?"

"Except for the rape of Susie." Martha rushed on before Jake could interrupt. "Hamel's youngest daughter, a stunning California blond. You know, the one George always described as easy on the eyes. Susie stood up at the ceremony and blamed her father's death on George. Halfway through the reception, she was seen running through the kitchen area, she seemed high on something…her clothes were torn."

"And that's when she got pregnant? Went to Europe, the private girl's school?"

"Yes." Martha hesitated. "Jake?"

"What?"

"We've got to get out of here, you've got to quit. This place, this man—there's evil here."

"We've got to hang on a little, Martha. We have lawsuits, we need to hang on." He reached across for her hand. "I can't get another job right now, George's right about that. I don't know what else to do."

"I worry about you."

"I'm all right."

◎⊗✠

At the local timber company, the most limber of the tree cutters would scale the gigantic sequoia trunks and attach a rope near the top. To guide its fall to earth. But this day, the cinching rope had slipped. The trunk broke loose and a middle-aged father of eight, working two jobs to support his family, had his cranium trapped and crushed. It was immediately evident in the ER that the tree cutter helicoptered in had sustained hopelessly severe and irreversible brain injury. Huge clumps of cortical material were seeping out from beneath the open fractures in the skull. There was no brain activity either on thorough neurologic exam or EEG testing.

It was for Jake a spiritual time in which he grieved for the family and its loss, but summoned hope in the knowledge that the man's organs and other priceless gifts could be harvested and used to help others live. He spoke at length with the distraught family who, with that quiet courage so often given by quiet living people, agreed to the organ donations. Jake secured all of the required verifications necessary for the regional transport coordinator to evaluate, then made the needed arrangements. Before leaving the hospital that Saturday afternoon, Jake gathered the necessary documentation to certify that the patient met all of the official established criteria for brain death. After bidding their final farewells, the family went home to mourn.

It was in the soothing quiet of his own home that Jake got the frantic phone call. Senorita Gomez, a Spanish immigrant serving as evening nurse supervisor at the hospital, could barely get her words out in English.

"Dr. Gibson, I don't think anyone has spoken to the family about this!"

"Of course we have, I spoke to them myself. They agreed to everything. There's no problem."

"Oh, thank God. I was concerned. Things seemed to change direction. You know, sometimes Dr. Black doesn't let families know—"

"Dr. Black?" Jake's stomach caved in.

"He rushed the patient to surgery!"

"What do you mean, he took the patient to surgery? What does he have to do with organ harvesting?"

"Dr. Gibson, Dr. Black canceled all that. He's got the man in the operating room for an emergency craniotomy!"

When Jake slammed the phone down, it slipped free. Martha picked it up.

"It's Black. He's performing a craniotomy on a dead man."

Martha's hand went to her mouth. She recovered enough to drive him back to the hospital.

Jake pushed through into the operating room and watched George Black work on a brain dead patient. The violence to his soul was beyond description.

"George, what the hell are you doing?"

George let his bloody hands drop away from the body. "What am I doing? That's pretty obvious, isn't it? I'm trying to save this man's life."

"For Christ's sake, George! This patient has a flat EEG and no brain activity! Why in the world would—"

"Why? I'll tell you why, Gibson. Because in this day and age every head-injured patient has a right to an operation." He pointed his finger, blood dripping. "What a total fuck up you are! Now I guess we all know why you got your ass kicked out of Minneapolis."

Jake stared at the madness.

"You have no right to be here!" George screamed. "You are interfering with a life saving procedure! I'll have you brought before the state license board. Now get the hell out of my operating room before I have your ass thrown out!"

Martha watched him carefully as they walked to the car. He was going down, and there wasn't anything she could do to stop it. Beyond the car, Mount Pleasant offered its first evening lights. The scent of pine mellowed the air.

12

Operating rooms and courts of law are different worlds. In one, Jake moved with assurance, with consummate skill and discipline; he made incisive decisions based on instinct and training, and yes, hunches; but hunches born of a brilliant mind and personal faith. Here in the Minneapolis courtroom, he was essentially adrift, a victim of his own naive faith that right will see one through, that truth is its own defense. Moving from one world into the other at a time when his mind and heart were under assault did not bode well.

Jake sat at the defendant's table with his lawyer and looked across at those who condemned him. There was Mitch Malone, apparently fully recovered, elegant in an expensive suit. A batch of lawyers were gathered around him, deferential, tentative, waiting, stacks of file folders at arms length. Seated were Malone's daughter, Shannon, and another partner in the firm, M. L. Auclair. Auclair was known to Jake by reputation. He was a balding man, going to fat around his middle, he had a permanent suntan acquired in tropical places. The crocodile boots were famous in the lawyer trade. Behind Mitch Malone's table were others he knew who spelled trouble: David Hudley, former associate Alex Al-Fassad, and the sleek and dangerous Everett Salig. Scattered around the audience were colleagues and friends: Vincent Wilson, although after having read his letter to George Black, Jake wondered how much of a friend he was. And beside him, there was Midge Stone. Jeanne wasn't there; she and Ben no doubt attending to the new baby. Jake remembered sitting with Jeanne on the couch, that special touch of her belly, the mix of a doctor's reverence for the life inside her, and the man's melancholy for a love denied and forever beyond his touch. But life had gone on, and Jake had Martha, a gathering strength as their marriage moved forward through troubled times. And something else: he looked back at her, seated just behind the defendant's table, smiling at their secret knowledge. Martha was pregnant. Their joy now centered on whether or not they would have twins. They would know today. Just a phone call back to Mount Pleasant and the obstetrician. Their secret, their love for each other, insulated Jake as he sat in the courtroom. There was malevolence here, and duplicity, and ugliness; but there was in Martha's presence goodness and hope and abiding faith.

The trial had gained national attention. Evidenced by the huddled reporters inside and satellite trucks outside. Video cameras were in place overhead. Jake frowned into one—at the soap opera aficionados around the country tuned into the civil justice system. Just for entertainment.

The chamber door opened at precisely 9 A.M. and Judge Abigail Tillman swept in. The bailiff's announcement carried across the courtroom. Approaching sixty, silver haired, resonant of voice, her composure in her floor length robe immediately dominated the proceedings. Formal words, cold yet elegant phrases, were a prelude to the hearings. Then it all began, the potential jurors moved like puppets by the lawyers as they maneuvered for a favorable jury. Jake looked back at Martha. He watched the small smile, the hand patting her belly.

During opening remarks, Jake scanned the faces at the opposing table. Sworn incriminations, grotesque in their distortions, skewered him. But he kept his face neutral. As the sun moved across a high window, slanting light across tables and polished floorboards, Jake saw the case shaping against him. And he had to admit that some of it was his own doing: a trust in speaking the truth, simply; and an adamant request that Martha not be drawn into the proceedings. During that morning's preliminaries she would lean forward, her words encouraging, her love ever-close.

Lunch was graveled. A two-hour recess. Jake and Martha headed for the door. It was then that they saw Martha's ex-husband, Howard. His glare was for Martha.

"Let's find a phone," Jake said. "Check with your doctor."

Martha made the call on a pay phone. Jake stood close by, conscious of curious people staring at them, these trial gawkers. He waited.

Martha hung up the phone and went into his arms. Her words were warm against his ear, lifting his grief at George Black's obscene surgery, lifting his anger at Jim Wright's crippling of a patient, buttressing his confidence as he faced his trial. "Twins," she murmured.

Jake's lawyer Callahan was waiting for them.

"We have a settlement offer."

"What?" Jake put his hand on Martha's arm.

"It's Mitch Malone. He'll dismiss the case without prejudice for half a million dollars. The insurance company is prepared to accept this."

"So, what's the catch?"

Callahan's eyes glinted behind his studious glasses. "The catch is you must surrender your medical license and agree—"

"No way!"

"—and agree to never again practice medicine in the state of Minnesota."

Martha's hand found his. "No."

"Okay. Then I must tell you that legally, from this point on, your insurance company is responsible for only the first half million in damages. If we go through this trial and you lose big-time, everything in excess of $500,000 is your responsibility."

Jake stared incredulously at his lawyer. "Hey wait, now. You mean my multi-million dollar umbrella coverage all of a sudden is only worth $500,000?"

"That's right."

"That's ridiculous." Jake turned his back. "Wait here. Martha and I need to talk."

They found a quiet corner, a wooden bench.

"We can lose everything," Jake said. "Be financially smashed for life."

"I know. But I support you, Jake. You're in the right. We'll fight to win, and if necessary, take what comes."

"There's the baby—twins, I mean."

"We're family, Jake. We face it together."

"We fight, then."

"We fight."

Shannon Malone began the initial presentation of her father's side of the story. While she played to the cameras now sited around the room, she did have a special look for Jake. It echoed back to her meeting him outside the depo room and thanking him for saving her father's life. She spoke confidently and moved with poise. She was the focus of attention in her tan jacket and skirt with its soft cream lace blouse. But her presentation was brief, and Jake watched as plaintiff's attorney Auclair took over. The crocodile boots stepped methodically over the sun slanted floor boards. Notes were held against his thickening waistline. Dr. Hudley was called to testify.

"Dr. Hudley, would you please review for this court the events following the arrival of the plaintiff, Mitch Malone, onto the neurosurgery service at the University Hospital?"

"Yes, sir. Shortly after the patient was—"

"Excuse me, by patient you mean Mr. Malone?" Auclair said.

"Yes. After Mr. Malone was admitted to the hospital by Dr. Gibson, he and I discussed how we should proceed with treatment. The patient—I mean Mr. Malone—at the time was gravely ill, and Dr. Gibson instructed me not to do anything."

"You mean not to treat him?"

"No. Yes. Well, sort of—I mean he told me not to use aggressive measures, like administering steroids or applying full resuscitative measures."

"You mean, Dr. Gibson gave you an order to give up?"

Callahan was on his feet. "Objection."

"Overruled."

"Well, that was the gist of it."

"Did you have the feeling that Dr. Gibson expected Mr. Malone to die?"

"Objection!" Callahan said. "Leading the witness."

"Overruled, but be careful with the phrasing of your questions, Mr. Auclair."

"Thank you, your honor. Tell me, Dr. Hudley, what conclusion did you draw from these directives?"

"I felt that Mr. Malone was expected to die."

"Anything else?"

"Yes. That he wanted Malone to die."

"Objection!"

"Overruled."

"Can you share with this court why you came to such a conclusion?"

"Yes. It was his attitude. You see, Dr. Gibson always pushed absolutely every button. He was always on a mission, a crusade of some kind. Even in hopeless cases he never gave up."

That brought a wry smile from Jake as he remembered giving up on a brain-dead patient and the madness that followed.

"But in this situation," Hudley went on, "he didn't do that. It wasn't his usual all-out attempt to perform a miracle. Consequently, I knew right away that something was different."

"Dr. Hudley, were you aware that the defendant had come to know Mr. Malone before he brought to the hospital?"

"Yes, everyone knew that. Mr. Malone handled a big malpractice suit against Dr. Gibson and the hospital several years ago. I believe it was for his negligence in the care of a woman who committed suicide. The scuttlebutt around the hospital was that it was one the largest malpractice awards ever. We heard he got hit for over $5 million!"

"Your honor!" Callahan jumped to his feet.

A smattering of oohs and aahs could be heard around the courtroom. Cameras zoomed in on Hudley.

"I withdraw the question."

Jake glanced at Callahan, relieved that he had finally scored a point.

"So you are convinced that the prior suit had something to do with Dr. Gibson's attitude about taking on Mr. Malone as a patient?"

"Objection!" Callahan was up again.

"Okay, I'll restate the question." Auclair tapped his notes. "Dr. Hudley, in your opinion based on working with Dr. Gibson for a number of years, and based on what you told us about the events of that day surrounding the treatment of Mr. Malone, did Dr. Gibson willfully withhold proper treatment from this patient?"

"Yes. It's my belief that he did."

Jake stared at the table. He ran over in his mind Hudley's unprofessional conduct, the frequent absences, the abrasive behavior, the mediocre skills.

"Okay. Now, Dr. Hudley. Tell the jury about Dr. Gibson's reaction the next morning, when he discovered that Mr. Malone had improved."

"Well, he seemed absolutely shocked."

"Could you be more specific?"

"Yes. I was there that morning with the patient—I mean, Mr. Malone and his wife, when Dr. Gibson arrived. I think he expected him to be dead or close to it. Instead he was awake and talking."

"What exactly did Dr. Gibson say?"

"Something like, 'I can't believe this'."

"And what did he do then?"

"He decided to immediately go ahead with surgery."

"Is that standard practice?"

"No, not exactly."

"What do you mean, not exactly."

"Well, most surgeons would wait for a patient who had suffered severe bleeding around the brain, like Mr. Malone, to further recover before proceeding with a difficult and dangerous operation."

Auclair nodded. "Is that what you would have done?"

"Certainly. I would have waited at least a week or two. As I said, until he had completely recovered."

"Do you think Dr. Gibson's rush into surgery was an attempt to harm Mr. Malone?"

"Your honor!" Callahan stood rigid. "I object."

"Objection sustained."

"All right, Dr. Hudley. From a medical standpoint, based on a reasonable degree of medical certainty, did Dr. Gibson's action jeopardize the life of Mr. Malone?"

"Yes. In my opinion it certainly did."

"And as you sit here today, Dr. Hudley, do you think that Dr. Gibson knowingly, willingly, and deliberately performed surgery in order to jeopardize Mitch Malone's life?"

It was clever and rehearsed. Hudley deliberately turned to make eye contact with Jake, the doctor of integrity facing a bad practitioner of medicine, the doctor standing up for what was right. "Yes, I do."

Hudley answered the question before Callahan could object.

As Jake watched Hudley, he tried to conceive what had triggered such a vicious lie. Surely his associates in the courtroom would not go along with these falsehoods. Yet, looking around, Jake could read their faces.

"Now, Dr. Hudley, let's turn our attention to the events surrounding the operations. Let's begin with the first surgery. I assume you were there?"

"Yes," he nodded. "I assisted Dr. Gibson with the procedure."

Jake scribbled a note to Callahan. *Ask him why he dropped a piece of Malone's skull, which I caught before it hit the ground.*

"Did everything proceed normally during the surgery?"

"Yes—well, that is until one of the aneurysms ruptured and bled."

"How did that occur?"

"As Dr. Gibson was placing a clip around the larger aneurysm's neck, it suddenly blew out."

"Any idea as to why it 'blew out', as you put it?"

"The clip was too short."

Martha leaned forward and pressed a reassuring hand on Jake's shoulder. Jake glanced at her, recalling her in the OR, her surgical mask, her competent handling of instruments.

"He used a clip that was too short?" Auclair's finger pointed at Jake.

"The use of a clip that's not the correct one—is that something a competent surgeon such as Dr. Gibson might commonly do?"

"No. A surgeon of Dr. Gibson's experience should know just how long a clip should be for any situation."

Auclair retreated to the plaintiff's table. There he dramatically held up an ordinary lunch bag and withdrew a borrowed aneurysm clip applier. Holding the delicate lifesaving instrument like a dagger, he paced in his crocodile boots, building tension as he appeared to be formulating his question. "Did this rupture and bleeding caused by the improper clip endanger Mr. Malone's life?"

"Well, yes, of course! We all thought he would likely die, right there in front of us."

"What did Dr. Gibson do when the aneurysm started to bleed?" Auclair twirled the instrument in the air, letting it catch the slanting sunlight.

"He got real nervous."

"This was obvious to those watching?"

"Yes."

"Can you tell us anything more?"

"Well, it looked to me like Dr. Gibson had suddenly realized that everyone in the room could see what he was trying to do. It was as though he had second thoughts about what he was doing, and so he was trying to correct things."

"So it's your testimony, Dr. Hudley, that Dr. Gibson behaved as if he had been caught red-handed?"

"Objection, Your Honor! This is preposterous!" Callahan waited in agitation.

"Sustained."

"Dr. Hudley, I will restate my question. In your opinion, did Dr. Gibson's actions in the OR that day indicate to you that he purposely placed a clip that was too short along the base of the second aneurysm causing it to bleed uncontrollably; and then, realizing what he had done, in full view of everyone in the room, did he try to conceal his action by replacing the clip with a properly-sized one?"

"I believe that is exactly what happened."

Martha's eyes were begging Jake. She had been there, handled the clips, let me testify! Jake shook his head. He looked around the jury, studying their faces. They were believing every word Hudley was dishing out. For the first time, he began to doubt his faith in truth being its own defense.

"Dr. Hudley, Dr. Gibson operated on Mr. Malone a second time later that evening. Can you tell the jury, in your own words, what happened that night, and what led Dr. Gibson to perform another procedure?"

"Yes. Well, I wasn't really involved in the second operation itself. Dr. Gibson performed that on his own. We were all concerned though, about the way he was behaving that evening. I believe he had been to a ball game—and may have been drinking."

Jake watched the jurors.

"He seemed to be distracted and in a big hurry to operate. I was worried about him. I didn't think he was capable of making decisions that evening, so I suggested to Mr. Malone's wife that perhaps a second opinion was a good idea."

Hudley's answers were following an obvious route.

"But Dr. Gibson didn't wait for the second opinion, did he?"

"No, sir. He did not."

"Dr. Gibson rushed Mr. Malone back to surgery, against the objections of his wife and family."

"Yes, he did."

"And against your advice as well."

"Yes." Again Hudley's eyes found Jake. "He sure did."

13

Suffer not thy mouth to condemn when something happens to a physician, for everyone has his evil day.

Isaac Israeli
(9th–10th Century)

When Callahan cross-examined Hudley for the balance of the afternoon, it became apparent that he lacked the skills of Auclair. He did not have the dramatic pause, the timing that imbued sometimes mundane comments with a sense of hidden meaning. Auclair could take the routine and render it fraught with menace against the patient's well-being. Callahan offered only a digging of facts and rephrasing of them that revealed no new insight, no forward movement. It was, Jake realized, a poor presentation of who he was and what he was all about. The $5 million dollar suit against him, slipped cunningly into the jurors' minds, dampened any instinct to think well of him. Jake looked around for his father and found him off to the right, halfway back. He nodded reassuringly at Jake. Thank God they were staying with his folks in that warm loving home. A sanctuary. Good will. Love. Kindness. Jake smiled at his father.

Just as Judge Tillman ordered a recess for the day, Jake was handed a message from the bailiff. He was to call the Mt. Pleasant Hospital. Martha and Jake said they would see Jake's dad at home, then they made their way to a pay phone.

He was connected to Carol McTegg. Head nurse of the intensive care unit.

"Dr. Gibson, Mrs. Chiodini isn't doing well." She had concern in her voice. "I'm sorry to bother you there, but I didn't know what else to do. Dr. Vierling, her internist, said to call the neurosurgeons."

"Did you call Dr. Black?" Jake's pulse pressure widened.

"I tried, but he's at the clinic today. I spoke with him—twice." Nurse McTegg sounded aggravated. "But all he did was tell me not to worry about it."

Jake glanced incredulously at Martha over the phone.

Two weeks earlier, Jake had operated on the sweet, elderly lady for a small surface meningioma. The cause of focal seizures. The tumor had been simple to remove. If it weren't for her diabetes, she would have been home a couple of days after surgery. And yesterday she had developed a blood clot in her leg, like her diabetes, being managed by her internist.

"Has she been put on blood thinners, Carol?"

"They were started yesterday."

"Ok, tell you what—" Jake stared at the graffiti on the phone panel. "Let's order a CT of her head. And keep calling Black. Somebody needs to get over there and take a look at her."

◎⬦✠

The ride home was uncomfortably quiet.

"So, how're you feeling?" Jake forced a smile.

"I'm fine, Jake. And I should be asking you that."

He nodded. "Rough day. And now this."

Martha hesitated. "Callahan doesn't have it."

Jake avoided her eyes.

"Look, I could testify and—"

"No! I said no and I mean it, Martha." Jake's voice carried a hot edge.

"But I was there, the clip size, Hudley's poor techniques—dropping a piece of Malone's skull for chrissakes—"

"No. I mean it. No. Howard Crane will chew you up. Auclair and Malone, they'll crucify you—it's no go, Martha. We'll rely on truth, straightforward truth. I'll get through to the jury."

The silence was cold and ugly. Martha's arms went over her belly.

"Sorry, darling. That came out too hot. Maybe it's that call from Mt. Pleasant, I don't know. I just want you safe, I—"

"I support you, Jake."

That was all she said.

When they pulled into his parents' driveway, his father's car was already there. The house offered warm lights, and the front door opened, his mother beckoning. Boxes of spring decorations, Easter baskets and plastic eggs were stacked in the hall, ready to be put to use. And there was another message from Mt. Pleasant.

Jake telephoned Nurse McTegg back.

"Dr. Gibson. Our CT is down for repairs."

Jake collapsed into a nearby chair.

"Mrs. Chiodini is getting worse, she's beginning to straighten her arms and legs to stimulation," Nurse McTegg reported.

"Jesus, she's posturing. Hasn't Black been there yet?"

"Nope. Haven't seen him."

The rest of the blood drained from Jake's face. "Christ in Heaven, call somebody Stat! Tell them this is a life-and-death emergency."

Jake slammed the phone down while his parents and Martha stared at him.

He paced by the phone for over an hour. He couldn't eat his favorite meal, specially prepared by his mother.

He called the ICU again. Black had arrived.

"Jake, I don't see where there's anything to worry about. I'll take another look at her tomorrow."

Nothing to worry about? Tomorrow? Jake pulled the phone closer to his mouth. "George, the lady's slipped into a coma. She's probably got a hematoma in the tumor bed, from the anticoagulants." He words were pointed. "There won't be a tomorrow if nothing is done now."

"Well, I don't happen to see it that way, pal. I say we sit tight and see what happens." Black hung up the phone.

Shuffling from chair to chair, Jake stalked the phone all night long.

At 6 A.M., a final call from Nurse McTegg informed him that Mrs. Chiodini had been pronounced brain dead. Her respirator was being turned off.

The courtroom was dull under electric lighting, no sunlight moved across polished wood. Jurors were settled in their seats, Judge Tillman sat forward in her robe, the plaintiff's lawyers were in motion rustling papers and files and legal pads. Auclair was pinstriped and wearing a too heavy dash of cologne. Malone was quiet, his eyes everywhere but on Jake. The careful orchestration of individuals embroiled in Malone's care and treatment was carried out. It was Shannon who addressed these subpoenaed staff members. She moved flawlessly, relating without antagonism to these persons, projecting a mood of only wanting to get at the truth, and how appreciative she was that they were there. Jake regarded all of them as loyal friends and trusted associates. As they spoke, sometimes glancing quickly in his direction, Jake nodded. No ill feelings. Just tell the truth.

The tough part began with Auclair's calling of one of the plaintiff's expert witnesses, Dr. Alex Al-Fassad. Jake had expected it. In fact Callahan had some preliminary notes on him.

"Listen to him carefully, Gibson." Callahan said. "Anything amiss, anything not quite right, tell me immediately."

Jake nodded while looking at Callahan's notes on Al-Fassad. Although he didn't need notes on this dismal track record. Jake watched as Al-Fassad settled into the witness chair. He looked out and around him from under bushy eyebrows. His nose was beak-like with large nostrils. All told, he was a menacing and unpleasant looking man, and there was no gentle spirit or impish humor to offset his looks. No inner light overcame his features. One surgery episode stayed with Jake. Without discussing the case with anyone, Al-Fassad had scheduled surgery to remove a metastic tumor. For some unknown reason, he attempted to excise a deep, more difficult lesion rather than approaching a more superficial and easily asscessible one. The result was that the patient was left in a greatly compromised, barely responsive state. The man was left with paralysis of his arms and legs, skew deviation of his eyes, and no speech. To compound the dilemma, Al-Fassad had failed to locate or identify the actual tumor, such that no firm diagnosis could be reached. The patient was hospitalized in a devastated condition for months before he finally succumbed.

Jake had confronted him on this and his high complication rate in surgeries. Al-Fassad had his own views.

"I don't think these are bad outcomes at all! If you read the literature, you'll find that I'm doing quite well compared to many others. In fact, I've reviewed all of my results with notable experts around the country and they have agreed that I do nothing except first quality work."

Jake, whose own professional reading was cutting edge, challenged him. "Alex, I really don't appreciate the bullshit. Do you think anybody's that stupid? Someday you'll come to realize that the mark of an unfit surgeon is an inherent inability to honestly evaluate his own results."

Jake had recommended to the university hierarchy that Al-Fassad be asked to vacate his position.

◉◈✦

"Now tell me, Dr. Al-Fassad," Auclair was saying, "is it correct that you were associated with Dr. Gibson for almost five years in the practice of neurosurgery?"

Nostrils flared. "That is correct."

"By the way, were you asked to leave that practice?"

"No, sir. I left on my own accord."

"All right, then. Would you say that over that five-year period of time you came to know Dr. Gibson quite well?"

"Yes, I worked for him on a daily basis."

"Okay, Doctor. Having worked with Dr. Gibson for some years, could you give us an overall description of him, especially his character? What kind of person was he during the time you knew him?"

Jake waited to see how it would be presented. There had been careful coaching of Hudley with the studied look at Jake, the slipped in comments that were 'withdrawn' but which remained in the jurors' minds. He guessed that Al-Fassad will have been cautioned to be moderate. That way his criticism would carry more weight.

"Dr. Gibson is an exceptionally skilled surgeon. He taught me a lot about technique. I can't say enough about his overall ability as a surgeon."

Jake waited. Here it comes.

"But as far as his character is concerned, he is among the most rigid and uncompromising meddlers you'll find in medicine. He always has to have everything his way, and when threatened by someone he never stops at anything until he destroys him. After a while, I personally couldn't take his relentless arrogance any more. That's the main reason I decided to abandon the surgical position at the university and start my own practice."

"Can you give us an example of something he did?" Auclair said, smoothly heading off Callahan's objection.

"Certainly." The doctor pulled dramatically at his long nose. "There was one particular patient that I remember vividly. I was forced to operate on him as an emergency for malignant tumors that had invaded his brain. Dr. Gibson blamed his eventual death on me, and distorted the facts to make it seem as though I had messed up his surgery."

"Why do you think Dr. Gibson would do something like that?"

Dramatically, Al-Fassad faced Jake. "I think he was profoundly afraid of me. I believe he thought I had turned into too accomplished a surgeon, and he didn't like the competition."

You can look away now, Jake mused to himself. The cameras got it. But he went on.

"He did his best to drag me down. You know, there have been quite a few physicians over the years who couldn't tolerate his tug-of-war stance, his arrogant second guessing. So they left the department."

Auclair nodded. "So what you are really saying is that no matter what, Dr. Gibson always finds a way to get what he wants?"

Callahan was up. "Your Honor!"

"Sustained. Please restate your question in more acceptable courtroom terms, Mr. Auclair."

"Yes, Your Honor. Dr. Al-Fassad, do you think Dr. Jason Gibson ever deliberately distorted facts to get what he wanted?"

"Without question, sir." The large nostrils flared. "I know for a fact he has in the past—and I believe he would do it over again without hesitation."

Jake felt his fatigue closing in. Too long under tension. Too little sleep. He was jarred awake at Martha's touch.

"The man's a butcher," she said. "All he wants to do is cut. I've been in too many operating rooms with him."

"We'll get our turn." Jake said.

Leaning forward directly against his ear she said, "I don't think Callahan can turn this around for us."

"We'll get our turn," he said again. "And there's only Salig left."

Professor Everett Salig, stealer of manuscripts, appeared precisely groomed, his mustache neat, his demeanor poised from countless appearances as an expert witness as part of his professional duties. He spoke confidently, engaging the jurors, moving his manicured hands for effect, his eyes now warm, now cold with indignation. He was a master. It would take a professional newsman to catch his subtle play to the cameras. He created a mood of ease and self-evident truth, of considered options and carefully found answers. The jurors hung on his words.

Salig testified that he had personally been present at the second operation, and that the surgical procedure appeared to have been unnecessary. It was his belief that Dr. Gibson had for years overestimated his own skills and expertise.

"Dr. Gibson has so much gall and such a big head that he truly presumes his ideas to always be right."

It was cleverly said. Plain talk for the down home folks.

"For years he has refused to listen to anyone else, and in this situation, his mind was obviously closed to the possibility that a second opinion would be of value. Throughout this entire case, it seems to me, he proceeded with haste and nearly caused the death of his patient. It is clear to me in fact that Dr. Gibson is guilty of gross negligence. I should add," Salig went on, "another patient of Dr. Gibson's, one that he recently operated on in another state, died last night because, once again, Dr. Gibson was too bullheaded to listen to anyone."

Jake vaulted from his seat. "That's total crap, Salig, and you know it."

Callahan grabbed hold of his arm, to return him to his seat.

Then Callahan was up. "With respect, Your Honor, this is completely out of order, I believe this court is to decide on any matter of negligence regarding Dr. Gibson's medical practice."

It was a good response but too little too late. The plaintiff's case was concluded by mid-afternoon. It was now Jake's opportunity to take the stand and relate his side of the story.

"Jake?" Martha stood next to him.

"Yeah."

"Are you up for this? I saw you nod off, or at least—"

"I'm tired—I've missed sleep before, what surgeon hasn't? I'll make it through."

In the event, he did his best to address the jury with a clear mind and honest heart. He answered each question put to him candidly and completely. Without slandering the names of prior witnesses, his colleagues brought in on subpoenas, Jake told his story forthrightly and unadorned. It was not good camera copy. He could only hope the jurors would recognize his words for what they were. He spoke to them the way he talked to his patients, as intelligent people who could understand truth however painful and deal with it.

But there was Auclair, crocodile boots stalking the floorboards. Jake had to admit the lawyer's cross examination was highly effective. He made it seem effortless, the way truth should sound uttered from innocent lips. Systematically, he dissected Jake's character, doing it with such delicacy that few detected its true savagery. In the court of law far removed from the world of the operating room, Jake was borne down on fatigue and judicial analysis. Truth, in the final analysis, not only did not work for him: it was irrelevant.

14

Catherine Gibson stood at the front door window looking out. "They're out there now, the news people. Must've followed you home or something."

"Ignore them, Mom, it'll all be over soon, maybe tomorrow."

The telephone blared, intruding into the quiet morning, with its smells of breakfast and second cups of coffee. Jake watched his father answer it. He didn't look at Martha.

"Your lawyer," his dad said.

Jake took the phone. "Yes."

"You've got another settlement offer from Malone."

"What?"

"But he wants a private meeting before closing arguments."

Jake stared at the front door and what waited beyond. "Martha and I have talked, we plan to tough it out."

"Well at least hear what the man has to say. Can you get down to the courthouse now?"

"Yes. We were just about ready anyway. We've got a couple of news teams outside."

"Bull your way through. Don't respond to any question."

"Hadn't planned to."

"See you there, then."

Jake hung up and looked from Martha to his parents. "We have another settlement offered. Better get down there." He kissed his mother and hugged his father. By that time Martha had her coat.

Mitch Malone was fresh in the morning, a good cologne, a well groomed appearance, and a confident manner to kick off his day. "Jason, my boy. This lawsuit goes before the jury today, and I think it's pretty obvious what the verdict will be."

"So, why are we here?" Jake watched him, studying the professional eyes as they took in those around the table.

"Ah. A good question. Frankly, it cuts two ways. On the one hand I feel sorry for you with your idealism, with your naive faith in truth and society's unerring ability to do what's right. And not just that. There's your reputation for steadfast integrity, the people who swear by you. But the fact is, Jason, you're an oddity, a utopian do-gooder. You're what this shallow society of ours spawns once in a while: a visionary hero, gimlet eyed, charging at truth like it's one of Don Quixote's windmills."

"So why are we here?" Jake said again.

Malone's face sobered. "Because you saved my life. That's the other way this thing cuts. I could right now be in some nursing home drooling into my cereal. But I'm not; I'm practicing law, the only thing that's meaningful to me."

"I'm sure Shannon will appreciate that."

Malone's face reddened. "Don't push me, Gibson."

Callahan cleared his throat. "Why not lay out your offer, Mr. Malone."

The lawyer leaned forward, a familiar body language from countless confrontations. And wins. "I want a signed declaration that you'll refrain from the practice of medicine in the state of Minnesota for the next twenty years."

The small conference room was deathly still. Outside in the hallway people began moving toward the courtroom.

"That's it?" Jake kept his face expressionless.

"That's it."

Callahan couldn't contain himself. "No monetary stipulation?"

Malone ignored him, his eyes on Jake.

"We need a few minutes to talk it over." Jake said, glancing at Martha.

Malone nodded and stood up. "See you in court." He turned on a waft of cologne and stepped out into the hallway.

Callahan was all over Jake. "If you decline this offer you could be held responsible to pay a settlement of several million dollars."

"I know. But when will I ever be able to practice medicine in this state again? Or any other for that matter, once they publicize that I voluntarily gave up my license?"

"No, you don't get it!" Callahan was twirling his Cross pen agitatedly. "The agreement he's proposing has nothing to do with your formal license to practice medicine. Don't give that a second thought. Your pledge to Malone is a mere legal formality, an unenforceable written promise, for God's sake!"

"Mr. Callahan." Jake's measured words calmed him down. "I need a few minutes with my wife."

The eyes blinked behind the glasses. The Cross pen disappeared into a pocket. "Yeah, sure. But court starts soon. Get back to me quick."

When they were alone in the small conference room, Jake looked at Martha. "Penny for them."

"Malone's cologne is still here, like he's here."

Jake shook his head. "No. He's gone. It's just us."

Martha reached across and pressed her hand over his. "What is it, Jake?"

He took his time answering. "Memories. Bad memories that stay with me."

"Like what?"

"Hear Malone go on about me?" Jake said, ignoring her question. "A utopian do-gooder."

"He also said steadfast integrity." Her hand pressed down. "What is it, Jake?"

"Truth? I'm thinking about mistakes, the times things went wrong."

"No, Jake, not now—"

"Yes, now! I'm facing charges for performing good surgery, for saving lives—even Malone's, you heard him. But what about bad surgeries, Martha, those that give me bad memories and haunt me?"

Martha straightened up. "Okay. Tell me. Get them out."

Jake rubbed at his jaw as if gathering his failures to him for review. "Mr. Robert Foster, brought in with stroke-like symptoms. Seventy, looking fit, planning a trip to Florida with his wife. A first year resident, I was to perform an arteriogram, maneuvering the catheter through the aorta. Standard procedure, you know the routine."

"What happened?"

"The catheter dislodged a piece of plaque from one of his brain arteries. A massive irreversible stroke. Dr. Wilson took over, talked to Mr. Foster's wife…"

"But, Jake, these—"

"And little Michael Moore, seven years old. I was a second-year neurosurgery resident and I placed a breathing tube in the child's trachea to assist with his air exchange." Jake looked at her. "They checked the accuracy of tube placement at the morgue. It was lodged within the esophagus." Jake rubbed at his jaw some more. There were other memories of course. They lined up in review, some grotesque parade. "Thomas McVay toppled down a flight of stairs fracturing his neck in several places. I was a third-year neuro resident by then, and I was placed in charge of surgical intervention—a straight forward neck fusion. When the patient woke up he had complete quadriplegia—total inability to feel or move anything from his shoulders down—"

"Jake, stop this."

Jake stared at the table. "Gregory Walker, Bryan Smythe, Larry Schweizer…"

"Jake…"

"Katie Lutz, Bridget…"

"Jake …"

"Keeping it all filed away in a bad memory bank. And all the stuff that's gone on the last few months—"

"Yes?"

He looked at her, his eyes wet. "It gets to you. It's a load."

"I know. But now it's a shared load."

Jake nodded. "They come to me, Martha, sometimes across long distances. And I can't help them. They come with inoperable brain tumors, invasive brain cancer, cerebral hemorrhages—"

"And you can't help."

"No. I can't help."

"But you have the successes, so many successes, Jake."

He wiped his eyes. "What else did Malone call me—a visionary hero?"

"Yes, by God! And I hope you go on jousting at windmills. Someone has to!"

Jake smiled, the first that morning. "Guess we'd better get in court."

They flew to Mount Pleasant that night, a long droning ride that offered an electrical storm at the horizon. Jake sat quietly and stared out his window. Martha was glad of the quiet. It gave her time to reflect on the courtroom session and bumping into her ex-husband Howard as she left the ladies room. She did not mention the encounter to Jake.

Their return to Mount Pleasant offered little respite from pressure. This time they faced the hostility of Doctors George Black and Jim Wright. Jake set about establishing his own practice, to provide good treatment to those who needed it. But he no longer had the safety of the courtroom. In court his naive views were offered a forum; his idealism could be heard even if he presented it badly. But here in Mount Pleasant there was no forum, no sanction; only the venemous hate of two healers who themselves were in need of medical care. In a matter of weeks they destroyed his practice.

Jake subleased a tight, four-room upstairs office on the grounds of a small Catholic hospital in Red Bluff, a lower class neighboring town. It was a seedy place with by the hour motels, but it was also a place where good people struggled to live good lives, earn a wage and raise families: a place that needed medical care. But Red Bluff had resisted the overtures of Black and Wright. The town had denied them staff priviliges. Now Red Bluff and Jake were too much of a target, a focal point of anger for the two doctors.

George Black began the assault by bringing weekly charges against Jake with complaints of impropriety. Jake was contacted by one medical staff committee or another which was compelled to investigate all charges. Black kept Jake on the defensive. It did not take long for the assault to have Jake lose his operating privileges at the Mount Pleasant main hospital. Since Black and Wright had control over the boardroom decision making, the ousting went smoothly. The next stage was to destroy Jake from within his office walls. George Black paid informants to stand outside Jake's building. These informants would cause trouble by confronting patients as they entered or left. Within days, only a handful of patients would turn up for appointments. Cash flow dried up. Jake was barely making his rent and the full time secretary was reduced to part time. George Black's tactic was cunning: Jake would be starved out, treating a fallout of patients who couldn't pay.

But it didn't stop there. George Black sent a promising patient, an attractive woman about twenty-five years old who said she was a model from Seattle. She was in town visiting friends and "got this pain…" She was quick and smooth, which is what George Black paid for. It took only moments for her to strip, to wrap herself around an offguard Jake. She was all over him as he called for his rented secretary, Georgia. The rented secretary did not respond. Following Jake outside the examing room the woman screamed of assault. She brandished ruffled clothing. There was a scratch on her cheek.

Jake got in a call to Martha before the county sheriff handcuffed him. He was hauled to a waiting police cruiser, then released hours later when the woman from Seattle failed to show up to press charges. An acquaintance later told him that she was seen at the airport being hustled onto a plane by the rented secretary.

Doctors Black and Wright finished him off with a lengthy list of allegations formally submitted to the State Medical Commission in Seattle. Jake was accused of unprofessional activities, highlighed by the fact that he had voluntarily surrendered his license to practice medicine in Minnesota. After review, the Board wanted to hear Jake's version in person.

He couldn't fight it. His presentation could not overcome the relentless chronological record in front of the commission members. His explanation of why he had surrendered his license in Minnesota carried no weight. Jake found himself on five years probation, his Washington State medical license under five years of scrutiny.

Martha was there for him, the joyful promise of twins was a balm for his taut nerves, but the final attack took away his priceless skills: a string of personal injury suits, eleven in all, were brought against him over a two week period. This forced his malpractice insurance company to terminate coverage. Jake had to give up surgery. The whole process of putting Jake out of business took six months.

During the ensuing weeks Jake and Martha took refuge in each other and found hope in their dreams. Gradually, for the first time in his career, Jake began to loosen up, to involve himself in the simple pleasures around him, far away from the life and death rigors of medicine. They went on summer hikes through plush mountain meadows, they rode bikes along old mining roads, they flew Chinese box kites on buffeting breezes. There were picnics and quiet conversations and shared dreams. For the first time Jake found himself not thinking about Jeanne and her marriage to Ben and their new baby. Martha was his world now, and he would watch her against a backdrop of lush meadow and mountain, quiet stream and swaying wildflowers. And Jake improved physically, his skin toned by sun, his eyes bright, his nerves rested, his spirit healing.

They decorated the spare room for the twins' arrival. Martha handpainted the walls with wilderness scenes. There were stuffed animals. For Martha's thirtieth birthday he gave her a cut glass slipper filled with candy kisses. They waited on the twins. They were due in a month.

The one activity Jake had that kept him in medicine was a neurological clinic in Susanville, a remote mountain town high in the Cascades. He would fly back and forth from Mount Pleasant, a thirty minute trip each way. The visits to the lumber community kept his hand in and was helpful to the residents. It was during one of these visits that he received an unexpected message from Martha: she had made last minute plans to meet him for lunch.

The airport was quiet. Nearby an ancient volcanic lake

offered its deep blue presence. There was a freshness to the air, and pines contoured themselves against the landscape. A smallish fox crept from its hiding place in the woods and dashed across the runway. Jake watched the small plane slowly descend toward the runway, its wings rocking slightly, feeling out cushions of cool air. When the explosion came it was a flash of bright yellow light followed by a cannonade, a rolling of thunder across the airfield. Jake stared, frozen, as burning shreds of airplane fluttered to the ground on ugly trails of black smoke.

15

A contemporary has rightly said that the only deeply religious people of our largely materialistic age are the earnest men of research...

My religious feeling is a humble amazement at the order revealed in the small patch of reality to which our feeble intelligence is equal.

Albert Einstein
(1879–1955)

Martha and their unborn children were laid to rest at the Gibson family plot, in a flower-laden gravesite close to the ball field. Jake was lost inside a shell, unreachable by family and friends. He promptly returned to Mt. Pleasant. The loss of Martha and the twins was unbearable, and for a doctor who healed broken bodies their loss was an exquisite torment that prowled his empty nights and endless days. He did what was left to him: he worked. He worked one hundred hour weeks tending the sick and spending the rest of his time buried away in the house, trying to ignore photos and bicycles, picnic hampers and nursery items. In the end, he buried it all away in the garage.

He found private rituals. At night he read favorite books, pushing back the bright yellow light and oily wreckage that fell behind his eyes. He worked around the house, finding jobs to be done but not jobs he and Martha talked about. Other jobs, out of the way, backwaters of energy and the dissipating of time. That was when he found the orange ball blocking the downspout. He held it in his soiled hand. The kids next door. Laura.

Laura had been a good friend to Martha over several months of sharing as housewives. Someone told Jake she had been at the funeral but he didn't recall any of that. What he did recall was Martha alive, her laughing across at Laura as she and Jake readied the bikes for a jaunt into the mountains. Laura pleasant, smiling, arms akimbo as she watched them set off. 'I'll soon be too big for this,' Martha had called. Laura had waved.

Jake turned the ball in his hand. He wiped away the dank smear of rotted leaf and twig. And there had been the offerings. Over the last three months Laura had stopped by, not enough to intrude but just to be there. Covered dishes. Pies. She had discouraged talk, only offering the plates with their soft linen coverings. Then she had gone back to her house next door. Jake squeezed the orange ball, climbed down the ladder, and walked over to her front door. He knocked once then stood there, dirty and sweaty, the ball bright in his hand.

When the door opened Laura looked at him but did not smile. She would not intrude like that in response to this effort from him. Because she knew it was an effort. Her eyes found the ball. "Jake?"

"I think this belongs to the kids."

"Yes, yes it does." She waited.

"I found it on the roof. In a downspout."

She offered a first tentative smile. "It looks in good shape."

"I cleaned it up."

A flurry of birdsong came from across the yard.

"Would you like to come in?"

"I'm a mess. Need to get cleaned up."

"Come in. Do that at the sink."

Jake went in. He washed up. He sat down in the den and accepted an iced tea. He watched as Laura sat down across from him. Slender but muscular, just like Jeanne. He couldn't think of anything to say.

"Are you managing okay?" Laura asked. She sat on the edge of the rocking chair. "Yeah. I keep busy with patients. Don't sleep much."

"How do you handle the nights?"

"I read. I'm going back over favorite books. They're predictable and comfortable." He managed a smile. "And I keep getting these meals from next door."

Laura leaned back in the rocker, slowly relaxing. "You owe me a few plates."

"I'll return them."

It was quiet in the den, warm with a life lived well.

"Jake?"

"Yes?"

"I have something to say. Perhaps now is not the time to—"

"Say it."

Laura wiped at her apron and stared at her hands. "That morning she left to join you in Susanville…"

"Yes?"

"She seemed frightened."

"Frightened?"

"We were chatting in your kitchen over a cup of that special herbal tea she made. There was a phone call." Laura looked at her hands again, as if they would shape her difficult words. "She talked for a long while. It got heated. I thought it best if I leave, give her some privacy. Later she knocked on my door to say she was leaving for the airport. She tried to be bright about it, joking about a surprise lunch with you, but it was a front. She was frightened."

Jake carefully set his glass down on a coaster. His eyes probed hers. "Did she say who had called?"

"No. Not that I remember. I was trying to be polite, support her because she was upset and—wait a minute. Yes. It was Horace or..."

"Horace? How about Howard?"

Fear shadowed Laura's face.

"Yes, I think that was it."

"Howard's her ex-husband. Was her ex-husband."

"We talked a lot, Jake, but she was private about some things —"

"That's okay."

Laura rocked forward and stayed still, her own eyes troubled as she looked at Jake. "You think there's a connection?"

Jake stood up. "I need to go home. Take care of a few things."

"I understand."

"Laura?"

"Yes?"

"Thank you. For everything."

She nodded, watching as he left.

Howard Crane picked up on the first ring.

"Howard, this is Jason Gibson."

"What the hell do you want?"

Jake thought back to the trial, Crane's glowering at Martha.

"I need to know something."

"You need to know something. Gibson, just where the hell do you get off asking me for anything? First, you steal my wife— "

"You lost her way before I came on the scene—"

"—then you get her killed in some plane ride. Now you want information."

"Howard, why did you call Martha that day?"

Silence spun down the wire. Jake could hear the heavy drawn out breath.

"I have no idea what you're talking about. The last time I communicated with Martha was at the trial. She didn't give a damn about me."

Jake slowly hung up the phone. Why would Howard Crane lie about a simple conversation with Martha? Maybe it wasn't so simple. It was enough to have Laura concerned about Martha's well-being.

When the knock came at the door he thought it was Laura. Still thinking about Howard Crane he went to answer it.

"How are you, doctor?" Midge asked.

Jake stared at her, this nurse from another life, a destroyed life.

"Jake? Gonna say hello?" Midge's perfect teeth shone in a familiar smile.

"What? Oh, sure, sure. Come in, Midge. What in the world are you doing here?"

"I'm on vacation. Thought I'd drop by for a visit."

"Let me have your rain jacket." Jake tried to hide his look. "Like a drink, a soda?"

"Not right now. Just sit, let me look at you."

Jake was uncomfortable under her gaze.

"Not so good."

"It's been tough."

"We were all sorry to hear about Martha, Jake."

Jake nodded.

"Not a finer nurse anywhere." Midge cast around for words. "I wanted to call but I didn't know what to say, I—"

"'s' okay."

"I know how much she loved you, how much she meant to you."

"Midge. I appreciate your thoughts but why are you here? You didn't come all the way from Washington just to—"

"I quit."

"What!"

"I quit the hospital. Since you've been gone things just haven't been the same. So last week I up and quit."

"I see." Jake managed a wry grin. "Look, Midge," he said carefully. "I'm no good to anyone right now. I put everything I've got into medicine."

"That's good. I'm glad of that." She composed herself with a small shrug. "How about a soft drink? You say you've got coke?"

Wordlessly Jake got a couple of drinks from the fridge and came back and sat across from her.

"Good," she said, after a swig. "That's good."

Jake waited.

"Look, Jake—that is okay, isn't it, if I call you Jake?—I've got some things to tell you."

"Okay. So tell me."

"Things went on just before and just after you left the university."

"Like what?"

"Jake, you're not making this easy—"

"I've had a bad few months, Midge. Like what?"

"Okay, remember the night Mitch Malone was admitted?"

"Of course."

"Do you know what David Hudley was doing that evening?"

"Yeah, yeah, I do. I confronted him, as a matter of fact. He was supposed to be covering the ER that day." Jake thought back, tracking the events. "Turned out, all along he was down in the cafeteria eating dinner. Apparently he didn't hear his pages."

Midge rummaged for a cigarette. "Mind if I smoke?"

"No."

"You can forget the cafeteria story. As I was getting ready to go home that afternoon, I saw him get out of a car that had pulled up to the side entrance. You know, over by the loading docks?"

"What time would that have been?"

"I'd say it was about 5:30 or so. I remember because one of the ICU nurses was late getting to work that day and I had to cover for her till a little past five."

Jake thought back to the parking area. There had been a Rolls Royce, silver, sticking out like a sore thumb. "What kind of car was it?"

"Luxury job, English looking, big radiator—like a Rolls, y'know?"

Jake thought back. "Huh…"

"What, does that mean something?"

"A silver Rolls was in my spot after I came out from the second surgery. You sure it was Hudley?"

"It was Hudley." She hesitated. "I also remember the license plate: EJS-1."

"Everett J. Salig." Jake murmured.

"Also my dad's initials, which is why I remembered them. There were a lot of strange things going on that day—really for that entire weekend. I brushed it off as one of those hospital warps, but after what happened I began to think about it all. For one thing, didn't you think David Hudley acted very peculiar? His whole relationship with Malone, and especially his wife, well, it was just odd. Odd enough to notice, to stick in my head."

"Odd how?" But Jake could guess her answer.

"Well, you know what a total asshole the guy is, his bad attitude, the way he bullied those under him, the constant complaining and whining. Yet with Malone, with Mrs. Malone, he was all smiles and deference, a regular guy."

"And always at the bedside." Jake said. "And following the wife around."

Midge stubbed out her cigarette and dropped it into the soft drink can. "Sorry, bad habit."

Jake thought back on his own suspicions, thoughts that had been buried under his loss of Martha and the twins. But now they were surfaced, in focus. Hudley's behavior had been odd. Right from when he had seen him with the Malones that first morning. The night Malone had gone into the coma, there was Hudley all chummy with Mrs. Malone. And she had kept referring to Hudley in conversations like he was some intimate confidant. Why was that? How had that relationship developed in a few hours? Midge was talking again.

"An orderly got it right. He said that David Hudley was acting like a waiter sucking up for a big tip."

"Something was going on. Something behind the scenes. I said as much to Martha."

Midge reached for her cigarettes then shoved them back in her purse. "Why was Hudley so mysteriously unavailable, Jake? We all heard the pages."

"Right. For the initial surgery, then the second." Jake's eyes were hard, a first anger mixing with the grief. "And at whose request did Salig emerge as the second opinion?"

Midge sat quietly, watching him.

"Have you discussed this with anyone else?"

"No."

"What's been going on with Hudley?"

"Well, I'm sure you heard, he was gone for a couple of months after you left."

Jake rubbed his temple. "No. I pretty much cut myself off."

"It was one of those fancy eight-week junkets around the world. He's now spending a lot of his time flying around the country testifying."

"Jesus."

"And he's doing a ton of work for Malone's firm. Did you know Al-Fassad rejoined the group?"

Jake stared, incredulous. "Hudley and Al-Fassad working together? Impossible. Those guys hate each other. I can't tell you the number of times they squabbled with each other in my office threatening to quit."

"Well, they're together and doing very well. Hudley just bought a mansion in Ladue."

"Two million at least."

"And Al-Fassad drives a brand new red Porsche."

"Shit."

"Other than that, they're the same old slipshods they always were."

16

Jake cooked the sirloin and salmon steak in silence while Midge sat on a kitchen chair. There was more to say and they both knew it, but for now they lost themselves in the sounds of sizzling steak and the comfortable familiar movements in a kitchen. It was a first for Jake. It had been months since he had gone to the trouble of preparing a fine meal. With the exception of Laura's linen covered offerings delivered unobtrusively from time to time, Jake had filled any hunger need with franchise meals. He glanced across at Midge and smiled. "Smoke if you want."

"Nah. I need to quit. Steak smells good."

"It's all in the loving care, not rushing it over a hot flame."

"That could be my love life," Midge said.

Jake ignored it. "So catch me up on anything else-especially things that worry you."

"Things that worry me... The department got FDA approval to market LEVIRA. Did you know that?"

"No." Jake was pleased. Shoving at the steak, he thought back to the preceding five or six years. A group of research assistants in the department, with his best friend Ben's assistance, had developed a device that permitted the precise localization during surgical interventions of abnormalities anywhere within the body. LEVIRA, or Laser Enhanced Virtual Resolution Apparatus, permitted surgeons to possess superhuman vision while they operated. The revolutionary and Nobel Prize-worthy invention had required years of testing and trial application before it finally gained FDA approval for routine use. "I'm glad I convinced the university hierarchy to sign over the commercial rights to a reputable non-profit equipment manufacturing company."

Midge stared. "Haven't you heard, Jake? God, so much has happened. The hospital is on the verge of being bought out—"

"What!"

"And I think Martha's ex-husband, Howard Crane, is leading the buyout."

Jake flipped the steak on the grill. "Go on."

"Well, there's talk of a lot of new faces, including Everett Salig's. He and Crane are tight. It's one of the reasons I left. Everything now revolves around bottom line accounting. Nursing staff don't count; morale is lower than wheel shit."

They ate a fine meal without enjoyment. The bottle of California red emptied itself into glasses. Jake and Midge watched each other across the table. "Everett Salig is a wild card, " Jake said. "I wish I knew how he fitted in."

"Is it true he stole your manuscript?"

Jake looked up, startled. "What?"

"The Salig International Classification of Brain Tumors."

"Who told you?"

"It's scuttlebutt. People are careful bringing it up. Salig scares a lot of people."

Jake watched her, but he kept his thoughts to himself; he remembered telling Martha about other scientists who had conveniently died just before Salig had published specific works that had built his reputation as consultant and lecturer. Jake shuddered and hoped Midge didn't see it. "Got somewhere to sleep tonight?"

"No. I'll find a motel room. Don't worry about it."

"Don't be silly. We—I—have a spare bedroom. Stay."

Jake lay awake that night, but not reading a comforting book. Instead he went over what he had learned from Midge about the hospital, the maneuverings. How was his former boss taking it? But Midge had clarified some of the events around Malone's two surgeries. The silver Rolls and Salig and Hudley. The affectionate relationships between Hudley and the Malones. Slowly he drifted off to sleep. For the first time no hideous ball of yellow flame seared his eyeballs, no thunder roll of the plane's explosion echoed across his brain.

◎▨✠

Over breakfast Jake asked Midge to accompany him on a quick errand. "I'd be glad to have you with me. Then you can be on your way." He smiled at her, sensing her attraction to him and trying to mask his own. It was complicated. He felt an attraction to Midge but it was for warmth, for closeness, not passion. But there was too much guilt, too much time spent in isolation. Too much of a burden after seeing George Black and Jim Wright destroy his medical practice. And fear. If he was honest with himself, there was fear. He was a healer, yet he was always on the outer swirling edge of violence, of menace. Events beyond his control. Emotions barely under control.

"So, where are we going?" Midge wiped at her mouth before standing up and carrying the dishes to the sink.

"The airport. I want to find out more about Martha's trip to Susanville that day."

Midge's lovely Scandinavian eyes darkened. Wordlessly she rinsed off the dishes and left them to drain. "I'll get my jacket," she said.

◎▨✠

It was a small airport. Aircraft engines droned overhead as small planes moved through the traffic pattern. There was a small reception building adjacent to the main hangar. In the hangar planes squatted in the shadows, some with engine cowlings removed. Cars were parked around the passenger reception building. Cascade Aviation had its own counter. A desk clerk was tapping on a computer keyboard. She got up as Jake and Midge approached. "May I help you?"

"I need information on chartered flights. You recently flew my wife to Susanville. There was an accident and she was killed."

"Yes, of course. I'm so sorry. But I don't see how I can—"

"Did my wife mention anything to you about why she wanted to fly up to Susanville at the last minute?"

Keys clacked on the keyboard. She brought up the flight record. "Mrs. Martha Gibson."

"And I'm Dr. Gibson."

"Yes, of course." Silence hung between them. Then, "I do recall she was in a hurry. It was her phone call to help arrange the flight. Very rushed, a bit agitated. But when she got here for the flight she seemed calmer—I guess because she had the flight booked."

"Was there anything else, anything a bit out of routine, anything unusual?"

The receptionist stared at the screen as if it would summon memories. Perhaps it did. "Well, the plane was a few minutes late taking off. She stood over there, by the window, looking out. She was watching the planes, the sky...."

Jake stared at the window. He saw her there. What was worrying her?

Midge gently interposed. "Why was the plane late taking off?"

"Oh, the gentleman accompanying her had to have his flight credentials okayed."

"What?" Jake turned, images of Martha pushed back. "What man? Was someone else flying along with her?"

"Yes." The receptionist's eyes grew uneasy, not liking where this conversation was going. "I spoke first with him. I assume it was the same guy. He inquired about getting to Susanville. He told me he and a lady friend needed to get there as soon as possible to handle a sudden family crisis or something like that. At first he wanted information about scheduled flights, but then he said he couldn't wait. So he asked about our twin-engine Seneca, but it was booked for the entire day. All I had open for rental that morning was the little Piper, and I told him none of our pilots were available. That's when he said he'd fly it, and we began checking his credentials." She looked from Jake to Midge and back again. "That's when your wife called, she said he was well qualified— look, the FAA investigators have asked me all this already—"

"Let me get this straight," Jake said. "A man arranged to rent the Piper. Then my wife called saying he had many hours of flight time. They could fly together?"

"Yes. I remember saying it would save them money."

Jake stared at the computer screen. "I'm sorry we've had to ask all these questions."

"We're just trying to piece together loose ends," Midge said. She was in her nurse's mode, projecting assurance.

"I really shouldn't be speaking to you, you know. It's the only crash Cascade has ever had."

"Why isn't the man's name on the screen?"

"Because he wasn't a passenger, he was the pilot. The FAA faulted us on that—"

"Can you tell us anything about him!"

"Don't raise your voice to me, Dr. Gibson!"

"Please understand," Midge said gently. "It's been very difficult for Dr. Gibson. If we could just get some closure—"

The receptionist was quiet a moment. "I just remember them by the hangar, Mrs. Gibson and this pilot."

"And they took off, later crashed, and no one knows who the pilot was."

"Sir—"

"Okay, okay. I'm sure the FAA went over maintenance logs, safety inspections, cargo lists—all those things?"

"Of course. And Cascade is strict on its safety and maintenance."

Jake got ready to go. He glanced at Midge.

"Dr. Gibson?"

Jake stared at the receptionist, seeing the tension there, the struggle in her eyes. He had seen it many times in patients. Patients who were holding something back because they were frightened. "What is it?" he asked gently.

She began to whisper. "I couldn't tell the FAA at the time. And later I never updated them."

"I understand. What is it?"

"A few days ago I was watching a TV program and it suddenly popped into my head." Her smile was brittle, self-conscious. "It works like that sometimes. The pilot's name was Howie Carr."

"Howie Carr."

"Please don't report me, Dr. Gibson. I'm so sorry about your wife—"

"It's okay. Thank you. Thank you very much."

Midge ventured a question, pushing at the receptionist's reluctance. "Don't you have receipts, a rental contract? Perhaps there's a credit card receipt—his pilot's credentials must be on record. It's a bit odd, I'm sure you'll agree—"

"They're missing." The words came out in a hiss, low and guarded. "The FAA wanted them. Everything's gone."

"Jesus."

"Please don't report that I mentioned all this, I shouldn't be talking with you—"

"It's all right. Just one more question. Was the pilot carrying anything? A briefcase, maybe. Think back: you saw him and my wife out by the hangar…"

She was crying. Tears rolled down her cheeks. "There was a small parcel that somebody dropped off. It was supposed to be in Susanville by one o'clock. When I went to lunch, I left it with our other secretary to see if the couple renting the Piper would deliver it to Susanville airport."

"And they took it?"

"Yes."

"And the FAA knows this?"

Tears rolled. "I forgot to tell them."

"Look," Jake said. "I want to talk with the other receptionist."

"You can't." There was fear now.

"Why not?"

"She was killed in a terrible automobile accident the day after the crash."

Outside Jake took a couple of deep breaths. He closed his eyes for a moment and stood quite still.

"You okay?" Midge asked.

"Nurse, what are you doing for the next few days?"

"Nothing. I'm unemployed, remember?"

"I need you, Midge. Will you stick around?"

"Of course." She nudged him and they began their walk across the tarmac. "Didn't the FAA question you, Jake?"

"Oh, yeah. But there was no talk of a pilot/passenger, no talk about a parcel."

"So, what do you want to do now?"

"Go see the FAA. They've got a field office around here someplace."

At the field office they were up against Officer Nick Calambini. No tears would flow here.

"The file on the crash is closed. It was determined that the accident was due to a fuel-line rupture, subsequent engine fire, and terminal explosion."

"Know who was flying the plane? I understand records have been mislaid at Cascade Aviation." Jake waited.

"We've checked missing person reports from across the country. Nothin'."

"What about parcels, packages, things like that?"

"Know nothin' about that. Although packages are sent back and forth all the time." The officer shuffled a stack of papers.

"So—"

He looked up. "Look, Dr. Gibson. I'm sorry about your loss, but we checked all this out. The file's closed."

"Okay, I understand. One thing, though, that might not be confined to your file."

"What's that?"

"A receptionist from Cascade was killed in a car crash the day after the flight."

"That's right. She lost control on Highway 101, went over the embankment. It was raining. One of those things. Killed instantly."

"Thanks for your time."

"Sure thing."

Outside Midge looked at him. "Now what?"

"Pack a bag for me, get your stuff, fly to Minneapolis. See a couple of people."

"Okay."

17

Ethics is the activity of man directed to secure the inner perfection of his own personality.

Albert Schweitzer
(1875–1965)

Howard Crane's corporate headquarters occupied both towers of a sprawling, thirty story, uptown complex. It held its own against Minneapolis' corporate skyline. Jake and Midge were back on old ground: for Jake, the pine trees and Swiss motif buildings of Mount Pleasant were far away. "I'm very sorry, Doctor. Mr. Crane is out of town and won't be back for another week. Perhaps you should have phoned first." The personal assistant's smile was practiced, a balance of concern and censure.

"Perhaps I should have. Still, now that I'm here, I'd like to set up an appointment for his day of return."

Well-shaped fingernails caressed a leather bound appointment book. "Yes, we can fit you in, Doctor—"

"Make the appointment in the name of Carr. Howie Carr."

She frowned. "Really, that's a little odd—"

Jake smiled. "It's a joke we have."

In the elevator heading down Midge said, "He might not know what that means, the Howie Carr thing."

"We're trolling. Let's see what we get. And it'll guarantee he'll see me."

The ornate doors slid back and they headed for the street.

"Let's go visit the hospital." Jake said.

"Now? Just like that?"

"Just like that."

"Anyone special?"

"The boss."

"Watch yourself."

Stepping back into the hospital touched something deep inside Jake. He let the familiar sounds and sights and smells impact on his senses. This was his world and he had been gone from it too long. He smiled and returned greetings with everyone he met. House-staff and janitors had supportive words for him, no furtive talk behind their hands, no secretive gatherings in corners which had been the prelude to his leaving the hospital with his professional reputation tarnished.

"Coming back, Dr. Gibson?"

"Who knows, Nancy."

"We sure miss you around here—"

"You, too, Brian."

Midge squeezed his arm.

Chairman Wilson's office was just the same. Jake remembered standing outside waiting for his mentor to return, the fatuous comment about his Washington D.C. trip: *sit on the beach*. But this time things were different. Sympathy and condolences about his loss of Martha saw to that. Jake nodded to the chairman's private secretary. "Is he in, Donna?"

She didn't smile. She just nodded. The first time Jake could remember her being caught off guard.

Jake pushed open the door and stared at Dr. Wilson, once mentor and friend. "Hi, Vince."

Dr. Wilson looked up, eyes sharp, then he settled back in his leather chair. "What are you doing here, Jason?"

"Coming in to see you. You know about Martha, of course."

"Of course. And I'm very sorry. But when you barge in without warning, you can't expect instant sympathy."

"You mean I'm rattling you, Vince?"

"What is it you want?" The lines in his face deepened.

"To tell you some things. I recently learned about some things going on here behind the scenes."

"Don't be ridiculous."

"Fact is, I assumed responsibility for putting you, the department, the whole damned hospital in jeopardy. I won't carry that load anymore. Understand, Vince. I'm going to find out what's been going on around here, and who's behind it."

"You're talking rubbish. The brute fact is that you nearly destroyed my department and the reputation of this hospital. It's not wise for you to be around here anymore."

"Here's an interesting question, Vince. Why were Everett Salig and David Hudley together about the time Mitch Malone was admitted through the ER?"

"Get out."

"One more thing." Jake took a much handled envelope from his pocket. He placed it carefully in front of the chairman. Wilson examined the signed but never submitted letter of resignation that Jake had been asked to sign prior to his court hearings. "I intend to get my privileges back, Vince."

The chairman set the letter aside and looked at Jake. When he spoke, his voice was remarkably calm. "Jason, why didn't you listen?"

"Listen?"

"Many times I asked. No, I begged. But you had to get out there with this knight in shining armor idealism of yours, pushing everybody's wrong buttons, pissing off the power players."

"Someone has to speak out."

"What, like you at that Congress speech? Inside twenty minutes you lost the President's support. And most of the ranking house subcommittee members, not to mention your colleagues on the commission. What did that cost us, Jake? How much did this hospital lose because you were on your self-righteous binge?"

Jake looked carefully at his mentor's face. Strange he had not noticed the cynicism, the etched in ugliness. When had that happened? While he was promoting his plans for the hospital, pounding the table, advocating God knew what in Wilson's face? He hadn't seen the change. Jake cast around for some way to anchor himself once more to his old boss. "Remember that Saturday morning, boss?"

"There've been too many Saturdays."

"The day we removed the door to the pathology lab, just so the man in charge could get his hands on the results of a late Friday afternoon brain biopsy."

"Those days are gone."

"You had fire, Vince. You talk about my idealism—what the hell happened to yours?"

"I warned you time and time again. Apply too much pressure, push too hard in the wrong places, and you'll make enemies. You pushed way too hard, Jake."

Jake nodded. "I guess the joke's on me. I learned from you how to be outspoken and tough minded when I was fighting for patients' rights. Now the guy I learned from doesn't exist anymore."

As Jake left the office, he came face to face with Alex Al-Fassad. The Iraqi gave a cold stare then pushed by him and went into Dr. Wilson's office. As Jake went to join Midge, he wondered if he had overplayed his hand with the chairman. Relating Everett Salig, David Hudley, and Mitch Malone had given him a lift, but had he now put someone else at risk? He had been foolish. Behind his eyes the yellow light bloomed, the oily wreckage fell earthward.

"Midge, can I borrow your car for a couple of hours?"

"Sure. What's up?"

"Thought I'd go see Mitch Malone."

Shadow moved across Midge's lovely eyes. "Be careful. And by the way, where are you sleeping tonight?"

Jake smiled at that. "Situation's reversed, huh?"

"My place," Midge said emphatically.

"Okay."

Another sleek office building. Everybody was doing well but him. Jake scanned the directory in the marble lobby. Mitch Malone's law firm offered itself—as did a neighbor on the same floor: Everett Salig. Jake filed that away and headed for Malone's office suite.

"I'd like to see Mitch Malone," he said.

Another well trained, stiletto cold, receptionist. "Do you have an appointment?"

"No. I'm an old friend. Mitch'll see me."

More well-manicured fingernails. She spoke briefly into the phone.

"I'll just sit over there," Jake said. "Catch up on *Sports Illustrated*."

The cologne fragrance preceded Malone. Jake gave him that: the lawyer worked hard, changing shirts, freshening up for the second leg of a fifteen-hour day.

"Dr. Gibson. What can I do for you?"

Jake tossed the magazine aside and stood up. "You're looking well, Mitch."

"Thanks to you. Come in. I have a few minutes."

"I knew you would."

Mitch Malone's personal office surprised him. Unlike the heavy-handed power-play furnishings of the conference room, the lawyer's office offered subdued lighting and one or two carefully chosen oil paintings. There was power here, too, but restrained. "Let's sit over here," Mitch said, making his way to a small intimate island of comfortable chairs. Well away from his antique desk, the mood in this corner was warm. Guards could come down here. Unplanned comments could slip loose on a complacent comfort. Midge's words came back: *Be careful.*"

"I went to see Vince Wilson. I told him I had evidence of behind the scenes maneuverings inside his department." Jake said, without preamble.

"Maneuverings?"

"LEVIRA. Bottom line medicine. Hiring incompetent surgeons."

"That was reckless, Jake."

"And you, Mitch. Hudley, for God's sake. You must've got him on the cheap."

"What do you want, Jake?"

"I took a lot of blame, Mitch. I got boxed in, took the fall, and now the behind the scenes stuff can come out in the open."

"So what does that have to do with me?"

"I want to practice medicine again, here in Minneapolis."

"You've got a hell of a way to ask for it."

"I saved your life, Mitch. Tear up that letter of agreement."

"In a word—no."

"Did you know David Hudley and Everett Salig were together just about the time you were admitted into the hospital?"

"You're losing it."

Jake leaned forward. "There seem to be a lot of unanswered questions about what happened around the time of your admission and subsequent surgeries."

Malone stood up on a second waft of cologne. "Look, Jake, I really don't have any idea what you're talking about. Perhaps you should have a talk with your attorney—Callahan, isn't it? As for your signed letter of agreement not to practice medicine here, the deal stands. But I wish you the best of luck with—what shall we call them?—your inquiries."

Jake left, fretting again that he had said too much. Perhaps Malone had that right: a pounding in the courts, the loss of Martha…not in full control.

◎❖✠

Back at Midge's, Jake knocked once and waited. After the second knock he used her key to open the door. "Guess who's in the same office building as Mitch Malone, Midge—Everett—"

The sap took him expertly behind the right ear, enough to knock him out, not enough to do permanent damage. He barely felt it. He awoke to find himself on the carpet with a bird's egg lump behind his ear. Total darkness. For a horrifying moment he thought he was blind. The light switch brought back his world. He stared around at the chaos: lamps and tables toppled, bookcases down on heaps of books. Wall pictures angled on the carpet. A splintered antique china cabinet surrounded by broken glass and crockery. "Midge? Midge!"

He made his way to the bedroom, walking like a drunk, dizzy and sick. Midge's waterbed had been slashed. Wall to wall carpeting sodden. When he heard the sound he doubted his ears, it was just one more noise in his pounding head. Then it came again. From the wardrobe. "Oh, Jesus…"

She was naked on the floor of the wardrobe, mewing behind duct tape, tangled in fallen clothing. He got her into a dry hallway and removed the tape. Her breathing was harsh, her mouth dry and cracked. "Midge, are you okay?" Surgeon's eyes examined her. Skilled hands sought out injury. She clutched his arm and nodded.

"I'll get you some water and a robe."

She sipped quietly, then gagged, pushing the water glass back at him.

"Take your time."

"I thought it was you."

"Yes."

"I went to the door hardly dressed, I was going to shower. There were two of them. One had a long ponytail. I thought I was going to be raped—"

"Easy—"

"But they were looking for something, they kept at me, where's the package, where's the package…" She reached again for the water, slower this time, wetting her mouth. "I think you scared them away." Midge's eyes, now dark with fright, looked around her hallway. "My clothes…"

Jake retrieved some jeans and a blouse.

"Okay, Jake. I'm okay now."

"Sure?"

"Let me see my place. See what's missing."

They went from room to room. "Christ, look at the china."

"At least you're okay."

She was still looking around. She found her purse. "They haven't taken anything."

"How about jewelry?"

"No. They wanted some kind of package." She looked at him, bewildered. "What the hell was it?"

"Are you up for a drive, Midge? I've got to get us out of here."

"Okay."

"Any suggestions?"

Midge managed a smile. "My fearless leader. Yeah, I know a place. An aunt of mine has a cabin out toward the Black Hills. I go there-used to go there—when the pressures of the ICU got to me."

"Fine. Let's go."

"Take Highway 90."

"Okay."

They spent the next few days trying to sort things out. Midge used a pay phone at a diner and called friends and co-workers at the University Hospital. Jake was not happy with the developing news.

"So Howard Crane is poised to buy the main teaching hospital." Midge said. "And some upper echelon administrators are already privately marketing LEVIRA. Some anonymous benefactor pledged several million dollars to the department of neurosurgery chair—"

"Vince is riding high—"

"And Al-Fassad is showing off another brand new car, a Ferrari this time."

"And Hudley?"

"He's gone. Left unexpectedly the night of the break-in. Somewhere out west."

"Christ, Midge. We really stirred up some shit."

Midge forced a smile. "So what's our next move?"

Jake looked out the cabin window at the snow, bright and clean in the sunlight. "You ski, Midge?"

"Yes."

"I say we take a little break from all this."

"Ok. Let's go for it."

18

The bright sun and dazzling snow lifted their spirits. Skiing took them out of themselves, away from the confines of the cabin and the uneasy mysteries: what was the missing package, what was happening at the hospital, why had Martha's plane crashed? They skied with a joy and exhilaration, curving through snow and crystals, freeing themselves. Jake watched Midge's face, the color back in her lovely Scandinavian complexion. "One more downhill?"

"You bet!"

They boarded the now deserted ski lift for the final run. Settled back in the chairs Midge looked out at the mountains which were now drawing down the setting sun. "It's just gorgeous up here, Jake."

Jake smiled. "Maybe we should've been park rangers, not—"

Without warning the entire ski lift halted, swinging and tipping the chairs now freed from the severed supporting cable. Midge fell, tumbling thirty feet to snow and rock below. Jake managed to grab the supporting bar. But he was hanging one-handed, skis and boots lugging at him, when the ski lift lurched forward, shaking him like a rat. He was going to fall. It was a matter of how soon. Looking back he saw Midge's body face down in the snow. Blood oozed from the side of her head. It spread into the crystal white.

Jake let himself drop towards a mound of fresh now, but it crusted hidden rocks. His skis fractured and he felt agonizing pain in both legs, then he was rolling forward. He came to a broken stop in powdered snow, lungs heaving, eyes searching out Midge. Then he was crawling and sliding on his belly to reach her. She was unconscious, and he braced her head and neck in his arms and carefully turned her over. Palpating the side of her neck he caught the weak pulse. But she was not breathing. Jake moaned, both in anguish for his friend and his own physical pain. He started CPR immediately, every once in a while looking around for help. Once he looked up and saw a colorfully clad snowboarder, long-haired, motionless against the exit ramp. Jake called out, screaming for assistance. Slowly the man lowered his goggles and sped away on the angled snow.

Midge's breath was spearmint. He smelled her distinctive perfume. He thought of Martha and her perfume, and in some grotesque kaleidoscope he smelled Mitch Malone's cologne, and then there was the ugly yellow light behind his eyes, and the oily falling wreckage. "Don't die on me, Midge," he said. "Don't die on me."

There was a gasp from her, then more, then slowly her pulse intensified. Blood leaked from her ear. He called her name, getting his jacket beneath her head. His trained hands examined her body. Fortunately, she appeared to have landed flat on her back in several feet of snow. "Thank Christ," he mumbled to himself, "Thank the good Christ." He straightened up and yelled for assistance, but his cries went out on echoing white silence. It was a difficult crawl between rocks and over coarse stumps and mushing across snow to get to the deserted lift operator's hut. His hand shook as he reached for the emergency phone.

The Med-Evac helicopter lifted smoothly into the air, its rotors sending up a cloud of snow. Midge was strapped onto a stretcher, Jake anxious beside the medical crew. "She's got a concussion and a basilar skull fracture."

The medic nodded. "Good to have you aboard, Doc. She your girl?"

"A good friend. A very good friend."

"How's your knee doing?"

"It can wait for the ER. I'm okay."

Midge was admitted to the neuro ICU for overnight observation, but Jake was heartened that the CT demonstrated she would likely be all right. In the ER Jake had a syringe of blood drained from his right knee and bandages wrapped around his shins. Then he walked gingerly to the charting station and the nurses gathered there. One swung a chair around for him. Gratefully he sat, staring unseeing at the several monitors. It was when he looked up to thank the nurse for an offer of a cup of coffee that he saw him: an unshaven man with a pony tail. He was exiting Midge's room.

The nurse followed his gaze. "Oh, that's Midge's brother—"

Jake was up on pain-jabbed knees, the chair swivelling out from under him. He ran as best he could towards Midge's room. There he found her sleeping peacefully. He ran again, this time towards the deserted hall, after the man with the ponytail. But the man was gone. And that was when Jake saw it. There are landscapes in medicine: everything is always in its place; in the OR surgical instruments are laid out with precision and discipline. For an anguished moment he thought about Martha, seeing her in his mind's eye, her surgical mask in place, her eyes bright. But here in the hall was a medical obscenity. It jarred on his senses and he stared at it. Careless, discarded on the floor. When he picked up the contaminated 25-gauge needle, his cry was an ugly sound.

In Midge's room he tore the plastic tubing from its insertion and stopped the flow of saline. "Get me another liter of lactated ringers!" The two nurses responded. "And send this one to the lab and test for contaminants—now, right now!"

Jake spent the night beside Midge. A nurse brought him that coffee. He stared off into the soft lighting of the room. Guilt had him now. Guilt because he was in something deep and he had dragged Midge into it. Mitch Malone, Martha dead, Everett Salig, David Hudley—what the hell was going on... He wondered if he and Midge would live long enough to find out. Jake jumped when the nurse burst in.

"Dr. Gibson, it's potassium chloride!"

"Dear God—"

"The technologist thinks there was more than ten times a fatal concentration."

Jake grabbed the phone. Then he stood by the window and waited.

Sunrise was lightening the sky when Martha's father drove up in his '65 Buick. He watched Harold park on the street. Jake got Midge out in a wheelchair, an overcoat draped around her. They got her safely placed across the back seat. Harold asked no questions. "Ready?" was all he said. Then they got out of there.

Back in Mascoutah, safe in the home of Martha's parents, Midge was confined to bed for several days with persistent headaches, nausea, dizziness, and blurred vision. Jake stayed close. It was Martha's mother who finally talked with Jake. Her words were at once a wound and a kindness.

"I hope you've found time, Jake, to visit Martha's grave."

Jake nodded. "I have, Ann."

"I know how much you loved her, and I know you have great concerns right now."

"Yes."

Ann hesitated. She sat down beside the bed and watched the sleeping Midge. "They are connected, these things, aren't they? Our loss of Martha and this sleeping child."

Jake nodded. "We'll find out what's going on."

"But be careful, Jake."

"Of course."

"I–I have put Martha's things away in a special place. There're some childhood photographs I think you should have."

"Thank you."

Jake was removing his knee bandage and Ann was whipping up blueberry pancakes when the phone rang. Ann took it in a floured hand.

"Hello?" Ann looked from her husband to Jake. "It's for you," she said. When she handed the phone to Jake, her hand shook.

"Gibson."

"Jason? This is Mitch."

Jake listened, stunned.

"Jason, you there?"

"What do you want?"

"I'm glad I tracked you down, it was—"

"What do you want, Malone?"

Silence. It tore Jake's nerve ends.

"We need to meet."

"Why?"

"Look, don't make this any tougher than—"

"Okay. We'll meet. Eight o'clock, the America's Center. Near the carousel."

"Good."

"Listen, what—"

The phone clicked dead.

Jake looked to Ann then Harold.

"We'll watch over Midge." Ann said.

Wordlessly, Harold tossed him his car keys.

Jake wore an oversized gridiron Cardinals cap, a heavy woolen scarf and tinted sunglasses. He huddled over a mug of hot chocolate at a cafe table. From there he could see the carousel turning to its own music, its lights bright and cheery. It was another ten minutes before he spotted Mitch Malone. He kept to the store windows and out of the flow of people. He wore a full-length trench coat trimmed in bear skin. He kept pulling at his brimmed fox hunter's cap. Probably to hide his face. Apparently none of them were any good at espionage. Jake raised his mug of hot chocolate. Mitch nodded.

"Sorry I'm late," he said without smiling.

"Want something to drink?"

"What? No. Look, Jason, get this up front: if you try to use any of what I tell you publicly you're on your own."

"Okay." Jake waited.

Mitch looked around, agitated. "Okay. Here it is. I have in my possession concrete evidence that supports what I'm about to tell you. But as far as anybody else is concerned it doesn't exist."

"Get to the point, Mitch."

Mitch stared at him, weighing him up. "The day I suffered the hemorrhage," he began slowly. "I was litigating a case against one of the local Expercare hospitals and their head physician in the emergency room. The doc had failed to properly treat a patient with a ruptured aneurysm."

Mitch waited, but Jake just drank his hot chocolate.

"Anyway, the doc failed with his treatment of an aneurysm much like mine. The guy ended up dead."

Jake slowly put down his mug.

"This happened nearly a year to the day that Expercare took control of that hospital. By the way, you aware that University Hospital has been bought out?"

"I'm aware."

"Then let me get right to the point. Expercare, Inc. has a longstanding agreement with a nationwide consulting firm called ER DOCS, Inc. They are to furnish fully trained emergency room physicians for its chain of hospitals around the country. The terms of the contract call for a sufficient number of certified ER docs, each fully accredited in advanced trauma and cardiac life-support..." Mitch's hand went inside his jacket and slipped out a folded document. He unfolded it like a treasure map.

Jake waited.

"You'll never guess who heads this lucrative enterprise? An old collaborator of yours, I believe."

"Who is it?"

But the lawyer was going to milk it. "Actually, I've been deeply involved with him myself for many years. We've worked together on probably a hundred litigation cases. As far as I'm concerned, he's as close as one can get to the perfect expert witness. On the plaintiff side—"

"So who?"

Mitch looked around, apprehension clouding over his excitement. "Everett Salig."

Jake masked his own emotions. Everett Salig. The name jarred on him, but it made sense.

"His fees are astronomical," Mitch said, leaning across the table, talking softly. "For court appearances he generally gets $5,000 per hour plus expenses. Believe it or not, though, the guy's worth every penny. I never wound up on the losing end when I brought him in."

Jake's gaze was cold. "I know. I've been there."

Mitch ignored it. "It's going to get tough as hell to replace him. Think about it: Hudley's a certifiable idiot, and your buddy out west- that George Black fellow? Well, I think we both know what makes him tick!"

The lawyer hunched forward. "Look. Just recently I remembered something that had happened the day I became ill. I bet you didn't know that there are several ER docs practicing in the Minneapolis area who don't have proper credentials."

"Bullshit."

"Okay, here's more. A couple haven't even passed a certified CPR course. Put it another way—all kinds of vital documents have simply been made up! They're fraudulent!"

"Suppose I agree it's happening—" Jake began slowly.

"Oh, it's happening, bet your Buster Browns."

"If it's happening, is it localized to Minneapolis?"

Mitch looked anxious again. He glanced around at the strolling people. He watched the carousel. "There's about a hundred others around the country."

"What!"

"And every one of them is employed by Salig's firm."

19

Life is short, and the Art long; the occasion fleeting; experience fallacious, and judgement difficult.

Hippocrates
(5th Century B.C.)

Mitch Malone nodded at Jake's hot chocolate. "Think I'll get one after all." He looked around before standing up. "Back in a minute."

"A hundred or so," Jake said, when he returned.

"And you didn't get it from me." Mitch slurped the hot chocolate. "That's good, hits the spot."

"Without proper credentials."

"And all Salig's boys."

Jake watched him. "So who forged the documents?"

"Salig himself, seems like—to meet various state licensure requirements. And he's been doing it for years."

"Now look." Jake leaned forward across the table. "I'm no fan of Everett Salig but this is difficult to believe. What about state medical boards? An investigator somewhere. Somebody would have caught up with him. You know how agencies are about credentialing physicians. And why would anybody take the risk to do something that stupid?"

Mitch wrapped his hands around his mug. "Pretty surprising isn't it? Look how it plays, Jason: one of the most well known and highly reputed surgeons in the country. His word's as good as God's. Nobody ever questioned him."

Jake rubbed his brow, massaging the beginnings of a headache.

"There's more."

"I'm sure there is."

"Don't you want to know how I discovered all this?"

"Yes, I do."

"Salig was scheduled to be my expert witness on the stand for rebuttal that afternoon, the day I became ill in court. We'd gone over to Cunetto's for lunch. I wanted to review his testimony. Well, I was going through his file and I found this memo mixed in with a bunch of deposition papers from his office." Mitch waited, enjoyment in the moment overcoming his anxiety.

"A memo," Jake said.

"It was handwritten by Salig himself. It listed those Expercare docs from around the country who were working for him on doctored credentials."

Jake looked across at the carousel. It was decked out for Christmas. How soon the seasons roll around. He thought of Martha and knew a profound sadness. "Anything else?"

"Yeah. One name was highlighted, the one he was supposed to testify against that afternoon." Mitch took out another folded piece of paper, but this he did not show to Jake. "He was going to double-cross me, put my legal career at risk. So I had no choice, I told him right there I had to remove him from the case."

"Lemme see," Jake said, reaching for the unfolded paper.

"No. I told you. You'll just have to take my word on this."

"That's tough to do."

Mitch smiled. "Something else you'll be interested in. I have it safe and sound: a notarized affidavit from the retired dean at the Las Vegas Med School. Actually, I got it just yesterday afternoon. The document outlines an interesting inconsistency in Salig's own credentials." Mitch waited again, sipping his hot chocolate.

"Okay, so what is it?"

"Seems Salig never completed a residency training program."

Music lifted from the carousel. Kids had their happy faces.

"Unbelievable, isn't it? The director of his training program at LVMS died quite unexpectedly when Salig still had more than a year to go with his training. Yet, for some unknown reason, this same chairman on the very eve of his death, agreed to certify Salig and another resident at the time…your buddy, George Black."

A first fear moved through Jake. He kept it down, deep in his vitals, while he watched Mitch.

"All this puts me in a tight spot, Jason. Naturally, as a reputable plaintiff's representative, I can't afford for it to become widely known that my oft-used expert isn't qualified." He leaned forward. "Cited for contempt, maybe even disbarred if this got out."

"That's why you let me off the hook with the suit?" Jake asked.

"Hardly. I thought Salig would quietly resign from his court appearance on that last case and that would be that." Anxiety returned to Mitch's eyes. "I underestimated the man."

"Me too. More than once."

"No, listen: I got sick right after the noon recess. I was cross-examining the other side's expert. Salig was seated right behind our table. I remember I had a pretty sore throat that afternoon and the good doctor offered me a lozenge."

Jake stared intently, knowing what was coming.

"A few minutes after I put it in my mouth, I got the worst headache and things went fuzzy. Then the lights went out." Mitch tried to smile. Instead he looked frightened. "Is it possible that he could've laced that lozenge and caused me to have a cerebral hemorrhage?"

"Oh, yeah. Any potent vasopressor or strong cardiac stimulant could've been added, which would've caused a sudden increase in blood pressure. A high enough dose might result in a cerebral hemorrhage." Jake managed a smile to bolster his spirits. "But Salig didn't know you had those two aneurysms."

The lawyer looked sick to his stomach.

"What is it, Mitch?"

"A few years back, I went to see him for a pain I was having in the back of my head. In the end he said it was just tension-related, but he did order a scan as part of the workup." Mitch's hands gripped his mug. "He did say something about a weakspot somewhere..."

"I'm sorry, Mitch."

Mitch nodded. He was silent a moment. "Remember when you came to my office a couple of weeks ago? You told me Salig and Hudley had talked? I began to put two and two together. Salig must have figured I removed something incriminating from his file. He may very well have seen me put the memo inside my suitcoat. After I got sick there was a big commotion, of course. My briefcase was left, my files were left—everything unattended in the courtroom. One of my paralegals saw Salig going through stuff." Mitch's gaze began its compulsive sweep around the cafe, the carousel and strolling people. "He must have figured I had it on me."

Jake nodded. "So he needed somebody on the inside at the hospital."

"That's it. Somebody who could move around freely and retrieve the memo."

"Dr. David Hudley."

"Oh, yeah. Notice how friendly he was towards me at the hospital? Actually, at the time, I was impressed. He was all over me, all over my wife and daughter, ever helpful."

"But he didn't find anything." Jake said.

Mitch smiled, an honest smile, free of fear, a celebration of self. He opened his flashy overcoat and demonstrated a hidden compartment on the inside of his jacket. "I hadn't worn this since it came back from the cleaners. It's the one I wore that day. You'll never guess what I found in this hidden pocket."

"The memo."

"Damn right. I must have had some memory loss from all that happened, but once I touched the memo in that pocket it all came back."

"Bad luck for Hudley," Jake said.

Mitch winced. "You know, I had him doing all kinds of legal work for me, the slimy bastard. It was only recently I got a fix on his surgical skills, the incompetence of the man."

Jake smiled a little, but he saw something in the lawyer's eyes. Fear prowled again. "What is it, Mitch?"

"Well, let's just say I'd have been a lot less trouble to Salig if I'd not survived surgery."

Some kids ran by their table holding balloons, heading for the carousel.

"You're saying," Jake said slowly, "that David Hudley deliberately sabotaged the operation?"

Mitch finished the hot chocolate. "Listen, my daughter mentioned to me the other day about some things she had noticed during my stay in the ICU. Hudley was always snooping, looking for something."

"Shannon's nobody's fool."

"That's for sure. Anyway, that's it. What do you think?"

Jake was quiet a moment. "First, why did you drag me into court? Put me through this long agonizing trial? Be on the verge of winning a huge verdict from the insurance company, then settle out of court for virtually nothing? And why are you still so interested in keeping me out of practice in Minneapolis?"

Mitch grinned. "Apples and oranges, Jason. You want it straight? I was paid five million dollars to get you out of Minnesota. So you gotta stay out."

Jake rubbed his brow. The headache was on with a vengeance.

Mitch got up to leave, his eyes sweeping the walkways and stores. "I have to go, Jason. I'm glad we had this talk. I hope it helps you get through things."

Then he was gone, moving again next to store windows, out of the mainstream of strollers. The fox hunter's cap was distinctive. Jake was expressionless as he adjusted his own cap and scarf and watched him go.

Howard Crane. It all made sense now.

The gunshot was distinct above the music and festivities. People stopped walking and looked about. Jake was up and running towards where he had last seen Mitch Malone. Other people were surging forward but Jake bulled his way through. The lawyer was lying in a deepening pool of fresh blood. Jake reached inside the coat around the single bullet wound to the heart. Frantic fingers hunted the hidden zipper, then he had it. He grabbed the bloodied papers with the bullet hole drilled through them, got them into his own pocket, then he was up and pushing through the crowd. They would know him, be able to describe him, he realized. Even with cap and sunglasses. Imagination rode him like a Valkyrie and he waited for a bullet in his back.

None came. He reached the garage, struggled into his car and drove out. He kept the speed down while his nerve ends shrieked. Logical reasoning returned. Driving down a street, turning at random, he thought through what he should do. First off, he couldn't return to Martha's parents and put them and Midge at risk. So he sought out a run down motel and checked into an upstairs room. There he double locked the flimsy door and dragged a weighty dresser in front of it. Then he phoned Martha's parents collect, instructed them to stay away from windows, to be on guard, to take care of Midge, and that he would call again tomorrow. As usual Harold just listened, but he took it all in, and Jake knew a first relief.

Then silence closed in. The stained walls, the dirt. The press of the seedy mattress under him. World class surgeon. The room mocked him. Images roiled. George Black, bloodied gloves, standing over a brain dead patient. Midge, bloodied and spread eagled in the snow. Mitch Malone, by turns smiling and anxious as fear took him in ugly rhythms. Martha dead, the oily wreckage.

Jake wept.

The television slowly warmed up, casting a slanted washed-out image across the screen. Swirling images. But the sound came through well. Jake jumped at the sound of his own name. He played with the knobs to stop the rolling image and then he saw his face, distorted, twisting on the screen. The words were relentless: prime suspect...eminent attorney's murder...

Jake got his things together. The bloodied papers were now dried out, the bullet hole a crusty ellipse. He left the room, exited by a back stairwell, made his way to the car and slowly drove away. For the first time he worried about the old '65 Buick and its distinctive appearance. At an all-night market he purchased some postage stamps, looked up an address, and used a street corner mailbox to post the plain manila envelope. The big Buick pulled away into the night.

The mansion offered its bulk to the darkness. Lights were on in several rooms, thick curtains draped out the ground floor windows. Snow layered across window sills and gutterings. Shadows slanted from brick and bush. Security lights haloed the snow. The front door was ominous, holding back the frivolous and unwanted. Jake stared at it through the windshield. He had crossed that threshold. He knew the bulky chair that dominated the study, the elegant staircase where Martha had stood in her silk jumpsuit. *How would you like to meet the President of the United States?*

So long ago.

Jake maneuvered the Buick behind a snow bank. The car was hidden from the street by piled up snow and from the house by its winding driveway and landscaped shrubs and trees. Jake settled back to wait.

20

He was awakened by a newspaper van. He watched the newspaper arc across the driveway. Who would come out to get it— servant or Howard Crane? Jake rubbed the sleep from his eyes and massaged his stiff neck and shoulders. Oddly, he had slept soundly for several hours. No dreams, no nightmares, no bloodied bodies. It had been the sleep of the exhausted, when all energy was gone, when even his own tormented brain had nothing left to work with. He waited, warming his hands with every breath.

Howard Crane stepped out into the driveway. He stood in the crusted snow, his business suit elegant, his shoes polished in the early morning light. Jake got out of his car and walked forward. It took a moment for Crane to look up from the headline which had engrossed him and to sense Jake's presence. He didn't run. He didn't shout for a servant.

"Well, well." Crane gestured with the paper. "You made the front page."

"We need to talk, Howard."

"Really? I don't see why." His eyes monitored his plants and shrubs. "Park over there, behind the snowbank?"

"Let's go inside." Jake said.

"If you insist."

Jake walked behind him as he moved towards the door. Fear and survival instincts tightened his gut. This was all wrong. Crane should be frightened, he should be terrified that Jake would shoot him the way he had shot Malone, right? It was all over the television, the newspapers. But Howard Crane was calm, he was contemptuous. It tightened him up still more, but now they were crossing the threshold. Jake's nerve ends were raw.

"Don't expect me to ask you to sit down." Crane's smile was ugly.

They were in the study. Howard walked behind his desk and sat down in the leather chair. He stared up at Jake, his fingers steepled. "Well?"

Then the pieces began to fit into place. Careful...

"Where are your servants?"

"Only two. I had them take a few days' leave."

"Right after you heard about Mitch's death."

Howard laughed. "Heard about? I did it, for God's sake!"

Jake stared. He watched Howard open a drawer and take out a .41 caliber two-shot derringer.

"I got him with this. Small, easy to carry. Packs a punch. You should have seen his face..."

The derringer pointed at Jake, its over-and-under barrels black holes leading into the depths of the world. "It's not mine, of course." He let it slant in his hand, the nickel plating gleaming in the desk lamp. Then the barrels were on him again. "It belonged to Mitch. Salig found it in Mitch's briefcase, when Mitch got sick." That smile again.

Jake had it now, the pieces in place. "You were expecting me."

"Of course."

"You're going to kill me."

"Of course." Crane's smile disappeared. "Nobody takes Martha from me, you sonofabitch."

Jake's back stiffened on instinct. "You had Martha killed because she left you?"

"I wouldn't think about it, you cocksucker!" Crane perched the gun closer.

Jake backed off.

"She was mine."

Jake gestured with an upturned palm. "So how does this play?"

"It's simple enough. Mad murderer comes looking for me after killing Malone. There was a struggle. I got the gun. I shot in self-defense." The twin barrels waggled again. "It'll have your prints all over it, of course."

Jake's mouth went dry. His options were down to nothing, a mere twitch on the derringer. All he could think of was to play for time, to do what he had come for.

"Have a nice chat with Mitch, did you? Listening to carousel music?"

"You watched."

"Christ, Gibson, you're so naive. Let me tell you, when Mitch gave a surprise visit to Salig and me, we knew he was on the road to figuring it all out. We watched him. And when he met with you, documents on the table, well, there was nothing else to do, was there?"

"And Martha, the plane blowing up?"

"That was bad—and unexpected. She had this old friend, you see. And the friend had a husband who was a doctor—an ER doctor. He kind of figured it all out. Well, of course, we couldn't take the chance—"

"What do you plan to do, kill everybody who figures out what's going on?"

Howard leaned forward. "There's too much at stake here. It's bigger than any one of us. We're talking about the future of medicine here."

The laugh slipped loose from Jake. It carried a madness to it. "You're doing all this for the noble profession of medicine?"

The first bullet drove into his chest and Jake twisted against its impact. The second grazed his temple. He fell down into blackness.

For some, a hospital is a place of fear and dread. Somewhere to go and give up your life into the hands of others, while you are held hostage to fears and stories you have heard. And somewhere to go and die. It happens. Despite the mighty efforts of dedicated people who work behind surgical masks amidst chrome and light, pulsing monitors and gleaming instruments, people die. It assaults the souls of medical brethren. It requires of them a balancing of skill versus wound, of what they can do and what they cannot. Of their own striving against nature's calamities upon the human body.

This was Jake's world. He moved with a commanding presence that was earned from skill and insight and occasionally heroic efforts. But now this world was turned inside out. He was viewing it from a stretcher, a concave world of peering faces and careful, skillful hands. But he should be up and among them looking down. His hands, his hands...

He knew them. Sharon, Raelynn, Dawn, Patty, LaVonna, Sue. He had encouraged them through difficult certification exams; he had joined them in happy hours; he had gone to their weddings. A short-acting IV drug was placed. Someone fussily elevated and extended his head for the breathing tube. The sound of adhesive tape unrolling, the breathing tube, there...there...Jake fell away on the wings of drugs, but words conjured and offered themselves, something Howard had said. Who was Howard? He slept.

Pain woke him up as an icy file cassette was shoved beneath his chest. Standing alongside the x-ray machine, button in hand, was Terry, no smile on his bearded face. Jake had operated on him nearly a decade ago for a subdural following a serious skydiving accident. He flinched at the stinging pinch along his forearm and he looked at the always somber Dana. The lab tech stared back. He had removed her occipital AVM just before being named a full professor. Out of the corner of his eye he saw Nathan, a vast bulk of a man, trailing an EKG machine. His median and ulnar nerves had been severed a couple of years before in a terrible fall through a plate-glass window. Both had been repaired with a nice return of function. Jake closed his eyes. He had no choice but to go with the soothing drugs, but part of him acknowledged those around him. He was safe.

The bright light pierced his eyes and he saw Martha's plane explode. He groaned, trying to get away from it, while second year neurosurgery resident Kevin shone the small penlight through his pupils. Jake fought his way back and looked around. There were friends around him, and fellows, interns and staff. They milled around like a disturbed beehive. Then as his pressure bottomed out Jack McCulloch, chief of cardiovascular surgery, bulled his way through. "Okay, everybody, we need to open his chest, right here and now! Let's have the thoracotomy tray and seven-and-a-half gloves. Suction please! And get some blood up here stat!" Before he faded again, Jake felt the wooden crucifix in his hand, held by a loop of string around his wrist. The crucifix given to him by his grandfather and carried in his baggy pants since medical school. He retreated on a fog of light and sound, finding the darkness comforting.

Pain took him and he writhed against it. A piercing ache in the middle of his back. Monitor alarms banged out their warnings, there was an accelerating whoosh of a bedside machine that gorged his chest with intense discomfort. Then the heavenly figure. He gripped his cross as he drifted away on the dose of IV morphine. He came around later and stared at the chest tube draining bright red blood from his side. His faculties came back too, and he realized the severity of his wounds.

A woman's voice. "He also got you in the head."

Jake's head turned in the direction of a friendly voice. *"Jeanne?"*

Midge smiled broadly. "Always knew you had a thick skull."

He felt around for his crucifix.

She replaced it in his hand. "Here it is."

He grabbed her hand and struggled to speak.

Midge pressed his hand and smiled. "Nothing to do now but rest. I'll be outside the door."

Much later Jake awoke to find Midge seated nearby and Jack McCulloch untying his arm restraints. "Hold onto your cross if you want. Gonna take your tube out, okay?"

Jake nodded. Almost immediately he wanted to cough and gag. He grabbed his chest in agony as the garden hose was deflated and yanked from his windpipe.

Jake sucked air and gagged for a moment. "Damn!" he managed. "So that's what it feels like." He tried to smile at Midge as he looked around the room. His eyes settled on the police sentry posted outside the door. "Midge—" he began, but an oxygen mask was placed over his mouth and nose. He tried to pull it down.

"Leave it alone, Jake." Chief McCulloch said.

Midge came to the bedside. "You're under arrest, Jake."

"Skip that stuff," McCulloch said. "Jake, you were shot in the left chest. The bullet transgressed the upper lobe, barely missing the aorta, then caught a rib. We were able to clean things up pretty well. We hope to get the chest tube out tomorrow or the next day, just as soon as everything dries up. You also took one on the side of the head, you got creased as the cowboys say." McCulloch patted his arm. "It didn't penetrate the inner table."

"Howard Crane shot me." Jake said. He peered up at them, the oxygen mask heaving against his face.

"We know. He claims self-defense. Leave it alone for now, Jake."

"Thanks for everything, Jack."

"Owed you one, right? My father's lumbar canal stenosis?" Jack patted his arm again and headed for the door. "I'll leave you two alone."

The next morning Jake was permitted to sit up in bed and was given apple juice and orange jello for breakfast. Midge hovered around the ICU. Later that afternoon, he caught a glimpse of Chairman Wilson looking in then quickly looking away. Midge joined him when Ben and Jeanne arrived. It was a brief visit, but Jake was glad to have Jeanne near him. He would be the first to acknowledge their mixture of loving friendship and platonic intimacy. He had loved her, then distanced himself in caring for Martha, then Martha was lost. Now there was a new relationship to sort out, some new and tactile way to relate. When he looked at Midge, he found her eyes fixed on Jeanne.

Each day saw a return to freedom for Jake, the slow return of control over his own body. Connections to infusion bags were removed. Drainage containers removed. His crucifix stood against a tissue box. The day came when he was to be transferred from the ICU to a locked jail ward and the thought sickened him. He needed Midge to talk to, but oddly she wasn't around. All that morning he waited. Old fears came back, but they dissipated when around lunch time she turned up.

"How are you, Jake?"

"You okay?" Jake said.

"Of course, I'm okay." She leaned over to kiss his cheek which surprised him until he heard her words. "Gotta get you dressed as quickly as possible."

"What's going on?"

"We're leaving. That's what's going on."

"Midge—"

"Now."

Jake glanced at the guard, just beyond the door, rocked back in his chair.

"I thought you might need these," Midge said, waving a pair of plaid briefs.

Jake got into a favorite flannel shirt and a pair of jeans. Socks and shoes followed. "How come he let you bring these things in here?"

"Who, the guard? Don't you worry about him. He's asleep."

"No way."

"A victim of his liking for fudge sundaes. I got him one. He was getting bored out there." Her smile was impish. "Xanax capsules. He'll be out for as long as we need."

Before they headed for the elevator, Midge covered Jake in a heavy hooded overcoat and dark glasses. He grunted in pain as he got into the rear seat of her convertible. The crucifix stuck into his leg inside his jeans pocket but it was a welcome sting. "Where we going?"

"Back to your in-laws. After that, other plans."

21

I have in the corner of my heart a plant called Reverence which I find needs watering at least once a week.

Oliver Wendell Holmes
(1809–1894)

It was a country estate with idle farm machinery about a mile from town. The owners were away and Martha's father Harold was keeping an eye on it. Jake and Midge looked around its generous expanse of cedar and scenic windows. Harold hid from sight Midge's distinctive sports car in an old barn. In his usual quiet way, Harold spoke a word of encouragement and left. "The refrigerator's stacked. But I'd be careful about the phone. And stay away from these big windows. Check back tomorrow."

Jake looked around. He'd put his head down in so many different places; fancy resort towns, hospital chairs, jail cells. He went to the window and studied the large wall posters of North American birds. Every type, shape and color. Jake picked up the binoculars and looked around. What was out there—Wood

Duck, Wild Turkey, A Yellow Warbler, maybe? He had the birds on the poster but not the seasons...

"Binoculars any good?" Midge asked.

"Seems good to me. I'm no expert."

"Might come in handy." Midge came and stood beside him. "What are you thinking, Jake?"

"Lots of things. I'm worried about the media and my mom and dad. If they were being bothered before, it must be hell now."

Midge nodded. "Anything else?"

Jake had to smile at her. "What is this, competent nurse finding stuff out?"

"Yes, frankly. It is. What do you want to do now?"

"Rest. Watch the news on my John Dillinger status—"

"Hey, bigger than that!" Midge said. "How can I put it? Nationwide celebrity, an internationally acclaimed neurosurgeon, placed at the scene of the murder of a famous malpractice attorney—"

"I get it."

"—nearly shot by his next target—that was sloppy of you, Jake—held captive by the sheriff's department during a hospital convalescence—"

"The media wouldn't use 'convalescence'. Too much space."

"And then, after drugging the guard, daringly escaping with the help of an unwitting accomplice."

"I don't see you as unwitting."

"I'm your moll."

This time Jake couldn't smile.

"What is it, Jake?"

Jake rubbed at his jaw, remembering. "Before Howard Crane shot me, he said something, just a casual line, but I sense now it was important. But I can't remember what he said."

"It'll come. Don't push."

"I need to go back to Martha's parents' house. Check some things out."

"Okay, I suggest we wait until nightfall—"

"Look, Midge, no offense, but I want to go alone. Look around her room. Things like that."

"Sure." Midge hesitated. "Who's Jeanne?"

"Jeanne?" Jake hesitated. "You met her. She's Ben's wife. They came to the hospital."

Midge nodded. "But when you were coming out of the anesthesia you looked at me and called me Jeanne."

"Ah."

"She's something—special, right?"

Jake nodded. He sat down and fiddled with the binoculars. "She was. Still is, I guess. But it's different now, because I had Martha. Martha buffered my emotions, distanced me from Jeanne."

"You were in love with her." Midge said.

"Yeah. But Martha got me through it." Jake looked up. "Jeanne's married to my best friend. She and I tried very hard to keep it on a friendly level, and we did quite well at it too. She truly was a good friend I could talk to."

"I think you're still in love with her."

"I've lost my wife, Midge."

Midge colored. "I'm sorry. That was thoughtless of me."

Jake hefted the binoculars. "I'll take these with me when I hike over there. To her folks. Remember, no phone calls. For all we know there's a surveillance set up by now."

"You sound like a veteran spy."

Jake remembered Mitch Malone bobbing around in his ridiculous hat and coat, the bloodied chest. "Oh, no. Far from it."

They watched television for a while. It was painful. Talk show hosts had picked through his life and found classmates, gas station attendants, even his extended family. Offers were made: exclusive interviews, book deals. Money was offered in the tens of thousands. And Jake was right about his parents. He leaned forward and watched the screen. Their faces were pinched and gaunt, their eyes moving restlessly around at the jabbing microphones and videocam lights. He watched his father ease his mother back inside. His father tried. It was foolish but he tried. He withstood the assaults—"fugitive from justice", "should be strung up"—then he too went inside the safety and quiet of their home. Jake stared.

"I'm sorry, Jake." Midge said.

"Gotta get out of this, Midge."

"You will. We will." She reached across and squeezed his hand.

Jake stood behind a big oak, a few hundred yards from Martha's house. It was dark. It was cold but clear. Perhaps a night like this had seen Martha coming home late from school, piled up with homework, living her young life and not dreaming how it would end. Jake studied the house through the binoculars. He scanned the parked cars. The binoculars were good, they gathered the night light and allowed him to see into the cars. He stood there for a moment, then walked in the shadows along the street, his footsteps crumpling over the packed snow, then he turned abruptly into the driveway.

Ann let him in. She looked around nervously. It bothered Jake how many lives his actions were affecting. But then, this was Martha's mother. She was involved, and she and Harold wanted closure in their daughter's death.

Martha's personal affects remained roughly the way they had been for years. Her mom hadn't given away or changed a thing. Not even after she had left forever. There were homes like this, Jake knew. A captured moment in time. An enshrined remembrance. He turned to Ann. He didn't say anything.

"It's hard, isn't it?" Ann said. "I should move it all out, that's the healthy thing to do, it's what Martha would want."

"When the time is right," Jake said softly.

"Is there anything special you hope to find?"

"I don't know. I have a question that's not giving me any peace. I have to start somewhere."

"Yes, of course."

What was it Howard had said? Just before the bullets had hit him?

"I wonder if this will help." Ann said, walking over to a vintage wicker secretary. "I've not touched it, not wanted to…it's from Lisa…"

Jake took the letter. It was unopened. It was probably nothing, just some part of Martha's daily life now rendered meaningless. He tugged at its seal with a fingernail. Handwritten letter. Top edges frayed, as if torn from a spiral notebook. And there was a computer diskette. It fell into his hand and he stared at it.

Dear Martha,

Sorry I haven't been in contact since we got together at Christmas. With the kids and all… Hope you'll enjoy your new city and new home…Jake sounds great…

Look, I must tell you this—I'm afraid to call, and I don't know who else to contact… Howie has been missing for over three days now… The sheriff thinks it's related to the strain of his work. I don't think so. I've got this terrible feeling he's not coming back… He left suddenly, but gave me this computer disk. If I didn't hear from him by today, I was to give it to you immediately—

Jake checked the postmark: the letter had been mailed right there in Mascoutah on September 12th. The day Martha was killed. When Howard Crane's words came back to him he felt sick: *She had this girlfriend, you see. And her husband was a doctor.* Holy God. He tried to keep his voice calm.

"Is anything wrong, Jake?"

"No, Ann. Tell me, were Martha and this Lisa close?"

"Oh, yes. Since they were schoolgirls. Her dad used to own a hardware store downtown but he died years ago. Lisa went away to college and became a nurse, just like Martha. She ended up marrying a doctor from over in Jefferson County, just north of here."

"Do you know where her husband went to school?"

"I'm not certain. Ann picked up a framed photo of her daughter and wiped at imaginary dust. "I do know he used to commute to Dubuque where he worked at an emergency clinic."

"Dubuque's quite far from here, isn't it?"

"Yes, but Howie flew his own plane. Then—"

Howie. That's what Laura had overheard. Short for Howard. "What's his last name?" Jake asked.

"Carr."

"Howie Carr!"

The name on the rental plane records. Jake suddenly couldn't think. Howard Crane's derringer was leveled at him, the bullets smashing into him.

"Jake, are you sure you're okay?"

"I'm okay, Ann." With an effort, he shrugged the nightmare away. "Tell me more about Howie Carr."

"Well, several years ago, he quit the practice up there and joined the staff at our local hospital. He'd been running the ER here ever since."

"Is he a moonlighter?"

"Moonlighter?"

"I mean, do you know if he was trained in emergency room medicine? Or was he just working there to make additional income?"

Ann shook her head, wanting to help, wanting to have some magic answer. "I really don't know. But he was a very good doctor. A couple of times I went by the ER and he gave me an injection and I didn't feel a thing." She laughed uncertainly, offering up her truth, hoping it would help.

"What's all this about him being reported missing?"

"Well, he disappeared suddenly. Right around the time Martha was killed in the plane crash—" Ann's words cut off abruptly. "Howie could fly! And both of them were gone—"

Jake went to her then and took her by the shoulders. "Listen, Ann. I want you to leave all this with me. Don't start worrying about it. It could just be coincidental, don't build false ideas out of all this."

"You must permit me to talk with Harold. We have no secrets—"

"Of course. Just don't either of you jump to any conclusions."

"And what about you?"

"Me? I need to think about it. Look, would Martha have Lisa's phone number handy? An address book or something?"

Ann withdrew it from the desk and handed it to him. He dialed the number.

"The number you have dialed...has been disconnected."

Jake put down the receiver. "Ann, do you think Harold would mind if I asked him to stop by her house and check things out with the neighbors? Perhaps he could talk to the police department and those in charge at the hospital."

"I suppose he can. We do worry, Jake, about our house being watched. I don't want Harold getting into trouble, even for—"

"It'll be okay. And I doubt if you'll be watched. You're not being watched now."

Ann's eyes hardened. "You checked?"

"Just being careful not to involve you both too much."

"Harold can help, but I don't know about the hospital. Everything's changed since it was bought out by that big conglomerate..."

"What?"

"I said everything's changed—"

"No, a conglomerate bought them out?"

"Yes."

"Remember the name, was it Expercare?"

"Yes. Expercare. That's the name."

Jake put his arms around her. They stood in Martha's room, surrounded by her world, amidst echoes of lost conversations and a young woman's dreams.

Jake spent most of the night on Harold's computer poring over the statistical records contained on Howie's disk. They were from the hospital in Mascoutah and a number of other hospitals around the country. The columns of numbers were frightening in their simple presentation. They showed death rates for various diagnoses following emergency room visits and short stay admissions. Simple columns of figures that offered the banality of evil. Jake felt sick. At around five o'clock in the morning, he finally turned off the computer. He massaged his sore chest area where tubes had pushed life into him. Then he wrote a short note and placed it with the disk in its white dust jacket. Then he put it all inside a stamped and neatly addressed envelope. He left it where Ann or Harold would spot it, next to the tea kettle.

The six a.m. bus rocked its way out of the station belching black diesel exhaust. The run from Mascoutah to Minneapolis-St.Paul would give him time to think. He would rely on Harold to look after Midge. He knew Midge would understand. Heat wafted up from a floor vent as the big bus moved along the quiet streets. Doctor's Day at University Hospital. A celebration to honor recently appointed members of the medical staff.

The crucifix was warm in his coat pocket, but the face of the former professor of neurosurgery was cold.

22

Jake was hidden away in the Memorial Hall elevated audiovisual booth. He had filched a university lab coat which now covered his casual shirt and pants, the downplayed clothing he used for hostile streets. The auditorium was filled. There was that informal hubbub as people settled. Jake looked beyond the glass enclosure and down to the gallery and stage. They were all there: Dr. David Hudley, Dr Alex Al-Fassad, Dr. Vincent Wilson—Jake felt a pang of concern for his old chairman- and there was Howard Crane, the keynote speaker, and Dr. Everett Salig as honored guest. Dr. George Black was an obscene presence. Jake ducked back as a couple of projectionists entered the booth. He listened to them as they played with the spotlights. Another quick glance out revealed Ron Brickle, the hospital administrator, heading for the podium. As camera lights flashed, Jake looked at the two formal paintings of his grandparents, Dr. Nicholas and Olive Gibson. Donors to the hospital, they looked out on the gathering. Occasionally spotlights swept across them as the projectionists worked.

Jake watched the men adjusting projectors, then stepped from his alcove. He waited until they noticed him. "Know who I am?" he said.

"Get outta here, Mac. This is a work area."

The other one nudged him, whispered.

"Holy shit."

"Just get out." Jake said.

Both men left quickly, looking back at him, probably expecting to get shot. Jake closed and locked the door and dragged over some A/V equipment to block it. The equipment looked familiar: the high-definition, three-dimensional video apparatus he had bought with his own money for the hospital. It was thick with dust. Jake stood quietly for a few moments. Security was obviously alerted. He would not have much time to say what he had to say. He waited, looking down, watching Brickle.

"Ladies and gentlemen, it is my great pleasure as president and CEO of the University of Minneapolis Hospitals, to welcome you to this very special presentation. As I'm sure you're aware, months ago Expercare reached agreement with the Board of Regents of the University to purchase and run our hospital. Today we are poised to hand over the keys!"

Camera flashes, polite laughter. Jake caught the sounds outside the audiovisual booth. Security was coming. And they believed him to be armed. Jake had to shrug the thought away. He planned out his speech. He waited.

"With over two hundred and fifty hospitals in its network across the country, fifty or so of them university-affiliated with more than twenty billion dollars in assets, Expercare is well poised to support the fundamental teaching and vital research of our university well into the 21st Century."

A scattering of applause. From beyond the barricaded door came the first exploratory shoving. He wouldn't have time. He was about to look spectacularly foolish and shamed. People looked up as battering began on the cubicle door and the small window was smashed. Then the miracle. Security Chief Joe Robinson peered in. He didn't waste time. "I can get you five minutes, Doc. After that, it's over."

Relief washed through Jake. Years before he had gotten an entry level job in security for the recovering alcoholic. Joe had worked hard and risen through the ranks. Jake said a prayer and maneuvered the spotlights and squelched the sound at the podium microphone. He cut off Brickle in midsentence: " In just a moment I'd like to turn the microphone over to Howard Crane—"

Stress took Jake then. Martha's plane exploded behind his eyes. The derringer fired, throwing him back. He shook his head and looked down. It was now or never. One of his five minutes was almost gone...

"Colleagues, honored guests, my good friends." He began. "I'll be brief. With the exception of Dr. Vincent Wilson, you have before you a pack of devious medical practitioners who will destroy our hospital. I'll spare you the fancy titles Brickle was about to deliver: you can look for David Hudley in some administrative capacity; and there's Everett Salig, positioned for a top post—what is it, Everett, professor and dean of the medical school? And up for the Chancellor's Medallion of Excellence? And the rest of them: Al-Fassad, Howard Crane who tried to murder me—"

A gasp went up from the auditorium.

"And George Black. Take a good look at that butcher."

A projectionist moved across the stage hauling wire and a microphone. He handed it to Howard Crane.

Howard Crane's voice carried across the floor. "I don't think we need to listen to this maniac any longer. This man is a brutal murderer of Mitchell Malone, and he tried to kill me by breaking into my home. There is no further need for talk here. This meeting is adjourned and I suggest we all file out of the auditorium. Please begin on the left..."

Nobody moved.

"Three minutes, Doc." Joe said.

Jake's mouth was dry as he leaned toward his microphone. "I have been the target of a great many false accusations. I've been hauled into court and ridiculed. I've been blackballed, and driven from my hometown; I've been shot at and nearly killed. I have been placed on the most wanted list…"

Jake looked down, trying to organize his thoughts. "But I hold myself at fault… I placed my trust in these men."

"Move out, please!" Howard Crane said to the rows of listeners.

No one moved, except to twist around and look up at Jake.

"Simple truth is, I care about people," Jake said. The words fell into a hall still echoing with high-blown platitudes. "I've wanted to be a physician since grade school. I remember my sixth grade teacher, Ms. Jacqueline Blue. She encouraged me to be the best I could be. And I remember writing on my binder—*Neurosurgery*." He paused and looked up. "If I have ambition in medicine, it is only to help expand our effectiveness as a profession to help others. But what you have on that podium is a gang of financial corsairs who have only their own bottom line in mind. Our traditional values are being suffocated under the likes of Expercare, which I can tell you is a criminal venture run by lawbreakers."

"Can you prove that, Jake?"

"Yes, I can! But I need time. I need your support!"

Seated in the last row, Mary Kay, long time nurse clinician on the Neurosurgery service, caught Jake's eye. She had seen so many residents through their training. Including him. They shared a quick smile. Then a tall skinny male nurse dressed in white and seated toward the back of the auditorium stood up. Slowly he began to clap. It was all there in that man's stolid clapping. You'll have support, Dr. Gibson. You'll have your time in the sun—far more than the desperate forum you've had today. More people began to clap, a rhythmic support that undulated across the gathering. Howard Crane walked from the podium. Everett Salig stared up at Jake, his eyes malevolent in the spotlight.

George Black and David Hudley were walking away. Only Vince Wilson offered a positive force far brighter than any spotlight. He too smiled up at Jake.

The door smashed open and Joe entered followed by security guards.

"Drop that gun!"

"Dr. Gibson has no gun." Joe said in a calming voice. "Dr. Gibson, we must take you into custody at this time."

Jake nodded.

It was Joe who frisked him lightly and handcuffed him. With much grace, he robbed both acts of their demeaning assault. "You did good, Doc."

"I garbled it. I didn't get it all out."

Joe stood and faced him. "You got it all out, Doctor Gibson. You did good."

Jake shook his handcuffs. "Now there's this."

"You've got friends. You'll get through this." Joe hesitated. "Is it true what you said, about Expercare, those guys on the podium?"

Jake nodded.

Newsmen and television cameramen swarmed as he was hustled into a police cruiser. The media people were ecstatic, moving from a dry hospital news piece to the capturing of a most-wanted murder suspect. At the municipal jail, Jake was stripped of his possessions, his wooden cross getting just a slight pause before joining his watch, wallet and keys in the container. After the fingerprinting and photographing, he was interrogated for several hours. Not asking for a lawyer was an act of rebellion. He told his truth quietly, deviating on nothing. Then he was placed in his cell.

Another foul-smelling cot in the corner of a dark cell. The odor drew a wry smile and he thought about the country estate where Midge was waiting. There he had reviewed the different places he had put down his head to get some sleep. And the bird posters. Wood Duck, Wild Turkey, Yellow Warbler. He'd never seen a Yellow Warbler. He lay quietly for a few minutes while he thought it through. He was all over the news. Midge was safe. She would get to him in time. And Jeanne? She had no place here, just in that private place of his reflections. Jake sat up and called for a guard.

"Yeah, what?"

"I have a right to a phone call."

"Thought you didn't want one."

"Now I do."

He was escorted to a pay phone. He called Shannon Malone.

23

The greatest trust between man and man is the trust of giving counsel.

Francis Bacon
(1561–1626)

Shannon Malone was waiting in the heavily guarded visitor's area. Morning sunlight slanted down from the high windows and caught her hair. She wore an expensive fox-fur trimmed suit, the skirt not too tight to offend a judge. Her face held some annoyance but also concern. Jake shuffled forward, his restraints jingling, and got into the seat facing her. They peered at each other through reinforced glass.

Jake smiled. "Still mad at me?"

"And good morning to you." She relented. "I was never mad. But don't ever do that again, Jake. Never let them interrogate you without legal representation."

"They offered."

"Of course they offered. You were a damned fool not to take it."

"Did you know I'd phone for you?"

Shannon shrugged. "I watched the tube like everyone else. When the call didn't come early—" She shrugged again. "Anyway, later we need to go over the interrogation. Right now you face arraignment and you let me handle that."

"Okay."

"I have to tell you, Jake. There'll be no bail. You're too sensational, too media sensitive." She reached into her purse and held up the newspaper headline: *Local Surgeon Arrested in Bloody Trail of Death.*

Jake winced.

"There's more."

"What?"

"I guess you haven't seen a television: Everett Salig was on Nightline. He chewed you up in elegant terms. You're young, rambunctious, and reprehensible. Worse, you brutally murdered an archenemy attorney." Shannon's face carried anguish. "That would be my father."

Jake pulled against his chains. "Look -"

"You didn't kill my father, Jake. I know that. Let's move on. There isn't much time."

"But we do need to talk."

"I know. Now, moving along. Howard Crane was also working the talk shows last night. He analyzed your actions as an attempt to send a false message to the health care industry. His subtext was we need more attorneys." She didn't smile.

"Look, about my family, Martha's family—"

"Christ, Jake, aren't you listening to me? They're hogtying you while you sit here playing jingle bells on your chains!" She relented a little. "Okay, I'll do what I can for your folks and in-laws. Now listen. Both Salig and Crane came to my office this morning and asked me to handle the case for them. Seems they want to bring a libel suit against you for defamation of character."

Jake's look was cold. "Howard Crane killed your father."

"Howard Crane killed—" Shannon Malone's face drained of all color.

"I went to his house. He took out the gun he'd used and shot me with it. Put my prints all over it."

"He was in my office." Shannon said. "That filthy bastard was in my office. He said how sorry he was that my father had been murdered."

Jake said nothing. He watched her lean back, absorb the horrific information, and recover her balance.

"Did you know my father started out as a public defender?"

Jake let her talk. She needed an outlet.

"He was married once before. Clare Elizabeth—called her Libby. Childhood sweethearts. He always had a picture of her in his billfold."

"What happened?"

"She died the night I was born. I found that out going through Dad's files. There was also a cover up surrounding her treatment and death. That's when my father quit being a public defender. He decided the public need a better defense against doctors and hospitals."

"That explains a lot."

"We need to move on," Shannon said. But the guard cut them short.

Jake managed to scribble Midge's telephone number. "She's holding back. She won't come here till she hears from me. Midge is no fool."

"Two things, Jake. You couldn't have killed my dad. You performed heroic efforts to save him. Second, I got these in the mail." She held up two letters, each addressed in the same hand in distinctive blue ink.

"Gotta go," the guard said.

"I'll be with you for the arraignment. Until then you talk to nobody without my being there."

"Okay."

Midge greeted Shannon at the door and showed her in. "Get into something comfortable, Shannon. We can begin work right now. How was the drive?"

"Fine." Shannon nodded to the scenic window and bird posters. "This is nice."

"If you don't watch television," Midge said drily.

"Show me where to throw my overnight case and I'll be right with you."

"This way. Like some coffee?"

"Yes, please." Shannon grasped Midge's arm. "We've got a lot to go over. Some of it won't be easy."

"I'm ready. I'll fix the coffee. Bathroom's down on the left."

Midge and Shannon hit it off right from the start. Shannon was persistent and thorough, filling page after page in her legal pad. They watched each other across their coffee cups while beyond the window the bad weather shaped itself in ominous clouds. They worked well together because each was a consummate professional in her own field. They got to the core of things.

"Tell me more about this Dr. Hudley." Shannon said.

Midge put her cup down on the coaster. "Hudley's a moron. As far as doctoring goes, he should never have been allowed to finish his training. Jake carried the guy, looking for a sudden spark, some sudden insight and motivation from working on a patient. Didn't happen. Martha told me he dropped a piece of your dad's skullbone. Jake got to it before it hit the floor—Oh, God, I'm sorry , Shannon. That was thoughtless staff talk."

"It's okay. So what about Hudley?"

Midge leaned back and thought about it. "Big thing is, he changed when your father was brought in. From a mediocre surgeon for whom everything was too much trouble, he became Mr. Helpful. He was all over your father and mother—"

"Stepmother. My mom died when I was born. I was telling Jake about it."

Midge smiled. "He does that, doesn't he? No matter what problems he has he always is ready to listen to others."

"A very good man. Why do you think Expercare would hire Hudley and place him in an administrative position to oversee the entire University Hospital staff?"

"Christ. When did that happen?"

"At the big meeting where Howard Crane was announcing the Expercare takeover. They all got plum jobs: Everett Salig, Hudley, Al-Fassad, Jake's chairman, Vince Wilson."

"Wilson's okay." Midge said.

"They turned him out to pasture with a fancy title and job security. I think they wanted to head off any potential trouble from him."

"Could be."

"So what about this admin post for Hudley?"

"A payoff for something. That's how the guy would work."

"Any way to prove that?"

Midge reached for her coffee. She told Shannon about the events that seemed to tie David Hudley to Everett Salig.

Shannon's pencil flew. "When did you first meet Salig?"

"I saw him with Howard Crane the day of your dad's operation. I was looking through some nursing journals down in the neurosurgery office when the two of them walked in to see the boss, Dr. Wilson."

"When was this?"

"The morning after your father came into the hospital."

"Are you saying that you saw Everett Salig and Howard Crane in Vincent Wilson's office while my father was undergoing surgery?"

"That's correct. I greeted Howard, actually. He was, after all, Martha's husband. That was when he introduced me to Salig. The jerk actually asked me to go out with him. Can you believe that? Incidentally, Jake told me that Salig has an office in Crane's building. Cozy, huh?"

"Cozy indeed. Salig and Crane... Huh... So, what about this Al-Fassad?"

"He's a sorry-assed clown. He was at the hospital for about five years before he got his butt kicked out of the university. When word leaked out that he was coming back I decided I'd had enough. He's one of the main reasons I finally quit."

"He's now director of the neurosurgical unit."

"Yeah? God help the patients."

"You say that with feeling."

"Look, Shannon. That incompetent jerk will operate on any difficult dangerous case at the drop of the hat. He knows he isn't up to it, but his ego blinds him to that. If he maims or kills someone, it's all part of the 'learning process'. That or he blames someone else. If he gets away with blaming someone else, he writes it all up for the medical journals. As far as I know, none of his work at our hospital got published, thank God."

"How do he and Jake get along?"

Midge leaned back and closed her eyes. "Dr. Jason Gibson. Jake. They don't come any better, Shannon. You're fighting in court for a fine man and gifted surgeon. He's totally devoted to his patients, to the ideals of medicine." Her eyes opened. "Sort of a throwback. Anyway, it ended up with Jake protesting to the university and Al-Fassad was forced to leave."

Shannon tapped her pencil on the yellow pad. "So we have mediocre Hudley now in a plum administrative job, Al-Fassad heading up neurosurgery, and Vince Wilson—"

"Set aside, into the backwater, I guess. He's been at the hospital since before I was born. A thoroughly decent man, Shannon. But caught up in things."

Shannon nodded. "Let's get back to this Everett Salig."

"There I think I can help. I have some facts. When Jake left here and went back to Minneapolis for that big powwow I began to do some checking around on my own. I've spent the last couple of days talking with nurses and a few docs I know around the country. All of them were either associated with him or knew about him." Midge's eyes were bright. "It ain't pretty."

"Talk to me."

Midge shuddered uncontrollably.

"Midge, you okay?"

She managed a smile. "I shake sometimes. There are medical words for it, but basically I shake."

"What's wrong?"

"Fear. You know Jake and I were nearly killed on a sky lift? And Martha's dead, and Jake got shot..."

Shannon glanced towards the kitchen. "Like some more coffee?"

"Yeah, but I'll get it." Midge got up. "There is one thing."

"What?"

"There's a gun in this house, I found it in the bedroom closet." She got clean cups and poured. "I don't know anything about guns. I see too much of the receiving end in emergency rooms."

Shannon got up. "Where is it?"

"I put it in the bedside table. Straight back." She watched Shannon head for the hall. "You know about guns?"

"I'm proficient. Not expert, but pretty good. What is it, an auto?"

"I couldn't tell you." Midge pointed at the drawer. "In there."

Shannon took out the Smith and Wesson .38 revolver with a six inch barrel. She broke it open and checked the rounds, then checked the drawer again. "A box of .38 special shells. Nice." Probing the drawer brought from her a pleased exclamation. "All right, a speed loader. This guy was ready to defend his house and home. Who is it, anyway?"

"Some friend of Martha's parents. He and his wife are away." She watched Shannon replace the gun and speed loader.

"This may come in handy."

"Come on, Shannon. Now you're getting me really scared."

"Let's just say it's good to have the gun. Now, how about coffee and your findings on Salig?"

"Okay."

They settled back in their chairs, taking up familiar positions. Shannon had her pencil poised over a fresh page of the legal pad.

"Everett Salig did his formal training as a neurosurgical resident at the University of Las Vegas. One of his co-residents at the time was none other than Jake's psycho partner in Mt. Pleasant, George Black. Apparently they were both considered excellent trainees with seemingly brilliant careers in front of them. That is, until the two of them got themselves involved in the death of a child." Midge sipped her fresh coffee. "As I was able to piece it together from a couple of good friends of mine who were out there at the time, the two of them concocted a scheme to make a few extra bucks by covering emergency rooms around the Bay area. What they basically did was organize a bunch of resident moonlighters—taking a handsome fee off the top, of course. Anyway, it seems they were able to cover their tracks for quite a while. Until this infant died with acute hydrocephalus. Herniated, for God's sake. Neither of them could be found for over three hours. From what I was told, they were on twenty-four hour call, in house. But they snuck out to cover a couple of neighboring ER's. They got caught."

Shannon looked up. "So what happened?"

"That's not clear, except the chief of their department was in a rage and all set to issue harsh reprimands—but seems a year shy of completing their training program, both Black and Salig received their completion certificates." Midge finished her coffee. "Then the chief had a heart attack and died."

"That's odd."

Midge nodded. "Talk to Jake. Too many people have been conveniently dying."

"So what happened once they had their certificates?"

"Black went to Washington State and set up a private practice that Jake views as a slaughter factory. Everett Salig went into academic medicine and rose up through the ranks. But his career's barbaric. Did you know he's credited with a classic medical text written by Jake?"

"No."

"Well, it's true. It's called the Salig International Classification of Brain Tumors." Midge grimaced. "Should've been the Gibson Classification."

"How do you know about that?"

"Martha told me. Martha was something else, Shannon."

Shannon nodded. "I'm beginning to see that."

"Want the worst for last?"

"Go ahead."

"Salig and Black are silent partners in one of the largest national health care corporations. They grow richer each year."

"Expercare?"

"That's the one."

"How did you find out?"

For the first time Midge's face clouded, a secrecy drawn across her Scandinavian eyes.

"Give, Midge."

"I—I overheard—"

"Bullshit. How did you find out?"

"Okay, okay! I went out with Salig. Just once. Before I knew what I was dealing with. He took me back to his place."

"And?"

"And he got this phone call. It agitated him a bit. He excused himself and went into another room and picked up in there." Midge hesitated. "So I picked up and listened in. I recognized the voice immediately. It was Howard Crane."

Shannon put down her pencil and stared at the carpet.

"I'm sorry," Midge said. "That was clumsy of me. You know, don't you."

"Yes. Jake told me."

Midge watched her. "He used that derringer."

"Well," Shannon said, forcing a smile. "You're getting to know something about guns."

"We'll get through this, Shannon. And your father will be avenged."

"That's not a word in a good lawyer's vocabulary, Midge. But I appreciate it. You know, Crane and Salig came to see me. They wanted me to represent them in a defamation suit against Jake. Crane said how sorry he was about my father's death."

Midge shuddered again. "Shall we keep going here?"

"Who's that!"

Midge's eyes darted towards the window. "It's okay, that's Harold, Martha's father." They watched him finish clearing the snow. The weather front grew ominous as the afternoon progressed. Harold came in as Midge unlocked the door and kicked off his overshoes.

"Ms. Malone, there's no way you can get back to Minneapolis tonight. Why not stay the night?"

"Thanks, I will. Actually I brought an overnight bag."

"Good." Harold looked at Midge. "A cup of coffee in a mug would go well for the ride home, Midge."

"Of course."

"Got to get back to Ann. All this stuff on the news, media people. Should be ashamed of themselves."

Midge watched him pull his overshoes on and then handed him the coffee mug. "Thanks for everything, Harold."

Harold's eyes found Shannon's. "Do your best, girl, to get Jake off. He's a good man."

Shannon nodded.

When he had gone, Midge and Shannon resumed their talk. There were quite a few yellow legal pad pages.

24

The phone call came shortly after midnight. A woman's voice, frightened. Midge's own nerves tightened up.

"What is it?" Shannon asked.

Midge listened, said a few quiet words, then gently replaced the receiver. She rejoined Shannon. "That was Lisa, Martha's childhood friend. Harold had been checking around for us. She heard about it and phoned Martha's mother. She's real scared, Shannon. She's coming over to talk."

Lisa arrived with fear etched into her features. Her eyes were bright from the cold and changing weather. She settled in quickly to tell her tale then leave. "You haven't drawn those drapes completely closed," she said.

Midge fixed them.

"Okay, here it is. I've been on the move. Someone's been following me and the kids for months. It started right after Martha was killed. We've relocated three times now." Her eyes skittered around the room. "I can't stay long."

"What do you want to tell us, Lisa?" Shannon asked quietly.

"About my husband. About the letter I sent to Martha's house. That diskette."

"Jake has played the disk, Lisa. He knows what's on it."

"Good. That's good."

Shannon waited.

"Okay, here it is…"

Early the next morning, Shannon received a call via Martha's mother from Jake. Her law office had relayed Jake's request that Midge be brought back to Minneapolis. Shannon was packing her overnight bag and looking out at the freshly banked snow now covering the roads.

"Ready when you are." Midge said.

"Be right there. Midge, all right with you if I take the gun?"

Midge flinched. The question brought home Lisa's fear and the ugly events going on in their lives. The gun was real, a tangible presence. "Okay."

Wordlessly Shannon closed her case, put it down, and went to the master bedroom. "Get me a clean dish towel, will you?"

"A dish towel?" When she didn't answer, Midge headed for the kitchen.

"Great," Shannon said. She laid it out on the kitchen table and carefully wrapped the revolver and speed loader into it. "This goes in the Bronco."

"Why are you wrapping it up?"

"Leather seats. Things slide."

"Oh."

Shannon smiled with a confidence she didn't feel.

"Should we take the box of bullets?"

"No. Let's not get too paranoid. Next we'll be towing a cannon along behind us."

Midge managed a smile. "I guess we can go then."

The Bronco ate up the miles, surefooted on the snow-covered roads. The sun was now bright and it glanced off the windshield. It was just inside the Minnesota state line that Shannon confirmed the tail. "We're being followed," she said.

"What? Oh, my God." Midge looked into her side mirror.

"The black Lincoln Navigator."

"Oh, God." Midge said again.

Shannon reached for the towel wrapped revolver and compressed it under her thigh against the car seat. "Could be nothing."

The Lincoln Navigator crept closer. Slush had clumped over a reinforced front bumper.

Their Bronco skittered a little. "Film of ice." Shannon said. "Roads are cleared but there's ice."

"Should we get off, find some place to stop, a crowded place?"

"Let's keep going." Shannon watched the rearview mirror.

The Lincoln Navigator timed it right, suddenly accelerating as the Bronco was closing on an 18-wheeler in the slow lane. There was a wicked dance on ice, a sliding pirouette, then the Lincoln's reinforced bumper caught it and sent it careening off the road and down an incline. A snow bank took the force of impact. The Bronco was well off the road, canted and hidden, a wheel slowly spinning in the air.

"I can't get my door open!" Midge screamed.

Shannon unwrapped the revolver and gripped the speed loader. "Keep calm, Midge. Wait. See what develops."

They did not have long to wait. There were two of them. Winter coats, Glocks. Shannon took a deep breath. The only advantage she had was surprise. They did not know she was armed. "Get on the floor, Midge."

Midge crumpled without a word.

Shannon tried to remember her defensive gun course. One weekend. That's all she had to call upon. The two men were sliding down the embankment. Soon they would have sure footing. They would spread out, increasing the angle of fire. It had to be now. Shannon braced against the car frame and opened the window, using the frame as armor to protect the brain, heart and femoral arteries. She carefully fired off two rounds at the nearest man.

"Shit, I'm hit! I'm fucking hit!" Red splotches on his coat. The Glock had fallen into the snowbank.

Shannon sighted on the second man who was bringing up his own pistol. Seventeen rounds were about to be unleashed on her. The revolver was nothing against the Glock. She fired again, hearing her instructor's words. *Stay disciplined, gain target acquisition, use only the front site, squeeze...squeeze...*

The Bronco lurched in the snow and fell onto all four wheels and shook itself. Panicking, Shannon fired the remaining rounds and fumbled with the cylinder catch. Empty casings jumbled out. She thrust home the speed loader and twisted, closing the cylinder with trembling fingers. She fired fast and erratically, pocking the snow bank around the two men. She watched them slip and slide up the bank, the second man helping the wounded man.

Shannon waited in fear for the fusillade of nine millimeter from the Glock, but no fire came. She stared. She watched the big Lincoln fish tail across the snow and accelerate away. She began to shake. "Dear God in Heaven," she said, fright pushing out the words like a prayer, which it was.

"Shannon! Shannon!"

"It's okay, Midge." Shannon managed, as she watched the snowplow haul its way to the incline.

"You okay, lady?"

"We're okay. Could use a tow."

"We'll figure something. Trouble with you women, always driving too damned fast for conditions."

The municipal jail interview room offered a harsh fluorescent light. The door was locked and there was an overhead video camera. A guard stood outside. Jake studied Shannon's face carefully. He said nothing. He waited.

"There have been some developments." Shannon said. "After you called my office to bring Midge back, I—"

"What? I didn't call anybody. Midge should be back at that farm house!"

Shannon massaged her brow. "That explains a lot."

"So she's here?" Jake pursued.

"She's ok, Jake. Safely hidden."

"God, what have I gotten you both into."

"We'll handle it. And I have some skin in this game, Jake. My father was murdered."

Jake watched the quiet resolution on her face, muscles tight, eyes steady. "Okay."

"Let's begin with Martha's friend, Lisa. Those letters you sent me."

"That one with the computer disk."

"Right. You've looked at it?"

"Yes. Computer records of accounting statistics, mostly emergency room stuff, and all of it Expercare, here and around the country."

"Right," Shannon said again. "Last night Lisa came to see Midge and me. She's very scared, she keeps moving, stays on the run."

"And her husband, the ER doctor—"

"Looks like he was the pilot who was flying himself and Martha to see you."

"He must have known his life was on the line..." Jake began.

"Lisa got a final letter from Howie, apparently written just before they took off. It was in a Cascade Airlines' envelope. There was a key in it."

"A key?"

"An airport locker at the Mt. Pleasant Airport. I flew out there and got it."

"And?"

"There was a briefcase filled with Dr. Carr's handwritten files. It's potent stuff, Jake. He documents a conspiracy to selectively eliminate elderly ER patients."

"Good God!"

"It seems Expercare has been very efficient in providing certain types of hospital care. According to the figures on the disk, they've dramatically reduced costs for acute hospitalization by simply reducing the amount of care required. See where this is going?"

"Fee reimbursement," Jake said. "Fees paid to hospitals to take care of the acutely ill, elderly patients…those likely to die within a few hours or days—the fees are the same across the board."

"Yes. So all participating hospitals receive the same amount per patient regardless of how much it might cost an individual facility to take care of that patient."

"So, if a hospital could find a way to reduce their costs…" Jake felt sick. He knew where this was going all right.

"The managed-care systems herded good hospitals and doctors like sheep. Paid them less and forced them to find ways to cut their costs. And if service declines, and patients don't get what treatment they need—?" Shannon's eyes were bright with anger.

"So what about Expercare?" Jake asked.

"It's obscene. Expercare emergency room admits had a fifty-fold increase of dying within the first hours of arrival."

Shouts came from beyond the locked door as some prisoner was being moved. It was ugly and lost against the cold bricks.

"Give me the numbers." Jake said.

"Okay. Around the country actual hospital costs on average for an elderly, acutely ill patient who has say, a large intracranial hemorrhage, are around $30,000."

"And for Expercare?"

"Less than 5,000. Seems their patients die a lot quicker."

"And Lisa's husband figured this out."

Shannon nodded. "It makes sense, doesn't it? He was an emergency room physician on the front lines. He must have suspected what was going on. Too many were dying off too quickly."

"So Expercare-owned hospitals across the country have been killing off the sickest patients to lower their overhead."

Shannon's mouth tightened. "Capitalism in action."

"A conspiracy, then." Jake said. "How far does it go? It must go to George Black, to Everett Salig."

"Tip of the iceberg, Jake."

"What?"

"Think about it: literally hundreds of ER physicians, they must know what's going on—so why don't they blow the whistle?"

Jake stared. "Your dad had the answer." He remembered Mitch Malone's prone body, the blood stained papers belonging to Everett Salig. "The ER physicians aren't credentialed."

"Some are, I suppose," Shannon said. "But Salig has recruited many who aren't, and who are locked into him."

"But even Salig couldn't—"

"Sure he could. Who would question this world class doctor and his records?" Shannon studied Jake. "Midge tells me he stole your research and published under his own name."

"Yeah, the brain tumor work."

"He's made a lifetime practice of it. And notice how people keep dying, Jake? Your fellowship director in Switzerland, Salig's and Black's chairman who qualified them?"

"I didn't know about that."

Jake rubbed his temples. "Look, even if all this is true, how are they pulling it off?"

"Ah, now we're getting to it. I came across an article in Dr. Carr's briefcase. It was written several years ago by Dr. Kevorkian. It described a revolutionary drug, something called Polyfisterase A."

"Oh, dear God." Jake murmured.

"You know it?"

"I know it. It's a potent poison discovered in Sweden. A mixture of compounds that when injected into the bloodstream will produce sudden heart fibrillation and death."

"And it's all natural substances," Shannon said. "It's impossible to detect in the system. The perfect hemlock. Your former associate, Dr. George Black," she went on. "He was a chemistry major in college. He worked one summer on a research project with a biochemist who was testing the drug in lab animals. Black actually coauthored a paper with him that described its rapid fatal effects. Of course, the substance was far too dangerous for any kind of practical use. And it's gone unrecognized for years, or at least that's what everybody thought."

"And Lisa's husband figured it out." Jake said.

"Right. He obviously figured out what Salig and Black were up to."

"But still," Jake said, "how the hell could they—"

"That turned out to be the easy part. They positioned the Expercare hospitals around the country to participate in a nationwide, NIH funded, experimental study. They were looking ostensibly for new steroidal alternatives. That's a good gambit, right? A steroid is something that would commonly be given to critically ill patients in an ER?"

"Absolutely. It's often administered right off the bat to patients who come in with head or spinal cord injuries, with tumors, and those in sepsis and shock—it's a helluva long list."

"Listen to how they do it, Jake. It's cunning beyond belief: the study is underway as we speak. They're testing several different classes of steroids in various dosages. Patients are—what do you call it?—randomized?"

"Oh, yeah, randomized into a double blind protocol." Jake said. "And only the project director knows which drug is being administered. Our sonofabitch celebrity to the medical world, Dr. Everett Salig."

"They're using Polyfisterase on terminally ill patients." Shannon's eyes were wet. "I'm so dreadfully sorry, Jake."

Jake stared at his chains. They shone in the harsh fluorescent light. "Dear God."

"Is it foolproof?"

"Nothing's foolproof in a hospital. Lisa's husband got onto it, for instance. But it is clever, it's infernally clever."

"How would it go, day to day, I mean?" Shannon asked.

"Simple enough. Some emergency room physician would call to enter his patient in the study. Salig is then supposed to assign at random the type of steroid to be administered. They're labeled A through F or something like that."

"So an ER physician never knows what he's giving, because it's a blind study."

"And all someone has to do is substitute the hemlock for one of the steroid drugs. Salig could easily decide who gets what."

"So the Polyfisterase is given to elderly patients who are given little chance of survival—"

"And terminal-care costs go down from $30,000 to $5,000 as per our example."

"Yup."

"And no one questions, because this is the world famous Dr. Everett Salig."

Shannon closed her eyes, feeling sick. "Black supplies the stuff. Salig uses it."

Jake sat quietly. "We've got to stop it."

"How?"

"Not by confronting Salig and Black, that's for sure." Jake looked across at her. "Mitch understood. When we met, your father was frightened. We sat there with hot chocolate, and he kept looking around."

"Just like Lisa." Shannon said. "These men have all of us in fear of our lives." Shannon told him then about the shootout in the Bronco.

"You're obviously okay," Jake said. "How's Midge?"

"She's frightened. I suspect she's at the end of her rope."

Jake nodded.

"Look, Jake. I have an idea. Maybe we can plant a little rat bait."

His eyes fixed on her, Jake smiled. For once, an attorney on his side with a devious and underhanded scheme.

25

*And he that saves one human life, of him the Scriptures say it is
as if he saved the entire life.*

Mishnah, Sanhedrin 4:5

Chaz Cova's vintage Italian bistro was built onto a granite
bluff overlooking the windy St. Paul River. They had a window
seat, sunny and scenic. Around them good wine chinked in
glasses, there were linen tablecloths and silver sticked candles. All
in all it was sleek, with a patina of Mediterranean flavor, but it
catered to the needs of an insular corporate elite. Shannon wore a
dark business suit with an elegant jeweled pin hastily purchased.
Her purse was new too, expensive and oblong, a shape that
accommodated the Smith and Wesson. Below her, she could see
the icy parking lot and the feathering of snow as wind blew from
the bluff. She tried to keep her face expressionless then realized
that was wrong, and she looked with attentiveness at Howard
Crane, this man who had killed her father.

"I'm glad you agreed to meet with me, Shannon. Things have been, to say the least, difficult. I considered your father a good friend, and he was a fine attorney."

Shannon felt his eyes on her, searching for the slightest suspicious look. "It's been bad for the family, for all of us." She said.

"Yes, of course. And now you're representing Dr. Gibson."

"I am."

"You'll forgive me if I say I find that remarkably odd. Especially since Dr. Salig and I had hoped to enlist your services in our defamation suit against him."

Careful… She sipped her wine. The phone call should come soon. Christ, make it soon. She bent over and lifted her purse to her lap.

"Doctors are different these days. Too much pressure, all this tremendous stress—"

The waiter carefully maneuvered their salads in front of them. "Will that be all?"

"For the moment." Crane dismissed him and picked up his fork, waving it a little for emphasis. "Take Dr. Gibson. A world class surgeon who's lost it, gone off the deep end. I'm sure he's given you his grotesque account of how I shot him." Crane's voice trailed off, the eyes dug into Shannon. "And Martha, of course. My beloved wife—lost to Dr. Gibson, I might add, with his amoral ways. And when she married him, and was killed…" The fork waved a moment then prodded the salad.

"There's still sentiment around town that Jake is innocent." Shannon said.

"Ah. 'Jake' is it? Yes, I've heard those stories: that he's been framed, that there's some vast conspiracy…I must say, when these doctors go off the deep end they really go!"

"And he has supporters at the University Hospital—"

"Yes, and they're interfering with our efforts to implement cost-effective methods of managing a modern teaching hospital—"

"Excuse me, sir, you are wanted on the phone."

Howard Crane glared at the waiter. "What?"

"The phone, sir."

"But nobody knows I'm, oh, what the hell." He stood up. "You'll have to excuse me a moment, Shannon."

"Of course."

"And when I'm back, let's finish this unpleasantness as quickly as we can. Please consider negotiating some sort of plea bargain between us and Gibson. We just don't want the medical profession dragged through this mess again." He leaned forward. "Let's avoid media hoopla, Shannon. And consider this: I've given a sworn statement to the prosecuting attorney stating that Dr. Gibson boasted to me, while he held me at gunpoint in my home, that he was the one who shot your father to death." He smiled, but it was strained. "When I get back, I'll finish that martini and order us another round—okay?"

"Fine. You'd better get that phone." Shannon watch him wind his way between tables. When he disappeared into the alcove, she removed from her purse the small plastic vial. She drew his martini glass to her and let it sit a moment while she looked around. Crystals dissolved into the martini. She swirled it lazily. Satisfied no one was paying any attention, she moved the glass back in front of Crane's salad.

Shannon was forcing down her salad when Howard Crane returned. She was not hungry but appearances were vital; he was already suspicious of her. Perhaps she should have been quick with a response about his sworn statement for the prosecuting attorney; or she should have said something about why she was representing Dr. Gibson. Why was she representing Jake? She had barely formed an answer as Crane sat down.

"Hung up, can you believe that?" He smiled at her but again the dark eyes were searching.

"About Dr. Gibson," Shannon said. "He saved my father's life. That's why I'm defending him now."

"My dear young woman," Crane said, "you remember the earlier trial, Dr. Hudley's testimony, how can you possibly think such a thing!"

Shannon allowed her features to take on a small cast of doubt. She stared at the table cloth and put down her fork.

Howard Crane smiled and drained his martini. She had cracked. This lunch would be worthwhile after all. "I'm ordering another. Care for one?"

"No, thank you." She watched him intently now, because she had only a few seconds to get it in. She caught his sudden wariness too, but he was way too late. "You killed my father, you disgusting animal. And I'm going to prove it."

By this time, his eyes glazed, his jaws had tightened. Whatever he had wanted to say went unsaid. He stood up, lurched against the linen table cloth, then turned and teetered a few steps. His fall to the ground knocked tables and sent candlesticks and meals sliding to the floor. At that moment, Shannon screamed for assistance.

The ambulance crew pushed through the restaurant towards Shannon who was bent over Howard Crane. The stretcher took Crane's weight, medical technicians busied themselves strapping him down, taking his vital signs, one of the EMT's talking into a two-way radio. Their activity headed off questions; they moved out quickly, Shannon beside them. Only one elderly man enjoying a plate of spaghetti and meatballs, a dish easily ruined but a joy when prepared well, wondered at the speed with which the ambulance team arrived. But it was after all none of his affair, and his meal was getting cold. Sirens died away as the ambulance reached the emergency room.

University Hospital was no more: a new sign in deep violet neon offered to the sick and injured: EXPERCARE UNIVERSITY HOSPITAL. The name bespoke care and competence, the dedication of trained professionals. Inside the Emergency Room were a dozen or so ER physicians and staff members in long white lab coats. Their faces were somber and rather strained as they gave full attention to Dr. Everett Salig. The presence of Dr. Al-Fassad added to the tension. Everyone focused on the dean of the medical center as Salig described his randomized steroid study, something demanded of all hospitals in the corporate chain nationwide. Dean Salig watched like a hawk as a physician rapidly performed the routine sequences of a thorough neurological examination on the newly arrived case: a shabbily dressed man with a grime smeared face and a stench of cheap wine on his baggy trousers.

"Notice both of his pupils are pinpoint, less than one millimeter, and barely reactive. He has total reflexive paralysis of both upper and lower extremities, and there's no response at all to commands or painful stimulation. Clearly this misfortunate seems trapped, irreversibly, in a deep coma. Note that his respirations are becoming somewhat labored." Dean Salig smiled a not unkindly smile. It was one he used in courtroom cases, a careful blend of the inevitable and the compassionate. "I think this old chap is nearly ready to check out."

A smattering of laughter went around the gathering.

With that brief but to the point diagnostic analysis, Salig removed from its jacket a CT-scan that had accompanied the patient. Without bothering to verify its authenticity, he inserted it onto a nearby view-box. He then solemnly addressed the doctors and nurses. "My lord, look here! There's a gigantic hemorrhage into the deep white matter of the brain stem. Surely, all of the vital consciousness centers have been permanently damaged." He glanced around as if to seek out a challenge. "Clearly, there's very little chance, if any, that this poor fellow will ever recover."

Salig placed a hand on the man's leg. But it was not to raise Lazarus. "I give him only twenty-four to forty-eight hours at the most."

Another restrained murmur from the physicians.

That was when a nurse's aid attending the dying man's essential needs clumsily bumped into the dean and spilled a chafe of warm urine onto the front of Salig's immaculate white coat.

"What in hell's name!—"

"Oh, I'm so sorry, Dean Salig! I'm so terribly sorry—"

Salig recovered. "It's quite all right, my dear. It's a story to tell your grandchildren, isn't it?" Everyone laughed.

Grimacing in disgust, Everett Salig slipped each arm in turn from his brine-stained lab jacket. Then he dropped it into the arms of an LPN, the message in his eyes quite clear: a fresh one immediately. As she pushed beyond the drawn curtain, Dr. George Black slipped in and responded to a brief nod from Salig. He reached into the back of the deep bottomed drawer of an emergency drugcart. He retrieved a single labeled, glass med-vial. While Salig and Al-Fassad kept the group's attention at the film view-box, he quickly reached inside a shallow top drawer and grabbed a 12cc syringe and a 20-gauge needle. He then drew up the contents of the disposable 10cc container.

"As you can see," Salig was saying, "this is an ideal candidate for our Steroid Randomization Study. According to the protocol, eligible patients must be elderly with an acute life-threatening illness." His hard eyes looked around as he shrugged into the new lab coat. "Data collection has been underway for almost five years. Double-blind randomization is accomplished through my office here in Minneapolis, as soon as the patient is admitted and pertinent data has been processed—such as age, admitting diagnosis, neurological status and the like—then the mainframe automatically provides the physician on the front line with the appropriate vial letter and number." Salig felt the syringe and other injection paraphernalia placed into his hand as George Black slipped by him. Salig then held up in the air a red-numbered vial labeled with the letter F for all to see.

"As ER staff, your job is to simply administer the drug according to the prescribed dosage regimen. I would strongly suggest, however, that a designated emergency room physician personally monitor each patient for a few minutes after the initial dose, though I can personally reassure you that up until this point in the study, absolutely no untoward side effects have been noted."

With that, Dr. Salig stepped over to the side of the barely breathing patient and promptly uncapped and inserted the needled syringe into the slowly dripping IV. Rapidly plunging the opaque, plastic syringe, he sent a bolus of a slightly discolored substance through the lengthy clear plastic tubing and into the distressed man's venous system. Then, with his features a display of regret and reverence, he decisively withdrew the beveled prong, detached it from the syringe, and disposed of both into a bright red contamination container.

"And there we have it, gentlemen—" Salig began, but was suddenly cut off by the most grotesque moans. The patient stirred, his eyelids beginning a rapid flutter, the corners of his mouth twitching. A shout came from the man, at first strangulated, then finding its strength on outrage.

"You son of a bitch!"

Salig swooped over the bed and placed an ear to the patient's mouth.

"You son of a bitch!"

Salig was knocked aside as the patient suddenly sat up and took him by the throat.

"You lousy son of a bitch—you tried to kill me!"

Physicians gathered in a small pack away from the struggling Salig and patient. Shouts came from them as they entangled themselves and aimed blows.

"You set me up! You want the data and results and you need me out of the way. Well, I got Malone and I'll get you!"

In some frightening surrealistic disintegration, the patient's hair came loose and slid from his head. Makeup and grime smeared around his wildly staring eyes. It was Al-Fassad who recovered first, then Black. They freed Salig and pulled him away.

"Howard?" Salig called out. "Howard Crane? Good God man!"

"I'm gonna kill you, Salig."

"What's the hell's going on?" Salig slid behind Al-Fassad and Black. "The scan showed a massive hemorrhage, I was following our agreed upon procedure—"

"Shut up, Salig." Black murmured.

"Too late," Al-Fassad said.

They looked around at the physicians who no longer were cowered by surprise. They looked with revulsion at Salig. Just then a nurse came in and offered a patch of sterile gauze to Howard Crane. He compressed it over the seeping IV site on his forearm. No one moved as Shannon Malone worked her way through the white coats and uniforms to Howard's stretcher. The videocam panned it all, slowly filming it, encompassing Salig, Al-Fassad, Black and Howard Crane.

As Shannon left, Midge retrieved a handful of intact labeled vials and the red plastic disposal container filled with contaminated needles and syringes.

"I know that nurse." Salig shouted, as Midge made her exit.

But it was all too late. Drs. Salig, Black, and Al-Fassad were alone with Howard Crane, who was wiping at his smeared face. He picked up the wig and crushed it in his hand before throwing it on the floor. "Consider yourself dead, Salig." Crane's words were softly offered. It made them all the more terrifying.

26

Jake sat quietly in the courtroom and watched Shannon Malone preparing her documents for presentation to the judge. She caught him looking and smiled. "It's different now, Jake. This is court work at its best: the clearing of an innocent man."

"Like medicine," Jake said. "There's a wasteland of talent, but you'll also find dedication and adherence to a noble cause."

"Exactly. In that regard our professions, at their best, are the same." She looked around. "Looks like your whole family's here."

Jake looked around. The front rows and gallery were filled to capacity. There were his parents, Paul and Catherine Gibson, Midge and Vince Wilson and other friends and colleagues. And Jeanne was there. He caught Jeanne's eyes and smiled. Their relationship had matured during the stress and violence of the last few months. Martha had helped accomplish that with her love. And Midge had helped with her loyalty. Jeanne and Jake now saw each other from that tender terrain of the heart which offered friendship and affection but which was somehow freed from feelings that were damaging to others. How odd, Jake thought, that it is here in a courtroom, scene of so many ugly indictments, vicious slurs, and unjust penalties, that he should first feel free to love again and rekindle his faith in his chosen profession. Shannon had it right: the ideals of medicine and law were the same.

She was speaking now, standing respectfully before the judge, eloquently offering the list of conspiracy, corruption, deceit and violence surrounding Expercare, the health conglomerate. It was a bravura performance, ending with the judge's own words: "Dr. Gibson, after discussion with the district attorney, I have decided to release you to the recognizance of your attorney, Ms. Malone, pending further investigation of this entire matter."

The courtroom surged as one voice. Jake reached for Shannon, then moved along the front row shaking hands. He could barely hear his father's words as he said, "Back to our house, everybody's welcome!"

"You mean lunch, Dad? Haven't had good food for a while."

"You know your mother—she'll set up a feast."

And it was. Jake sat quietly in a favorite armchair, one in which he had burned the midnight oil many nights as a young student, gently urged on by his parents. His father had offered the love of medicine; he had reflected in his life the humanity of his calling; and he had conducted himself always in the highest ideals of his profession. In this environment of learning tempered with humility, Jake had forged the foundations to his own professional calling. And he had almost lost them. Cynicism had held reign over him; he had been drained by predators like George Black and Everett Salig. He had in Mount Pleasant witnessed the medical arts transmuted into something obscene. Dr. George Black, his bloody gloves over a brain dead patient, was an image he would carry forever. Even prison was better than that; to be manacled and counted like some cipher, to be stripped of strength so that in the coldness of night you questioned who you were.

"Get enough ham and potato salad?" Midge asked, sitting down beside him.

"Sure did. Everyone is having a good time."

"Your mom's a great cook. I'm envious of her."

"Believe me, Midge, I didn't inherit the skills. Neither did Dad as a matter of fact—and he's the first to admit it." Jake watched as the others came in and found comfortable seats or places on the floor. "You know, I do have a few questions."

"For whom? Us?" Shannon said. "What can you mean."

"Come on—how did you pull it off?"

"Like the ambulance?" Jake's brother Steven asked.

"Yeah, for starters."

"Believe it or not you can find them in the yellow pages as rentals."

"You never could tell a lie with a straight face, Stevo." Jake said.

"Okay. Let's leave it like this: we had a couple of friends in high places. Now don't push it any more, Jake, or we'll land some folks in trouble."

"The ambulance was outside while Shannon and Crane were having lunch?"

"Yup." Shannon dabbed at her mouth with a napkin and set her plate aside. "And it was going to Expercare and nowhere else!"

Jake shook his head. "Okay. So, what pharmaceutical warfare did you inflict on Howard Crane?"

"Poor Mr. Crane." Midge said, her eyes bright. "He apparently got hold of some very bad deadly nightshade—and you know how upsetting to the system belladonna can be."

Jake pulled a face. "I'm damned glad you guys are on my side," he said. "All right. Last question. How could you be certain that Salig would give Crane a cholinergic antidote, and not administer the dose of steroid hemlock?"

Shannon stood up with her plate, ready to take it into the kitchen. "We—that is Midge—switched the drug vials in the whatchamacallit—"

"The crashcart." Midge said.

"Right, the crashcart. But we also had to be sure Salig didn't have a vial in his lab coat pocket—"

"So I peed for the cause!" Midge said, triumphantly. "Got the old goat with a bunch of it. An LPN had to get a new coat. Once he did that we knew we were home free."

"And the makeup, the wig?"

Steve smiled. "They really got into it, Jake."

Jake watched Shannon as she headed for the kitchen.

"Hey, let me give you a hand," Midge said.

"Those two work well together," Steve said.

Jake leaned back, content. "That they do."

Tension and stress slowly left him as he held court in the familiar chair. Only Shannon's and Midge's leaving roused him. "Hey, you're going?"

"Just for a while." Shannon said. "I'm fixing Midge up with a room at my place."

"Okay."

Shannon's face clouded. "And Jake, don't sell Salig short. We're still in this thing. He can maneuver like a cobra."

"I know."

The two women smiled as they said their goodbyes. Shannon had a special handshake for Jeanne, who had kept out of the general festivities.

"Stay in your chair, Jake," Midge called out. "You look like you're enjoying it."

"Gonna kick my shoes off."

"Good for you. See everyone later."

Jeanne came into the den and found a chair close to Jake. "You're blessed with good friends, Jake."

"That I am," he said, slipping off his shoes. "Jeez, that feels good."

"So what now?"

"Now?" Jake closed his eyes. "Catch a nap."

It was Jake called to the phone by his mom. "It's Vince Wilson."

"Jake, I just got off from a conference call with Salig and Crane."

Jake pressed the phone to his ear. Was this the news he'd been waiting for?

"Salig's one haughty son of a bitch. Totally denies the episode in the emergency room yesterday ever happened. And for Crane, his line is always the same. Blames everything on you." Jake took a deep breath.

"As far as Expercare is concerned," Wilson continued, "it appears to be business as usual."

Jake continued to listen.

"This whole thing has got me concerned. Salig alluded to—well, he made an inference that something was going to happen. He made it very clear that I should steer away from you for the next few days—"

Jake's pulse pounded.

"—and that goes for—"

The explosion when it came tore the front door off one of its hinges. Windows blew out and curtains lifted like banshees. Acrid smoke, broken glass. It cut at Jake's feet as he leaped for the door and outside. When he screamed, it was torn from deep inside him, ripped from him, something primal and terrible.

Shannon and Midge's car was chunks of torn metal surrounded by licking yellow flames. Black smoke plumed upward, darting and twisting on vile currents of air. The car and its occupants were totally consumed by some monstrous beast. No one could get near it. The beast guarded its prey as its flames roared, then were sucked down into an oily muck. Snow melted for meters around, fleeing in rivulets then pooling in gathering swirls.

Jake stood quite still, unaware of his father standing close to him, watching him. When Jake collapsed, his father was there.

The minivan rocked a little on the bumpy road. It awakened Jake who suddenly tore at the blanket wrapped around him.

"It's okay, Jake!" Jeanne yelled. "It's okay!"

Jake sat back, suddenly still. He watched the road. "Their car exploded," he said.

"Yes."

"Shannon and Midge are both dead."

"Yes."

Jake stared at the road. "My parents, the house."

"All okay. The fire trucks were quick."

He rubbed his face. He was sweating under the blanket. When he looked around, he saw the suitcases.

"I'm getting you out, Jake. Away from reporters and other media types."

"Your place?"

"For now. While we think."

"When I went down, who—"

"Your father. He gave you something. I don't know what. Then we bundled you into this van and we got out of there."

"I'm not crying."

"What?"

"I'm not crying. I should be crying."

"Try and rest, Jake."

Traffic picked up, drawing the minivan into it, rendering it anonymous.

◎◈✳

Once settled in Jeanne's den, she brought him a straight whiskey, no ice. He sat on the couch, sipping it, looking straight ahead but seeing nothing.

"We're okay here, Jake." Jeanne said.

"Where's Ben?"

"He went to his mother's with the kids."

Jake emptied the glass.

Her hand found his arm. "How are you doing?"

"Shaken up. I'll make it."

"You need to let it out, Jake."

He looked at her then. "What, cry? I suppose I should. I just—"

The phone rang.

"Hi, Ben."

Jake watched her.

"Yes, he got released. That Shannon Malone's some lawyer. When are you coming home? Okay…" She hung up the phone. "We have a couple of hours, anyway."

"So how are things—you and Ben, I mean?"

"They're good, Jake. You put in the effort, you realize what you have, who's counting on you, and soon it's not an effort anymore."

He watched her blue eyes.

"What about you?"

"Me?" Jake forced a smile.

"What are you going to do, Jake?"

Jake lowered his eyes. "I don't know. For someone who was always sure of himself, knew where he was going, this is a strange feeling. And the hurt and fear. And the loss: Martha, Midge, Shannon, her father…I can't seem to grapple with it."

"Jake, when was the last time you did something for yourself?"

He shrugged.

"Well, then. Maybe it's time you looked beyond all the ghosts wandering around in your head."

Closing his eyes, Jake shook his head.

"You're really beginning to piss me off!" Jeanne said.

Jake's eyes again found hers.

"Don't you see? Medicine isn't what it used to be. You devoted your life to a profession that put people first. Remember how it was practiced by your grandfather?" Jeanne gently brushed the front of his collar. "Isn't he the main reason that you went into medicine?"

Jake's face energized. "He was one of my idols. I still have a few of his patient logs. The day he went into the hospital with his heart attack, at age 82, he saw his last patient—a high school student who lived across the street from his office, needed a physical to play football. My grandfather examined him and completed the paperwork." He grinned. "You'll never guess his charge?" He shook his head. "One buck."

Jeanne studied his look. "Please don't tell me you're giving up on medicine."

"Jeanne, Grandad's been gone twenty-five years. It's all become money and plundering of broken and diseased bodies, right? Why stay?"

"What about your dad? I hope you won't say that in your folks' presence."

"No."

"So, what do you do, fight the likes of Howard Crane and the medical complex conglomerates. Or what?"

"No. I see only one way out."

Jake's eyes found the photo. "Nice picture of you and Ben and the kids. I don't remember it."

"We just had it done."

Jake sat quietly for a long time, long enough for Jeanne to start worrying. Then he slowly got up. "I'll be leaving now, Jeanne. Remember me to Ben and the kids. I noticed you didn't tell him about Shannon and Midge."

"There'll be time for that later."

"Yeah."

"Like another drink?" Jeanne reached for his glass.

"No. It's okay, Jeanne. I'm okay now."

"So where are you going?"

"I don't know. Away from here. Try and heal. Try to give back in some way. I am trained, after all."

Jeanne squeezed his hand. "Just remember. I will always be here for you."

Jake wrapped his arms around her. "I know."

"You'll call." Tears filled her eyes.

"I'll call." Jake kissed her on the cheek.

Shivering in the doorway, Jeanne watched him head off, suitcase in hand. Long after he had gone, his footprints filled with fresh snow.

27

The poor are the best customers, because God will be their paymaster.

Herman Boerhauver
(1688–1783)

The Rain Forest is lush and beguiling, alive with the cries of birds and insects. And there are primal voices of jungle cats, and the snuffle of furred animals making their way through dense undergrowth. Rains come and turn dead leaf and branch into a foul mulch on the forest floor. But there are traces of man, mostly primitive man, unless some engineer is there seeking out minerals or trees to be brought down for upscale neighborhoods. Man-made trails find their way through openings in the brush; they sometimes offer silvered twists from droplets of moisture caught by a distant sun high above the cupola of trees. But mostly the forest is dark and dank and dangerous.

Salomao is a primitive tribesman. He has trekked through the mountains and is now moving through the forest to reach the city of Belize. In his arms is his eight-year-old daughter. She is very sick. Salomao is a portly man not suited to a two hundred-mile journey, but he moves with a determination that along with this daughter is his constant companion. She is known to fall, and when she moves her arms it is in odd ways, as if they are not her own. So Salomao carries her, sometimes over his shoulder, sometimes in his arms, but always he moves forward unless he needs to tend to his daughter's physical needs and his own. They stop sometimes by creekbeds cut into ancient rock. Then Salomao will gather up his daughter into his arms and resume his walk towards Belize, for there he will find the American doctor...

The hospital was befouled, a place of sanctuary and healing set against rotting vegetation and relentless humidity that ate away at the stucco put up by the British army a half century earlier. Later, in the Sixties civil war power struggle, it was abandoned. In its decline, denied the attempts of occupants, the hospital deteriorated even more. That was when the missionary sisters found it. They fought against filth with pure hearts. But even so, the filth abounded. Stray animals roamed freely on the ground floor of the building. Hospital workers had to sidestep piles of feces and pools of urine as they steered the bed or wheelchair patients between wards. All around was the dreary damp of broken and boarded up windows, leaking roof overhangs, exposed wiring that threatened, and leaking plumbing that gurgled and swamped against the best efforts of its users.

It should not have existed, but it did. Working here to save broken and diseased bodies were the most remarkable, talented people. They worked miracles with supplies passed down from the member hospitals in the SSM Healthcare Network, the only surviving nonprofit chain of its kind that still spread across the entire United States. They breathed life into ancient instruments and their first-generation CT scan. They washing and rinsed and disinfected cloth and surgical mask, they processed surgical gloves, they maintained surgical instruments donated by other institutions and kept a wellspring of purity to any cutting edge, any stainless steel hinge or tired screw. Sister Susan had studied computer sciences in college and had developed an instinct for practical engineering and electronics. Nurse Irene was a wheat farmer's daughter who had been on her way to scuba dive the barrier reef, but had found herself in Belize, drawn to the hospital. Now she was the gas-passer who could work magic with a resterilized and rehoned IV needle. She could make an ancient piece of adhesive tape stick one last time. And there was an energetic senior medical student named Austin out of the University of Buffalo. It was supposed to be a six-week internship. He was still there. And because there was no paperwork, no endless filling out of forms, all of their attention was for the patient. It was all medicine, all the time, for all of them. Especially for the American doctor.

Salomao spoke very slowly and Jake listened. Occasionally he would ask a question in the Kekchi Indian dialect. But mostly he examined the girl. He used the ancient funduscope. His face was impassive behind the beard and sun darkened skin. His hair was shot with gray. Only his eyes were young, fired by some passion, and to Salomao who knew about such things, they carried a hidden pain. Or tiredness. Or both.

Jake was not surprised to discover the tremendously swollen and hemorrhagic optic discs. Together with typical signs of midline cerebellar compression, the marked intracranial pressure, there was one obvious diagnosis: severe obstructive hydrocephalus caused by a sizeable posterior fossa mass. He looked up to find Salomao's eyes fixed on him. "Your little girl is very ill. She has something wrong inside her head. There is bad trouble here."

The two men looked at each other from their different worlds. The Mayan tribesman who knew how to farm the marshy plains of north central Guatemala, who struggled to provide sustenance for his family on corn and sugar, and who was now exhausted from his journey. And the doctor, who knew how to mend broken bodies and cut out disease, who struggled with cast off instruments and wheezing machines, and who in the process had not closed his eyes in thirty-six hours and was now exhausted.

Jake showed the area of concern at the hind portion of the child's overly round cranium. His fingers held an exquisite touch as they moved through the child's silky black hair. "There is liquid here. It presses inside her head. It is very dangerous and we must operate- fix it- right away." He put a hand on Salomao's shoulder. He struggled for words in Kekchi that would soften the blow. "Or she will die."

"Aaaaaaah."

"Don't worry, my friend." Jake knew that outside were the worldly goods of this man, or what remained of them. He would have bartered them for food for his daughter and himself. Jake was always humbled by the courage and wisdom of the native peoples. In societies that could be brutal this man was an outcast, someone defiled. Yet, here he was, two hundred miles later. "You will sleep and rest in my bed," Jake said. He took him to the cell-like cubicle on the subterranean floor of the Catholic run orphanage which was adjacent to the hospital. Above the cot was Jake's small wooden cross. He watched as Salomao touched it.

Nurse Irene inserted the needle in the girl's forearm, applied a set of recycled cardiac monitor leads with adhesive tape, then she slowly began to drip liquid ether onto the absorbent cloth window of a rubbery mask that encircled the child's face. She kept close watch on the vital electrical blips flowing hazily across an aged cathode ray tube. She watched the child's rate and pattern of breathing, Irene's only reliable methods of monitoring the essential depth of anesthesia. She had no formal training in anesthesia. Yet she was responsible to assure that each patient was kept under and safely asleep for the duration of any surgical procedure. She had no benefit from sophisticated monitoring equipment commonly used in developed countries. She didn't even have a simple endotracheal tube or mechanical respirator.

Reggae music fell into the room, a rhythmic mantle as they worked.

Dr. Austin, Jake's right-hand man, made sure the child was securely positioned on the operating table on her side, with her head snugly in place within a donut-shaped foam cushion. He nodded at Jake.

The nape of the child's neck and a section of protuberant skull just above it were prepped by Austin, who was delinquent in the required year of post-grad internship but who had served for several years under Jake's watchful supervision. A small bit of overlying hair was shaved away with a rusty disposable razor and then, over a ten minute period, the site was cleansed by wiping it briskly with a series of small cottony sponges saturated in absolute alcohol. At this point, Jake retreated to a side room to scrub his hands and forearms to the elbows.

The voice was startling, touched with concern. "Dr. Jake? Dr. Jake?"

Jake looked up from scrubbing.

"Are you all right? You've been scrubbing your hands for almost twenty minutes. Are you awake? We're waiting for you to get started."

Jake pulled himself up from over the sink and forced a smile. He quickly began rinsing the soapy residue from his hands, dipping them repeatedly into a final water-filled, scummy basin. Had he slept, even as he washed his hands? He had an image of Jeanne sitting across from him, her smile, those sycamores in Ben's backyard. Jake shook himself, forcing himself to focus.

Nurse Maera, the clinic's Panamanian scrub, had completed the arduous task of cleansing by hand and sterilizing in antifreeze the surgical instruments. She was now poised over the footrest of a lengthy overhead table which had been hand made by local craftsmen. Instruments, tarnished and scratched, some indented, were grouped in neat rows. As Jake got ready, a brief thought of Martha filled his tired mind. He remembered her precision with the surgical instruments, how she flawlessly anticipated him during surgery. Then she was gone, pushed back in his thoughts.

Jake stood ready in his discolored green cloth gown spattered with a patchwork of stains and repairs acquired over the years, ready with his recycled latex surgical gloves to drape the back of the child's head. Here he would secure the perimeter of his intended approach with sterile towels. Ready, he was handed a scalpel and he began to execute in precise layers the scalp incision.

That was when the light, an overhead mounted spotlight, flickered then went dark.

"Okay, who forgot to pay the bill?" Jake's hands remained poised.

A young missionary available as an extra pair of hands pushed open the door to the mechanical room off the OR and prepared their alternate power. There was a series of bangs and knocks, then the methodical drone of an engine. Light wavered, rallied, then offered its best illumination.

"Well done, Sister."

Under intense scrutiny, although he was unaware of it, he defined and exactly incised the layers of the scalp, each in turn, with nary the loss of but a few drops of blood. He then used the hand perforator and forearm-powered Gigli saw to open the lowermost portion of the child's hindskull. Coaxed on the moan of the old generator, the operating microscope was brought into position.

Lighting wavered, then gathered force.

"You know what it is, don't you." Jake said.

"What?" Nurse Irene asked.

"Traces of sewer water contaminating the fuel oil." His head jerked up. "Didn't I just say that—am I repeating myself?"

"No, Dr. Jake. First time." Nurse Maera said. She glanced anxiously at Dr. Austin, then Nurse Irene.

"Good, 'cause I mustn't start repeating myself." Jake went to work around the beam of light. "No certifications, no cockamamie forms—right, Irene?"

"Right, Doctor Jake."

"Damn right."

It took two more tedious hours before the formidable neoplasm that had aggressively invaded the roof of the fourth ventricle was identified and completely extirpated. Dr. Austin painstakingly sliced away a few microscopic pieces from the excised tumor mass and prepared a stained slide for tissue analysis. Jake moved around mumbling to himself. All eyes broke away from their tasks to watch him.

"Okay," Jake said. He went to the ancient monocular microscope and studied the pathological slide. He cried out in triumph, but it was finely edged in hysteria. "A cyctic juvenile astrocytoma! Get that, boys and girls?"

"Excellent chance for total cure." Austin said guardedly.

"Give the man a cigar." Jake tied in sequence the hand-threaded sutures that Austin applied. His fingers spun perfect square knots but he was mumbling again. "There we go, you see. There it is…"

Sister Kathleen, head of the local order, banged on the OR door.

"Nobody home," Jake said, applying a clean dressing to the wound, just as the child began to grapple and cough as she came back from the depths of her sleep.

"Go see her, Dr. Jake." Nurse Irene said.

Jake walked over to the door and met Sister Kathleen. "It went well. Gonna tell Salomao. She's gonna be okay."

"I'm glad, Dr. Gibson, so very glad."

Jake squinted at her. "Something wrong?"

"Good news and bad news. Doctor—are you all right? You look asleep on your feet."

"Tired. That's for sure. What's your news?"

Sister Kathleen's face brightened. "Dr. Julia's returning. She wants to come back and work here permanently."

"Oh, that's wonderful." Jake breathed.

"You trained her well, Doctor."

"So what's the bad news?"

"There's word from home. A good friend of yours is very ill. A Doctor Vincent Wilson thinks you should know."

"Wilson? Vince Wilson?"

"Yes. It concerns a Jeanne—"

"Jeanne!"

Sister Kathleen did something then she had never done before. She took hold of Jake's arm and led him away from the door. "Doctor, you do not look well, you need rest desperately. With Dr. Julia returning, you can take a vacation, get away, restore yourself."

Jake stared at the floor. He thought it was his mother. Now Jeanne...

"How long has it been, Dr. Jake?"

"Twelve years. Maybe thirteen."

"Then go. Dr. Julia will be here in a week. Go!"

Jake went to see Salomao, his exhausted brain almost cracked open with thoughts from a forgotten life, a forgotten time. Over the twelve years, he had deadened his senses to all of it—Martha, Midge, Shannon, and Jeanne. He had walked away from her, suitcase in hand, and now she was ill. He had to see her. And he had to see the resting places of the women in his life who had died. What had happened with Everett Salig, Howard Crane, Al-Fassad? And Vince Wilson who had contacted him? It all cracked open and inundated his weary senses.

Jake found Salamao sitting cross legged in his cubicle. He looked up when Jake entered. "Your daughter will be well." He said.

Salomao hung his head over his crossed legs. When he looked up, his eyes were wet with relief. But in the end, he had words saved for the American doctor he had traveled two hundred miles to see. "You are very tired."

Jake managed a smile. "I'm hearing that a lot these days."

He fell across his cot and was lost in a drugged sleep from his demanding body. Salomao covered him with a sheet, then sat again on the floor, cross legged, patient. Soon someone would come and take him to his daughter.

The airport was alive with sounds offering a jungle of their own. Jake stood in line for the passport check, not quite sure what he would do about his expired passport. He was clean shaven, with a decided two-tone to his face where the beard had protected him from the sun. The suit was old and illfitting. He could not bear a tie tight around his neck. Slowly the line moved forward. Nearby were security guards in their flamboyant South American style uniforms. Everyone looked like a general, he mused. At the desk, he waited while the customs and immigration officer looked at his passport then up sharply at him. Brown eyes studied him, but not with suspicion. More a look of delicate decision making, of that need to walk the diplomatic tightrope and not lose his job or cause an international incident. "Dr. Gibson?"

"Yes."

"You are aware that your passport has expired?"

"Yes. I've been working in the villages and hospitals. Things have been busy. I haven't had time to—"

"Come this way, please." He shouted to another officer who took over passport and papers review. In a quiet room which was entirely bare of photos, pictures, or notices of any kind, the officer told him to sit down. He pulled out a pack of cigarettes and offered them across to Jake.

"No, thank you."

"Ah, a doctor knows about the dangers of smoking."

"Why I am in this room? It looks like an interrogation room."

"That is correct. But you are not here to be interrogated. We are both here for peace and quiet." He smiled amiably.

Jake stood up. "Look, I—"

"Sit down, Dr. Gibson!"

Jake sat down.

"Now."

"Now what?" Jake stared at this friendly but dangerous little man.

Smoke rose up in dirty acrid clouds.

"We think."

"We think?"

"I know of you by reputation, Doctor. The humanitarian work you do for our people. Many people know of your good works…"

"Yes?"

"So I want to help. But there are procedures which are not to be broken—my job would be at stake, you understand? You know how difficult it is to get one of these jobs, what I and my relatives had to pay to get me in?"

"I understand," Jake said. "But—" he waved his hand helplessly.

"Who do you know here who can help you, some consulate, some embassy, some politician?"

"I don't know anyone."

The officer smiled and flicked ash on the floor. "I understand, you are an idealist, it is all straightforward with you: tell the truth and all will be well."

Jake forced a smile. A customs agent came in with a printout. There was a fast exchange of street Spanish.

The officer waited until the door was closed again. He waved the printout. "You have an outstanding bench warrant against you."

"But that was long ago," Jake protested, "over twelve years ago—"

"It's still in effect."

"So now what?"

"We wait for Mr. Chang."

"What?"

"Do you know Mr. Chang?"

"No, there are many Changs, of course—"

"This one is the American consulate. Patience, Dr. Gibson. I think we can extract this pearl from the tiger's jaws."

When Mr. Peter Chang entered the interrogation room, he looked at Jake with genuine joy at seeing him. "Dr. Gibson! I am Peter Chang, many years ago you saved my little sister, Bridget?"

"Bridget..." Jake cast around desperately.

"You saved her life! My family thinks of you as a hero. Do you think I could get an autograph or something?"

"Bridget…" Then he remembered.

"She's just delivered her fifth child. You know, my brother is in D. C. A great job with President Claggett's White House team." He handed over a business card, then his face grew serious, adopting the neutral planes of the diplomat. "Now, I have some documents for you to sign to clear you through Customs here. I have another set—always so much paperwork—to cancel the outstanding warrant. The only proviso is that under no circumstance can you practice medicine in the United States. Is that understood?"

"Yes, that's fine."

"Because if you do, you will be arrested and there will be nothing I can do to help you."

"I understand."

A heavy silence filled the room as the Customs officer stubbed out his cigarette and reviewed the paperwork. All three men signed. Jake took out a travel folder and autographed it with a note to Bridget and the family.

"How's that?" Jake said.

Peter Chang smiled. "Thank you. I'm so glad I was able to be of service, Dr. Gibson."

"Me, too."

The Customs officer stood up. "Return to our country, Dr. Gibson. It is an honor to have you here."

"Thank you."

He received a courtesy escort to the waiting plane.

The cracked walkway leading up to the front door of his home had not changed. He still found himself dodging that uneven pavestone where once he had blackened a toenail. But he did hesitate at the front door. Now, twelve years later, it bore small marks of the explosion that had torn it from its hinges and torn away the lives of Shannon and Midge. It was difficult. He found himself standing undecided at the door. Then he heard his mother inside, and for a moment there was the tang of fresh baked rhubarb pie. He pushed open the door. "Mom?"

And he was home.

28

The EXPERCARE UNIVERSITY HOSPITAL sign still offered its deep violet neon, except the first letter 'I' in university had burned out. Jake decided to go in unannounced, take a look at things on his way to see Vince Wilson. There were new signs, new departments, so far removed from his Belize hospital. 'Genetic Engineering and Cloning Ward'. Didn't recognize the nurses' stations. And there were high-tech workstations that were new. As a doctor he felt the palpable coldness of it, the distancing from patients that this ultramodern setup must inevitably cause. The brightly colored furniture, the fluffy pillows and fresh flowers didn't make up for it. Somewhere in all this was Jeanne and he would find her. But common sense told him to check the terrain with his former chairman. When he found the old office the twelve year old lettering offering his "Director of Department of Surgery' was chipped and faded. Jake knocked lightly and entered. He was shocked at what he saw.

"I knew you would come." Vince said.

Jake tried to keep his face in a neutral smile.

"Yeah, I know. I don't look so good."

"Well, you don't look sick, Vince. Just exhausted. And I know how that is."

Vince picked up a pencil and toyed with it. "So how are your mom and dad?"

"Fine. Some things don't change. We spent last night with the photo albums. I caught up on all the nieces and nephews. They've grown like weeds in twelve years."

"Things change all right."

"You sound down, Vince. Not just fatigue. Something else."

"Don't you want to see Jeanne?"

"Of course."

They talked as they walked.

"It's been a bad twelve years. A relentless march forward to convert human function to a computerized one. This place is bloodless—does that make sense?"

"I've seen some of it, the nurses' stations. Cold as steel. No familiar clutter: the spread out forms, pens everywhere, patient charts, specimen bottles, rolls of tape—all gone. There's no soul to this place anymore. Nothing to tell me I'm in a hospital."

"Yeah." Vince offered a tired smile. "So how about you, the missionary medical work?"

"It's real, Vince. Tough, we've got desperately little by way of resources. But there's a dedicated staff of the old school. They perform miracles with spit and shoelaces."

"Sounds good. I'd like to see that. Participate in that. Remember your talk to Congress, standing in the well, reading the riot act?"

"I'm not so sure I have that fire anymore, Vince."

"You do, Jason. You do." They came to the ICU. "Be prepared for more of the same, technology-wise." He touched Jake's arm. "And Jeanne. She's not doing well."

"An inoperable tumor, you said."

"I'm damned glad you're here."

Jake recognized the room. He had occupied it himself recovering from gunshot wounds courtesy of Howard Crane.

"I'll wait outside here, probably have to head back and take care of a few things."

"Okay. Thanks, Vince."

Jake gently opened the door and stepped inside.

"Yes?"

"It's me." Jake stepped around the bed.

"Jake? Oh, God, Jake it's you." Her hand reached for his, trailing an IV.

He kissed her lightly on the forehead. "How bad is it?"

She smiled a little. "At times…other times I get by. Not too much—discomfort—right now."

A woman in spaceship garb came rushing into the room.

"Sir, I must ask you to leave. Visiting hours are restricted." She clamped her hand on Jake's shoulder. "I have to ask you to—"

Jake turned his face her way.

"I can't believe it! You're—You're Dr. Jason Gibson." She took a step back.

Jake nodded.

"Your picture used to sit in my mom's office. She talked about you a lot before…before she… She used to tell me stories…"

Jake caught her name tag.

"Jennifer Jadlot?…Of course, I remember your mother." He smiled. "Mary Ann and I worked together for years, before she became nursing director here."

Jake squeezed Jeanne's hand. "I've come a long distance to pay a close friend a visit. I hope it's okay?"

Nurse Jadlot smiled and left the room, quietly closing the door behind her.

"Oh, Jeanne." He looked deeply into her blue eyes. "Why didn't you let me know?"

"You've been away for a long time, Jake." Her eyes were wet. "I wasn't sure you were ever planning to come back."

Jake sat on the side of her bed. "All you had to do was call." She squeezed his hand.

"Dr. Wilson tells me that it's impossible to remove?"

"That's what all the doctors have been telling me," Jeanne wiped her eyes. "But I'm not so sure."

Jake frowned.

"No. I mean it, Jake. There's only one doctor I've ever trusted."

"I want to look at your chart."

She laughed then. "No charts, Jake. Everything gets gobbled up in the computer system. You get this weird feeling of limbo, like you don't exist, that what you tell them doesn't count, y'know?"

"Yeah."

She squeezed his hand together, not letting go. "Twelve years. So much has happened. I have this memory of you leaving my house, trudging off into the snow with a suitcase. And now you're here. What happened to your face?"

"My face? Oh, I had a beard up until a couple of days ago. I'm two tone now."

Jeanne's face turned serious. There was a brief spasm of pain, then it was gone. "We were making it, Jake. I mean Ben and me. The kids kept us close…"

"I'm glad. Ben's a good man."

"But now…what do you and I have, Jake? It's something, even after all these years."

"We have a deep friendship, a special blend of caring and admiration for each other. We're lucky to have that."

"Martha helped, didn't she?"

Jake nodded.

Jeanne closed her eyes.

"Look, I'm going to leave you for a little while. I need to check on some things. Then I'll be back."

"I'm glad you're here, Jake."

He kissed her cheek gently then left.

◎▨✠

He was surrounded by well-orchestrated, very high-tech computer work stations. He asked Nurse Jadlot about Jeanne's condition.

He was invited to take a position at the CCT, or client-care terminal, to access and review her pertinent medical records. He marveled that by only a few clicks of a mouse on a pad, every piece of germane patient data—organized, condensed, even summarized—was readily displayed on-line. And there were many radiologic images digitalized into 3-D. It took him only minutes. He was riled.

"All she's got is an uncomplicated sphenoid-wing meningioma! Jesus Christ! They've let this thing grow for five years?"

"We're told its inoperable."

"Of course. It's gotten so big now that it's causing brain compression. Looks like it's invaded the Sylvian Cistern and may even be encasing vital arteries. Holy Mother…"

"Dr. Gibson, Dirk Watts is the neurosurgeon in charge. I could—"

Jake was up and heading for Watt's office.

◎▨✠

"Well, if it isn't the famous Dr. Gibson." The present occupant of the chair in neurological surgery was sitting at his desk working some sort of ultra modern computer module. He stood to shake hands. Dirk Watts had a huge grin.

"I remember watching it unfold on T.V.—Malone, Salig, Why I—"

"Listen—" Jake took the seat in front of him. "—I came here to look in on a patient of yours, Jeanne Brooks. She's a friend of mine."

251

Watts returned to his chair.

"Mrs. Brooks, yes, she's a client of mine. We tried to get her operated on several times. I'm afraid there's nothing we can do."

Jake pushed forward, his hands on Watt's desk.

"You watched her tumor grow for five years, and you call yourself a surgeon?"

Watts face reddened. "Gibson, your license to practice medicine was revoked here years ago, wasn't it? What makes you think you can come into my department and push your weight around." Watts attention was quickly back to the video screen. Piped in from the OR. "What the hell is going on in there, people? Get that client off the table. Follow the damned protocol."

A response came back.

"Oh, hell, I'll be right there." Watts glared down at Jake as he rushed out.

Jake headed back to the boss's office.

Vince Wilson looked ill.

"Now I know why you look like shit!"

'You've been through the CCT, seen her records."

"I've seen her records. I've talked to that moron Watts. What's the matter with you, Vince! It's an uncomplicated sphenoid-wing meningioma, why wasn't she operated on years ago?"

"It's the computerized systems, the protocols. Watt's COBRA—"

"COBRA?"

"Computerized Brain Robotic Apparatus, all Expercare hospitals have one. It rules, Jason. It rules."

"Jesus Christ."

"According to the COBRA data bank volumetric analysis, Jeanne's tumor is just too extensive to permit it to be safely removed."

"Bullshit. You know it, I know it. Is that the company spiel?"

"The protocols don't permit that much margin of error."

"Vince, listen to yourself! You know as well as I what we're dealing with here. She needs to be operated on and right now."

Vince picked up his pencil.

Jake watched him. The man had lost it, he was gutted.

"What they say is this: Health care allocation decisions take every pertinent element into account. All significant factors related to a particular disease process are included in the data analysis. The end result for each and every client is an accurate, unbiased and statistically reliable determination of the most appropriate treatment solution." Vince glanced up from his pencil doodles.

Jake stared in horror. "Do you hear yourself, Vince? Do you hear what you're saying? God knows I've done hundreds of these operations, so have you. Yet now, you're beaten down by some fucking computer—"

"Enough! Don't you think I know? Don't you think I hate what I see happening? It's all so different, Jason." Vince's voice trailed off. "It's all so different..."

"So, we're into the 21st Century medicine are we, Vince? Flow chart mega-analysis, some computer chip as the ultimate decision-maker."

"It's how it is."

"COBRA replaced our LEVIRA?"

"LEVIRA is history now. Even COBRA is to be superseded by ARMADO.

And in the name of God what is that?"

"Advanced Robo-Magnetic Auto-Digital Oligospectrography. The latest thing."

"The latest thing. Son of a bitch, Vince."

"It's what's happening, Jason!"

"You didn't fight, did you, you didn't wade in there and say, a living and breathing surgeon has a place in this, has a place in this noble profession that is both an art and a science—all the good phrases—you didn't wade in and use them, did you?"

Vince raised his voice. "Listen, I'm behind a desk. They pushed me out of the OR years ago, remember."

"So, you just didn't do it, did you?"

Vince turned in on himself. "No, no, I didn't."

"Tell you what, Vince. I'm not about to sit around and let someone very precious to me die from this grotesque medical nightmare."

"What do you mean by that?"

"I'm going to operate. And you're going to help me."

"Now, Jason—"

"First I want to see this 21st Century surgery in operation. Look, Vince. I need you in on this."

"You'll be destroyed as a doctor. Finished. I've already been pushed aside, so—"

"And Jeanne will be alive and well for her husband and kids."

Vince sat quietly. "Ok...we'll need a gas passer. Remember Doc Schweiz?"

"Sure!"

"And I could pull in Karen Jacobs as scrub nurse, she's still around."

Jake grinned broadly. "Now you sound like my old boss."

"She's in her eighties."

"Who cares!"

Vince Wilson looked carefully at Jake. "I'm glad you came back."

"Me, too. And it was you who got me here."

"That bothered me. I knew you would be all over me when you found out what was going on here."

"Forget all that, Vince. The point is, we have a plan, we're going to save Jeanne."

29

I divided my life into three parts: In the first I learned my profession, in the second I taught it; and in the third I enjoyed it.

John Bland-Sutton
(1855–1936)

COBRA was a presence from the new age yet harnessed to the old. It moved on clattery, piston-driven gadgetry and offered combinations of revolving levers and mobile fluid joints, all of it hovering menacingly from the ceiling. The contrivance, for all that, had the appearance of the ultimate robot. It dominated the entire breadth of the operating room. The floor space beneath it was divided into numerous tomb-like chambers, each containing a black operating rest and attached client.

Supervising these functions through glass-encased portholes provided each tightly sealed cubicle, were teams of identically dressed operating-team members. Each team member had his own computer workstation. They sat quite still, diligently manning the complex array of controls. And there were specialists, including anesthesiologists, who were situated along the flanks of each contamination-free cubicle. They were personally directing the administration of intravenous medications and airway gases by using the overhead labyrinthine arms. These anesthesiologists simultaneously monitored innumerable physiological functions on brightly colored bar graphs and a series of digitalized readouts.

The attending brain surgeons and their sides, whose workstations Jake noticed were farthest from their respective patients' cranial compartment, commanded the most intricate control benches. Each neurosurgeon sat behind impressive, high-resolution, multi-dimensional video displays. Each used finger responsive gloves to command the intricate control mechanisms that in turn directed pairs of sleek robotic hands about the desired tasks.

The charge-operator and assistants donned 3-dimensional laser retinal displays. With these they could visualize in minute detail the entirety of the operative field. Their actions meantime were translated by the microsurgical surrogate—aloft and some thirty feet away—into highly precise, operative manipulations measured in microns.

"My God," Jake said from their observation port.

Vince nodded. "Our legacy from Salig and Crane and others."

"So what's up with them?"

Vince Wilson stared incredulously. "You mean no one has told you, you don't know?"

"Know what?"

"Well, Salig's dead. He finally passed a couple of years ago. Shortly after you left, he was found face down in a service elevator. Got his head punched in. Some janitorial employee was suspect, but it was never solved." Vince thought aloud. "Salig living out his life a vegetable in a nursing home. Not the retirement he would have planned for himself."

"And Howard Crane?"

"Expercare fell under federal controls with a host of new regulations. All the profit chains did. Howard Crane and his cronies were indicted."

"So Crane's in jail?"

"Always the idealist, Jason. No. Actually, he's a consultant to the President on health care, and he was recently appointed to a National Health Consortium."

Jake shook his head. "What about Al-Fassad?"

"He wasn't so fortunate. He finally got caught in one of his lies about a surgical procedure. Seems he operated on a young woman for a micro-adenoma and ended up blinding her. He apparently missed the sella entirely. Then he tried to falsify records, laying blame on a resident. The woman's husband pulled a pistol in Al-Fassad's office and shot him. Killed instantly."

"And Hudley and Black?"

"Hudley sold out his shares in Expercare before the federal takeover. He made millions and left medicine. Now runs a chef school in Chicago. Loves his work, I understand, and is pretty good at it. Found his calling," Vince added dryly. "Black came to a pathetic end. Remember Y2K? Well, somebody hacked into George's portfolio and cleaned him out. Since he had alienated everyone, he had no one to turn to. His creditors began pressuring him, and it looked like he and his family would be out on the street."

"So, what happened?"

"He sat in the bathtub Roman style and slashed his femoral artery."

Jake put his head in his hands.

"Sorry, Jason. It was all so long ago for us. We're used to it. It's old news."

Jake nodded. "I paid a price for shutting myself off in the jungle."

"Yes."

"God, Vince. It's all inanimate machines! There's no simple touch, no humanity; it's obscene isolation and abandonment of essential human needs."

"Great for the insurance though." Vince's voice was bitter. "After you left, there was a slew of lawsuits. Now the paperwork is always exact, diagnosis is always precise and bureaucrats are happy. Litigation is unheard of now."

To add to the sophistication of the robotic environment, each operative cubicle was entombed in an individual super-conductor such that a vast array of spectographic scans were constantly being made available. Nuclear radiologists monitored each client, their efforts producing honed, high-resolution images that were sequentially projected into the appropriate surgeon's field of vision. Jake looked into one of the monitors at the detailed pictures. They offered topographic surface views through the operating telescope at narrow and wide-angle views of the operative field. There were a variety of magnifications, pre-operative 3-dimensional MR and functional MR images, electrophysiologic images, and dynamic MRA images.

Jake felt sick. "I've seen enough. Let's get of here."

"You know what it makes me think of, Jason?"

"What?"

"Those reality arcades the kids play in shopping malls. All that virtual reality game playing."

"Our future brain surgeons."

"See over there?"

Jake looked.

Additional specialized workstations: each client's vital metabolic functions were being intensely monitored by organ-specified personnel.

◎✸✠

The purple neon EXPERCARE UNIVERSITY HOSPITAL shone into the darkness. The letter 'I' in university had been promptly fixed. Within the hospital walls, far removed from fluffy pillows and flower arrangements, piped in music and stylish furniture, things were happening in OR-1. All the robotic devices were stilled. Stainless steel arms were motionless, their open claws ready to grasp the midnight air. Workstations were abandoned, computer monitors switched off, their dulled monolithic eyes blind to the primitive events going on around them.

What Jake and Vince, scrub nurse Karen Jacobs was not as spry as she used to be. But she bustled about her duties, buffing her plump body up against tables, her pudgy hands moving with old skills. She laid out the antique instruments furtively gathered from the display in the hallway. But it was her eyes that told all. Bright, focused, intent on the resurrection of all her skills for this one last time.

What Jake and Vince, scrub nurse Karen and old Doc Schweiz were doing was illegal. But the skeleton crew worked as skillfully and meticulously as ever. Just like clockwork, at the top and bottom of each hour, a uniformed security guard would pass, shining his light through the full-length glass doors at the entrance to the operating theatre. They worked. They pushed away the sophistry that passed itself off as advanced medicine and offered their skills to Jeanne. They were, in a sense, in a time machine far more sophisticated than any electronic contraption around them, They were reaching back to Asclepius in BC, to Guy de Cauliac, Father of Surgery in the 14th Century, to William Osler in the 19th Century, and to Harvey Cushing, Father of Neurosurgery in the 20th Century—not forward in some grotesque distortion of honorable medical tenets justified by circuitry and pulsing lights and steel robotic arms. They had their place to be sure, but only when grounded in the imperatives of good medicine for the patient, above all, the patient.

They waited on Jeanne.

Without a simple suction apparatus or standard respirator, the silence in the room was interrupted only by repeated thrusts of Doc Schweiz's arthritic fingers on a primitive insufflation bag and the occasional thug, rap, or clang of an instrument being passed or the bipolar pedal pushed.

"How are you doing, Doc?" Jake asked the anesthesiologist.

"Don't worry about me, young man!"

Vince laughed from behind his mask, all of the cynicism gone from his eyes, his old fire returned.

"You tell him, Doc." Karen said.

"You look twenty years younger, Karen." Jake said, as they maneuvered the venerable Zeiss with its monocular sidearm.

"I feel twenty years younger, Dr. Gibson."

They moved together with the Zeiss, a ballet of coordinated movement.

For the briefest moment, Jake relaxed his hands from the operating field and looked beyond the makeshift anesthesia screen at Jeanne's peaceful face. "Won't be long now, dear heart."

In accordance with the rules of nature, the tumor he encountered was unusually nasty. One of the most difficult types. It crept along the lateral fissure to implicate the base of the skull in its growth. In the process, critical cranial nerves and vitally important blood vessels to the dominant part of Jeanne's brain had been gravely surrounded.

Long after the operation had ended, Jake sat by his patient's bedside. An orange glow making its appearance in the darkened sky.

"Jake, Jake." A mumbled voice came from the direction of the bed.

He went to her.

"How are you feeling, babe?" Jake took her hand.

"A little bit groggy, but I feel pretty good." Jeanne's eyes carried a light.

Jake kissed her forehead just beneath the bandage.

"You did a beautiful job on me. Thanks, bub."

Jake reached for her other hand. For a few moments, they remained attached to each other.

The graveyard was very still. It was bathed in mist and sunlight and offered its old and new gravestones in an elegant mosaic of the timeless, of the inevitable fate for all of us. The grass was greening in the spring rains, already a keeper faithfully mowed the acres, carefully avoiding the flower beds that would, in time, unfold their radiant colors. Her gravestone was still fresh after twelve years. It was in the Gibson family plot, next to his grandparents and the waiting places of his father and mother. His own resting place was there also.

It was a good stone. The lettering carefully recording who she was. And Martha's parents had agreed that she belonged with her husband. She was his third visit to a gravestone after Midge and Shannon. Jake spoke his words quietly. There were thanks owed. They had to be expressed. Thanks to Martha for loving him unconditionally; thanks to Martha for her faith in him during the disastrous days in Mount Pleasant, so long ago. Jake smiled. And walks in the mountains, and the bicycle rides, and their sacred communing which would have brought forth twins. Jake tried to remember the names they had selected. He couldn't remember…

He knelt beside her and got his words out, especially about Jeanne, how he still loved her so but knew the wrongness of it. How Martha had given him direction, a soft push against his heart. He told her that Jeanne was well now. She would soon be back with Ben and her family.

His eyes turned to a sound, a vaguely familiar sound, faint and off in the distance. He caught movement between the trees, bobbing silhouettes, in colors. It drew him in; he retraced his steps along that gravel path.

A group of boys were playing ball—tossing baseballs back and forth into leather gloves. He took a seat on the weathered wooden bench, his fingers probing the rough surface, still forged with initials of his era. He came across a pair that made him pause.

"Hey mister, you wanna play?" Several of the boys had walked over.

Jake looked up.

"We need one more player for a game. Can you throw?"

Jake smiled. It was then that he noticed.

Three men who walked towards him. One was a uniformed police officer, the other two obviously detectives. They stopped away from him, giving him some brief extra time to distance the kids.

"No, sorry, can't right now." He watched innocent eyes study him for a moment, then return to their game.

"Dr. Gibson?" A plainclothes detective said.

"Yes."

"We are here to arrest you for illegally performing brain surgery on one Jeanne Brooks, wife of Benjamin Brooks, at the EXPERCARE UNIVERSITY HOSPITAL."

"I understand."

"In doing so, you violated the special privilege granted you on return to this country from Central America—"

"I understand." His fingers grazed those initials in the bench one last time.

"You have the right to remain silent…"

Above him the sky had brightened. Birds swooped at the trees. A light breeze caromed gently from grassy glades and honed itself across the cyclone back-stop. Dust swirled around the player's feet. There was a message here, Jake realized. Here, surrounded by his youth. He offered no resistance as the handcuffs were placed around his wrists. Here was an abiding freedom in the creator's presence. Here was an abiding peace in the realization that he had done his best for his mother and father, for Martha and Jeanne. And perhaps himself. That he wasn't sure of. Where he would end up he didn't know.

What he did know was that he had been true to his calling; that having to choose, he had always chosen truth and shouted it out proudly. He had chosen truth in his country's Congress, in his country's courts of law, in the rain forests of a place where a man would walk two hundred miles with his sick child to search out that truth.

As they walked away, Jake smiled to himself. He would always have his truth, the love of all those close to him, the gratitude of his patients.

It was enough.

POSTSCRIPT

Medicine is an art which is difficult to master! If one does not receive a divine guidance from God, he will not be able to understand the mysterious points. A foolish fellow, after reading medical formularies for three years, will believe that all diseases will be cured. But, after practicing for another three years, he will realize that formulae are mostly not effective. A physician should, therefore, be a scholar, mastering all the medical literature, and working carefully and tirelessly.

A great doctor, when treating a patient, should make himself quiet and determined. He should not have covetous desire. He should have bowels of mercy on the sick and pledge himself to relieve suffering among all classes: Aristocrat or commoner, poor or rich, aged or young, beautiful or ugly, enemy or friend, native or foreigner, and educated or uneducated, all are to be treated equally. He should look upon the misery of the patient as if it were his own and be anxious to relieve the distress, disregarding his own inconveniences, such as night-call, bad weather, hunger, tiredness, etc. Even foul cases, such as nicer, abscess, diarrhea, etc. should be treated without the slightest antipathy. One who follows this principle is a great doctor; otherwise, he is a great thief!

A physician should be respectable yet not talkative. It is a great mistake to boast of himself and slander other physicians.

An Ancient Chinese Code

A few months after my twenty-second birthday, I completed my freshman year of medical studies. That August, a lifelong idol passed away, very unexpectedly. He also attended the oldest doctoring college west of the Mississippi, though in his era there wasn't even a specialty called "neurological surgery." Anticipated life expectancy in the U.S. when he graduated was 54 years, the more frequently encountered, life-threatening disorders being infectious diseases (pneumonia, polio and tuberculosis). Only about 3 percent of the gross national product in the U.S. was devoted to health care back then; perhaps accordingly, physicians earned on average something less than $4000 a year. At that time, a malady called medical malpractice had not yet been conceived, and managed care orchestrated by Wall Street executives—well, let's just say the entire concept was unimaginable.

After serving as a medic on the front lines in France during World War I, the key influence behind my ambition to become a healer returned to his Missouri hometown. He completed his internship at the old St. Louis City Hospital and set out to do what nearly all private practitioners were doing in those days; he opened shop as a respected neighborhood GP. During the depression he occupied a small office on the near South Side, sharing space with his older brother, Cy, also a capable general practitioner. With the advent of World War II, once again he volunteered his services to the U.S. government; whereupon, due to his age and paternal status, he was given the less than glamorous job of company doctor for a large ammunitions factory. For the duration of the war effort he commuted most every weekend across the breadth of the Show-me State. For as long as I remember as a baby boomer growing up in the '50s and '60s and 70's, the silver-haired medicine man kept a tiny, three-room upstairs office, accessible only by a steep and odorous flight of stairs. I can still recall the inspiring stories he would willingly tell, to anyone who would listen. His incredible experiences in medicine: the droves of newborns extemporaneously delivered at home, right in their mama's beds; the emergency appendectomies and amputations accomplished with only a handful of crude instruments; the T and A's, I and D's, and D and C's performed by the hundreds literally upon the kitchen table; the shattered bones set on the spot by hand; and so forth and so on.

Unfortunately, by the time I had arrived into premedical studies in college, he was into his upper 70s and had retired most of his cherished hospital privileges. Nonetheless, into his early 80s his first love continued to receive a major chunk of his daily attention. I can still envision the cluttered treatment room at his office, shelves and counters overflowing with all variety of drugs: antibiotics, antispasmodics, antiinflammatories, anti-hypertensives, etc. etc. To this day, I have a vivid image of him slipping a few dusty tablets or sugar-coated capsules of whatever was needed by a patient into a smallish white envelope, upon which he would then inscribe instructions, quite illegibly. Later, after spending an additional 20 or 30 minutes shooting the breeze, he would be paid for his services in cash, if that patient was able to do so; often a buck or two. (And that was as late as 1972!)

I finally graduated from St. Louis University School of Medicine three years after my grandfather had passed on. Life expectancy in the United States at that time had risen to over 72 years, with heart disease, cancer, and stroke firmly established as the leading causes of death. As a rookie intern I was encouraged to join the American Medical Association, which boasted of its 400,000 members, each of whom could expect to earn, on average, $75,000 a year. As evidenced by their newfangled, paid advertisements, a generation of aspiring personal injury attorneys did not let those figures go unnoticed.

Inspired by a paternal granddad's genuine spirit of compassion and generosity toward people and challenged by a devoted professorial father to carry on his deep fascination for the human brain, I proceeded to invest nearly a decade of my life to become the best neurological surgeon I possibly could.

Recently, in 2000, I quietly took note of my twentieth-fifth anniversary as a physician, and nearly my twentieth lawsuit. Life expectancy in the United States had further increased to almost 78 years, though the list of top-ten killers again included an infectious agent, HIV. That same year I earned nearly a 100 times what my grandfather had during the most productive years of his practice; and annual health care expenditures in the U.S. had exceeded one trillion dollars (nearly 15 percent of the GNP!).

The year 2015 will mark my 65th birthday and presumably witness my retirement as a doctor of medicine. If present trends continue, life expectancy in the U.S. for those afforded proper medical care should be well into the 80s. One can only speculate as regards the overall impact of health care upon the U.S. economy into the next millennium and the degree to which the present generation of corporate executives and health care administrators, politicians, and personal injury attorneys will fundamentally transform the decision-making role traditionally afforded physicians, such as my grandfather.

P.H.Y.

Check out these other fine titles by
Durban House at your local book store.

EXCEPTIONAL BOOKS
BY
EXCEPTIONAL WRITERS

MR. IRRELEVANT
by Jerry Marshall.

Sports writer Paul Tenkiller and pro-football player Chesty Hake have been roommates for eight career seasons. Paul's Choctaw background of poverty and his gambling on sports, and Hake's dark memories of his mother being killed are the forces which will make their friendship go horribly wrong.

Chesty Hake, the last man chosen in the draft, has been dubbed Mr. Irrelevant. By every yardstick, he should not be playing pro football. But, because of his heart and high threshold for pain, he perseveres.

Paul Tenkiller has been on a gravy train because of Hake's generosity. Gleaning information vital to gambling on football, his relationship with Hake is at once loyal and deceitful.

Then during his eighth and final season, Hake slides into paranoia and Tenkiller is caught up in the dilemma. But Paul is behind the curve, and events spiral out of his control, until the bloody end comes in murder and betrayal.

OPAL EYE DEVIL
by John Lewis.

From the teeming wharves of Shanghai to the stately
offices of New York and London, schemes are hammered out
to bankrupt opponents, wreck inventory, and dynamite oil
wells. It is the age of the Robber Baron—a time when
powerful men lie, steal, cheat, and even kill in their quest
for power.

Sweeping us back to the turn of the twentieth century,
John Lewis weaves an extraordinary tale about the brave
men and women who risk everything as the discovery of oil
rocks the world.

Follow Eric Gradek's rise from Northern Star's dark
cargo hold to the pinnacle of high stakes gambling for
unrivaled riches.

Aided by his beautiful wife, Katheryn, and the devoted
Tong-Po, Eric fights for his dream and for revenge against
the man who left him for dead aboard Northern Star.

ROADHOUSE BLUES
by Baron Birtcher.

From the sun-drenched sand of Santa Catalina Island to the smoky night clubs and back alleys of West Hollywood, Roadhouse Blues is a taut noir thriller that evokes images both surreal and disturbing.

Newly retired Homicide detective Mike Travis is torn from the comfort of his chartered yacht business into the dark, bizarre underbelly of LA's music scene by a grisly string of murders.

A handsome, drug-addled psychopath has reemerged from an ancient Dionysian cult, leaving a bloody trail of seemingly unrelated victims in his wake. Despite departmental rivalries that threaten to tear the investigation apart, Travis and his former partner reunite in an all-out effort to prevent more innocent blood from spilling into the unforgiving streets of the City of Angels.

TUNNEL RUNNER
by Richard Sand.

Tunnel Runner is a fast, deadly espionage thriller peopled with quirky and most times vicious characters. It tells of a dark world where murder is committed and no one is brought to account; where loyalties exist side by side with lies and extreme violence.

Ashman "the hunter, the hero, the killer" is a denizen of that world who awakens to find himself paralyzed in a mental hospital. He escapes and seeks vengeance, confronting his old friends, the Pentagon, the Mafia, and a mysterious general who is covering up the attack on TWA Flight 800.

People begin to die. There are shoot-outs and assassinations. A woman is blown up in her bathtub.

Ashman is cunning and ruthless as he moves through the labyrinth of deceit, violence, and suspicion. He is a tunnel runner, a ferret in the hole, who needs the danger to survive, and hates those who have made him so.

It is this peculiar combination of ruthlessness and vulnerability that redeems Ashman as he goes for those who want him dead. Join him.